"We could swing (asteroids into a nea..." said the cybertech. "But we get a much more comfortable margin for error if we grab a really large body. In designing the blowfish orbits, I came upon a propulsion system that may work. We could even bring down Ceres herself."

Grace studied the papers. "The plan requires a supply of thermonuclear devices. More than fifty-eight hundred, I see."

"Do you realize what this represents in terms of our national arsenal?" barked the Undersecretary of Defense. "You'd strip the country. We'd have to dock our submarines, ground the bombers, empty the silos."

"In view of the doom we all face in little more than five years," Grace said drily, "that doesn't seem to be an important consideration."

* * *

"An impressive first novel, going far beyond the usual disaster tale in scope and imagination—and solidly based on a real scientific possibility."

—Stanley Schmidt, Editor, *Analog*

THOMAS WREN

THE DOOMSDAY EFFECT

THOMAS WREN
THE DOOMSDAY EFFECT

BAEN
SCIENCE FICTION
BOOKS

THE DOOMSDAY EFFECT

Copyright © 1986 by Thomas Wren

A Baen Books Original

Baen Publishing Enterprises
260 Fifth Avenue
New York, N.Y. 10001

First printing, July 1986

ISBN: 0-671-65579-5

Cover art by David Egge

Printed in the United States of America

Distributed by
SIMON & SCHUSTER
TRADE PUBLISHING GROUP
1230 Avenue of the Americas
New York, N.Y. 10020

For my Father

Chapter 1

Grace Porter: PUNCH-IN

The AmAir jumpjet loaded with late Sunday traffic had just lifted from SFO. It was pinwheeling at 15,000 feet toward the coastside of the San Francisco Peninsula, where it would shoot up to 33,000 and level for the run to the south. ETA in LA was 5:20.

In an aisle seat back of the wing, Grace Porter spread her fingers across the layer of papers on her flipdown tray. These jumpjets were advertised as traveling "up like an elevator and off like a rabbit"—a federal regulation to suppress city noise levels, she knew—but the maneuver was more like a carnival ride. The takeoff made her paperwork slide, when it wasn't snapping her neck around.

Paperwork was one of Porter's eccentricities. Everyone else in business loaded summaries into their memoscribes and plotzed along on the high points. When Grace worked with a contract or a proposal, she liked to have the whole text in front of her. Of course, she read faster than most people. She also liked to use a real ink fluoromarker. That put her so out of style that she was almost stylish.

Grace Porter was a minister's daughter, raised in an Iowa town that could calculate to a tenth of a cent how much poverty was good for the souls of its

1

parson's family. She wore white cotton socks and poor-box polyester discards until she was sixteen. Drinking, dancing, dating—it was all sin. So was growing up to be as tall and archly beautiful as Reverend Porter's demon daughter.

A state scholarship helped her escape from the town. A corporate training grant took her out of the state. And she never went back. When she was still a young bizad with the ink barely dry on her legal certificate, she hit New York City at mach five. She did advertising on the Avenue: contract wrangling, some video production, concept and comp, mostly for freeze-dried foods and powdered wines. In three months she had picked up a $400-a-day cocaine habit and a shit of a husband. Grace broke with both of them in the same month. That was a bad month.

Then she headed for the Bay Area and high tech. After a couple of wrong starts she found Pinocchio, Inc., maker of industrial automata—vulgarly, robots. Selling steel-collar workers in a labor-hungry world was like hooking trout in a drained lake. She liked it. She stayed. And in fifteen years rose to become exec veep of marketing. She had only needed to stomp, stab, or bury enough bodies to fill the beds of a small convalescent hospital.

San Francisco was a hard town for a single woman. The ratio of straight gals to straight guys was four to one and climbing. The competition was politely homicidal. With her golden hair and haughty face, her bearing, her income, Grace had always been able to get nibbles just by trailing her fingers in the water. But now she had one foot on the big four-oh. No matter how good the skin or taut the body, the nibbles were moving downstream, toward the fashionable girl-children. It was a time when the men in Grace's life were wanting less and she was wanting more.

It was harder, too, in corporate life. She had made

her rise on vision and decisive action. But now she was at the top slot for a soft science professional, a non-tech, in a hard science company. Just being good wasn't enough. Everyone wanted more.

Take the Mad Russian in the seat next to her. Alex Kornilov was one of Pinocchio, Inc.'s four chief engineers. He was also a full project manager in the gigabuck range who had picked up the space option late in life. When other engineers were buying plots of grape land up in Napa and trading stock options for early retirement, Kornilov was studying null-gee structurals and taking centrifuge tests that would have had Grace puking into her hat. And he couldn't have been less than fifty years old.

Kornilov was hard science, and he'd maneuvered his career onto the right track: the growing space market. Although right now he was officially below her on the corporate ladder, Grace knew that Korny was presumed to be her equal. On this trip to nail the LiquiSteel contract, he had co-power of negotiation with her. In five more years he could be running Pinocchio, putting non-techs like her through the hoops. It would take an act of God for her to catch up—when she was already, on paper at least, ahead.

While Grace spread her papers, reviewed the specs and played patterns with the contract clauses, Kornilov shrugged his square, storklike body into a relaxed angle and ordered a double scotch from the flight attendant.

Was he worried about the deal they were going to have to cut? Was he concerned about building in-place automata for the Earth's first orbiting mini-mill? Not at all. He didn't seem to care if his head was clear or not.

When Grace politely probed him about risk assessment, for setting the escalation markers on contingency, he shrugged and suggested she pick a number. That was her country, he said.

The fly-guy came back and handed the big plastic glass of amber scotch across Grace. Korny turned to reach for it.

As the glass passed in front of her face, Grace tilted her head aside, so she missed the flash. She heard the bang, like a brick hitting a garbage can. And the crackle-zing, like a mosquito making a kamikaze dive past her ear at Mach 2. Then the lonely whistle of pressure loss in the cabin.

Korny dropped the drink. He dropped his—hand—into Grace's lap. It was there. In her lap. And his wrist was fountaining blood across into the attendant's bottle cart, splattering like rain on Grace's papers.

He said an "Uff" that turned into a sighing scream that rose right past the jet engines and seemed to go out of hearing range.

There was blood on *his* lap and blood on the fly-guy's apron, but on Grace there were just these white fingers and ice and scotch and the empty glass.

A bright yellow oxygen mask dropped out of the ceiling to dangle in front of Grace's eyes, and the world screamed like the crowd on a roller coaster going over the top.

A tenth of a second later, a star fell into the waters of Crystal Springs Reservoir.

This narrow chain of lakes in the hills of the San Francisco Peninsula provided drinking water (odd days or even days only) for more than three and a half million people. Fishing and bathing in the reservoir were prohibited by federal law, and it had been ten years since any human being had run a boat powered by internal combustion on a freshwater source in California. Eight-lane Highway 280 had been re-routed away from the reservoir to avoid further lead contamination. Armed Rovers patrolled the shoreline to intercept unauthorized approaches.

So no living person was on hand to see the spark of

light and vapor trail that streaked down from the western sky.

Rover 18 swiveled its photoreceptors toward the crackling sound and promptly had them burned out by a flash of ultraviolet. Radio interference jammed its brainboard. Three other Rovers within a mile radius froze up with electrical glitches.

If it had touched down anywhere else, the spark might have caused no more damage than this. Crystal Springs Reservoir, however, runs down a fold in the hills created by the millennial creep of the San Andreas Fault.

The fly-guy had backed up the aisle with a yelp.

"Call the pilot," Grace Porter told him, fighting the bile in her throat. "Get us down."

In the confusion, Grace was barely aware that the plane had stopped its smooth pinwheel and was into a violent sideslip. The babble of the other passengers was like a breaking sea that surrounded her and the bubbling fountain of blood from Kornilov.

He had started to curl around the severed wrist, hugging it to his chest. And Grace knew that was wrong: he'd never stop the bleeding that way.

She pulled at the scarf around her neck and tugged the clickpen from her inside pocket. "The pressure point is inside the elbow," she said under her breath. "The pressure point is . . ." It was a mantra for her panicking mind.

Korny was doubled over now. She put the scarf and pen in her mouth and tried to force him back with her hands. She ended up bracing her shin across his knees and heaving upward on his shoulder. He never stopped screaming.

A spurt of blood, bright red and arterial, came up from his left thigh and caught her on the chin.

"Jesus!" she swore. With the edge of her right hand she gave him a chop above the collarbone to numb what was left of his arm and constrict the vessels at skin surface.

Arm or leg, which to take on first . . . ? The arm was pumping faster. So Grace wrapped it with her scarf just below the elbow, tied it and twisted the pen to cut the flow. She hooked the pen behind his biceps to hold the tourniquet.

Now the leg . . . but with what? He wasn't wearing a tie or a belt. Holding him upright with one hand, she kicked off her sandals and used the other hand to wriggle out of her pantyhose. This was going to ruin a thirty-dollar pair of SparkelBrites.

She slipped the silverstrand nylon under his knee and worked it back up toward his crotch. The seat under Kornilov was soaked with blood. Jesus, was there a hole in the *back* of his leg too?

"Can I help you, Miss?" It was the chief fly-gal.

Porter tied the nylon as tight as she could, reached under the loop and twisted with her own hand to constrict the artery. She found a free hand to work one of the dangling oxygen masks over Korny's face. "Yeah," she grunted, "are we landing yet?"

"Uh . . . please be patient," the chief fly-gal said. "The pilots are doing the best they can. But there does seem to be some trouble with our systems. And we have reports of trouble on the ground."

Grace looked up at this glass-eyed robot doll, all coif and face paint, in disbelief. "We've got a man cut to pieces here. He's dying!"

"Well, as I said, we do have a slight problem," the woman said in her coolest professional voice. "There is a radio blackout on most frequencies. One of the pilots, however, did hear something about an earthquake."

"An earthquake?" Grace checked the pen at Korny's arm to make sure it hadn't slipped.

"Yes. There seems to be a lot of confusion."

"You're telling me. All right, help me find his hand."

"His *what*?" The fly-gal turned whiter than her nouveau makeup.

"It's down here somewhere." Grace pointed at the floor with her chin. "It slipped when I stood up. Find it and put it on ice till we get on the ground."

"Oh, we don't have ice in the galley. Just a cooler unit."

"Then put it in there."

"But it's just for liquids. I can't put a *hand* in it."

"Oh fuck! Just find the thing and keep it clean, will you?"

Grace changed position so she was sitting next to Kornilov instead of crouching over him. His head nestled into the hollow of her neck and he started to shiver. He was in shock.

She told the woman to stop groping around under the seat and get a blanket. The fly-gal nodded gratefully and ran off up the aisle.

"C'mon Alex stay with me fellah don't go to sleep we'll get you down. C'mon Alex stay with me fellah don't go to sleep we'll . . ."

It was another mantra for Grace to chant. Two in one day was some kind of a record.

From overhead Grace heard a moaning, like the wind at the eaves of an old house. She looked up and saw a scar in the fiberfab paneling over their seats. It was a star fracture about four inches across. She reached up her free hand and felt the cold sucking air escaping from the cabin. She snatched her hand back.

Just as the fly-guys were covering Korny with a blanket, she heard the engines dip to a lower pitch and the seat seemed to sag under her. Finally they were landing.

She hugged Korny closer and rubbed his back and side as best she could with her free hand. She remembered to loosen her grip on the leg tourniquet every few minutes. The arm she kept pinned: there wasn't much tissue left to oxygenate.

The Peninsula hills, the Bay, the city's arching skyline swung in rotation past the window. Most of the buildings seemed to be standing—although, like a boxer's crooked smile, there were one or two teeth missing. Still, it couldn't have been much of a quake, she decided. Not the Big One.

Their skimming approach to the airport told more. A lot of smoke and dust seemed to be in the air. The terminal tower looked kind of . . . lopsided. And half the planes at the ramps seemed to be nose down or on their sides.

As their jumpjet slid into the terminal bay, Grace saw a dozen trucks with flashing lights and caught a glimpse of ten thousand broken windows in the observation lounges. Well, she decided, an airport's built on filled land. It's going to rock and roll in any quake.

"Okay, lady, you can let him go." It was a white-suited medic, already jabbing a needle into Kornilov's good leg. "Heysoos, what happened to him?"

Porter eased back and let the two medics take his shoulders. "His arm. And his leg . . . an artery, I think."

"You cut him up with a knife or what?" The man didn't even look up as he rigged the IV.

Grace stared at the medic in surprise. "Did *I*—? I was just sitting here and he came apart."

"Sure, lady."

"He did!"

"Then it sure is a mystery, huh? Same as you two got right and left matching sunburns."

"What . . . ?"

Suddenly the right side of her face, under the crusty patches of Korny's blood, felt tight and scalded. But she hadn't been out in the sun for weeks. She looked at Korny's face and saw that, while the right side was pale from blood loss, the left was a faded purple-red.

The medics lowered him into their bundlebasket.

"You want to come with us, get that treated?"

"Um . . . Aren't you going to tell me I saved his life?"

The man looked up and shrugged. "Sure I will. If he happens to live."

And then they were going down the aisle at a run.

Porter started to follow and felt more pain. She had the impression that the whole side of her body, under her blood-clammy clothes, was sunburned.

There wasn't a better time to unleash an earthquake on the Bay Area than the end of a summer Sunday afternoon.

The towers of the San Francisco financial district swayed and cracked. Shards, knives, sheets of glass fell into the street until there was a glittering rubble three inches deep. If it had been a workday morning, evening rush hour or the noontime ramble, there would have been megadeath. On Sunday the glass fell in silence like a tree in the center of the forest.

At Ocean Beach the dogwalkers, sun bathers, sandcastle builders, surfers, surfer friends, windsailers and windsail watchers saw the waves retreat beyond the fringes of fog that hung around Seal Rock. Then the water came back with a six-inch dividend. A small lip of sand eroded into the waveslop.

So much for California falling into the ocean.

The crowd hardly noticed. Everyone's attention was distracted by the sight of the historic Cliff House—packed at the cocktail hour—somersaulting once again from its rock perch into the Pacific.

Inland, the cantilever section of the Bay Bridge lost its hold on Yerba Buena Island. And there more people fell into the water: the solid stream of traffic, returning from the casinos of South Lake Tahoe and Reno, slid with the bridge. More than sixty cars and camper vans shot toward the side of the island and into the Bay, leaving a shriek of rubber and a haze of tire smoke.

Evangelists would preach the punishment of sinners for at least three Sundays to come.

On the Golden Gate Bridge, four suspension cables parted from the deck and slapped sideways. All of them missed the light flow of traffic but one, and it flicked the oldest Volkswagen beetle registered in Marin County into the ebbtide going toward the Pacific Ocean.

Under the rivulet of fog that each evening slipped through the Gate, the main cellblock of the Alcatraz Museum collapsed with a final banging of steel bars. A late tour had just moved out to the rec yard, so no injuries there.

The lattice of the Sausalito Dome broke at a dozen joints and showered jagged fragments of Stresslite down into the hottest of California's hothouse cultures. But it was mostly tourists who bought a sudden and mangling death on the slidewalks along Bridgeway; the town's residents weekended at Stinson Beach.

The stands on the east side of Candlestick Park pancaked. But the Giants were at Pittsburgh that day.

The real damage happened along the Bay side of the Peninsula, from Belmont to Cupertino. If a structure stood higher than two stories or was founded on anything less solid than concrete on bedrock—and that took in ninety percent of the slum blocks and townrows in the area—it fell down a little or a lot. There were 100,000 deaths and half a million injuries—a light toll, considering that the population density of this semiurban district was almost three million.

On the foggy ocean side of the Peninsula the single-story houses, even those built on sand, may have walked around their foundations, but they stayed upright and on their lots.

Thirty-six minutes later, the "falling star" reappeared in disputed territory between Sinkiang S.S.R. and Tsinghai of the P.R.C. The former had been Chinese, was now Russian, and would soon be Chinese again. The latter was now Chinese and would soon be Russian. Which direction the border was traveling depended on your point of view.

The local time was 9:24 A.M. on Monday—bad timing, in view of how alert everyone was.

A gout of flame and a column of fire appeared out of the rocky soil two hundred yards from a Russian bunker. The column was half a meter across, so it was easily mistaken for an incoming rocket shell. In the confusion that followed no one remembered that, instead of coming down and bursting, the fireball arched almost straight *up* into the sky. The Russians only noticed that the smoke trail was angled toward the east.

A Soviet noncom sent off a *Mat' Narodya* in return and called for a full spread of missiles.

The Chinese general for that sector responded with a 300-millimeter *Shan Di Xiong* and called for his own barrage.

Whatever that first blow was, it released a blast of x-rays, ultraviolet, and UHF radio waves that blinded all radar, both handheld and installed, for 400 meters along the line. So both sides panicked and fired blind.

The fighting didn't die down for a week.

Eldon Richardson, associate news director of KSAS in Wichita, had the job of putting together the late scan on weekends. Sunday night was mostly sports— baseball and football scores and some local rodeo— because viewers wanted to put off Monday-morning realities like the commodities market for as long as possible. And nothing happened on Sundays in August anyway.

So Richardson had one eye on the news board and another on his editor. He was putting together clips for "Lens on Your Life," his own 6:30 A.M. feature feed on people and events. The name was his creation, even though his station used ninety percent more network stock, file tape with voice-over, and data feed than actual live lenswork.

The board was so quiet tonight that he thought about slipping in his cut from that morning on the Kingman man who had broiled and publicly eaten a neighborhood nuisance of a barking Afghan. Sort of a grim "man bites dog."

It was fifty-two minutes to air—they still said air, although all signals went by optical cable—when the first report on the San Francisco quake came in. The datanet just about locked up on that one, words so far but no pix. No live eye. No damaged buildings. No tear-streaked victims.

This was going to be duller than the farm report, Richardson decided, as he sorted the stream of details into a manageable story. Without visuals the scan would be merely the syntho of his talking head and a twenty-fifth data line for the deaf.

At fifteen minutes to air he started getting pix out of the local SF net, plus historicals of the great San Francisco quake of the last century from the national net. He went into high gear, his fingers flying over the keyboard, weaving the new data into some sort of package.

At eleven minutes to, some local yokel was pushing hard on a jumpjet brought down by gunfire that had to make an emergency touchdown at the ruined airport. Well, Richardson would weave it in.

At ninety seconds, with the autoboard chopping

frames on Richardson's rough cut so it could splice in commercials, the national interrupted with a priority story about border fighting in Sinkiang, wherever the hell that was.

The board lit up like a Christmas tree on methacoke and started restacking on its own.

Richardson screamed at it and began punching overrides, but it was too late.

So Kay-Sass, the Voice of Wichita, went out with its top slot pushing a words-only national cut on some firefight halfway round the world—while the story of the century, the quake that for thirty years California had been fearing and the Bible Belt had been praying would punish the Sinners of Sodom, heh-heh, went into the autochop and came out custard.

Eldon Richardson knew he'd have to account for this come morning. Even if it *was* the machine's fault.

Cincinnati Transport Company cab number 909 had the last word on it, as usual.

"In Ohio we got floods. In Kansas they got twisters. In California they got quakes. In Russia they got the Chinese—and contrariwise.

"So the quake kills half a million sunbirds at one time—but it only comes once every hundred years. Our river kills what? Eight, ten people every spring. Twisters yank up a couple hundred every year. And in Asia the Reds of both colors kill a couple hundred every day.

"Take your pick of disasters. One way or another, somebody gets shot out, mudded out, blown out, or shook out. So it all evens out.

"You can only die once."

Chapter 2

Ariel Ceram: 8.8

Ariel Ceram was thirteen years old again and dizzy.
She had locked herself in the bathroom after her
last-ever fight with David, her only and forever David,
who had just said he was going to study for the
*priest*hood. He said he believed in a *god* and wanted
a *high*er love that no one else understood, that she
didn't and couldn't, and he had said he couldn't love
a person like that but he would certainly try to save
her *soul*. She had taken two, no three of the gelcaps
and the rest were getting sticky in her clenched fist.
She was trying to make the dizzy get worse because
that would mean she was dying, but she didn't want
to take another capsule because they tasted like sour
milk and moldy peanuts when you chewed them and
she didn't want to vomit and be a mess when they
found her. She tried to arrange herself gracefully on
the floor but the toilet bowl was in the way. And
then there was a pounding on the door and her
father's voice calling her name, booming on the "Ahr"
and squealing on the "iiell." Pounding on the door
and rocking the bathroom floor until—"
  Ariel Ceram woke up from the nap with her head
bouncing on the pillows and cracking once painfully
on the oak headboard of her bed. She came awake to

find that the booming, squealing, and rocking hadn't gone away with the dream. Her bedroom pitched like a cabin on a steamer in rough seas.

Earthquake!

She rolled out of bed and tried to stand. When she was thrown to her knees, she decided it was better to crawl.

Ariel headed toward the sundeck but found the sliding glass door was jammed. Beyond the deck, the tips of the trees were thrashing as in a gale.

The deck offered no escape anyway.

Ariel lived on Grizzly Peak Boulevard, along the ridge of the Berkeley Hills. Her lot sloped away from the road at better than forty degrees. The house stood on stilts, with a garage pad on top, a stairway down to the living room and kitchen, more stairs down to the bedrooms and bath. With the trees below it all. Her back yard was her front yard and the whole house had a fantastic western view of the Bay, the lights of San Francisco at night, the necklace of the Golden Gate Bridge, and whatever else might be worth seeing from a window.

It was a stupid place for a professor of geology to live.

She had always known that the Big One was coming—if not on the nearby Hayward and Calaveras faults, then on the tectonic dividing line of the San Andreas.

The inevitable was happening around her now. She knew those groans and squeaks were the house stilts gnashing themselves to splinters. If she fled across the sundeck and jumped, then she'd be downslope—with the house coming down on her heels.

As she looked out, Ariel's car rumbled across the roof, broke through the carport railing and flipped casually down into the trees. But first it smashed off the edge of the redwood decking.

She got to her feet and staggered into the bathroom, where the side windows might let her out. From there she watched a river of rocks, earth, eucalyptus litter and saplings flow past in the twenty feet of land that separated her home from her neighbor's. His house slowly walked off its legs and collapsed into the flow with a billow of dust.

Up, she decided, and out through the top.

The shaking was still going on. Ariel climbed the stairs sometimes on her feet, sometimes on her knees. It was like getting kicked to death by a soccer team.

When she reached the living room, the bookcase exploded in her face, pummeling her with bindings and flying pages. She batted them aside with her hands and fled toward the next flight up to the carport.

In the entryway at the top of the stairs, the front door knob turned freely, but the door was jammed in its frame. Ariel clutched the banister and threw her shoulder up against the door once, twice. It budged but still stuck.

Then suddenly all around her there was silence: no rumbling, no creaking, no slithering of earth. And in that thick silence, she could hear a car horn wailing somewhere below. Hers? Smashed among the trees? She also heard the gurgle of the toilet caught in an endless cycle of flushing.

The silence grew, like pillows clapped to her ears, until it was undercut by a new sound: the clawhammer shriek of wooden beams finally giving up their bolts.

One last time Ariel lunged against the door and it popped open into the late afternoon sun that slanted into the carport. The force of her blow carried her diagonally across the gravel lip of driveway and out onto the pavement of Grizzly Peak Boulevard as the house slid away behind her.

She stumbled across the road into the drainage ditch and collapsed in a faint.

*   *   *

Ariel Ceram came to in about ten minutes, feeling like she'd been beaten with a stick. A spring, newly opened in the side of the hill, had wetted the ground under her. She was sitting in the weeds along Grizzly Peak, looking out at the Bay and the evening outline of San Francisco.

It was no time for a geologist to be sightseeing. She had to get to campus, to her laboratory.

All that was left of Ariel's home was part of the fence along the road. Her bicycle was still chained to it. The key to the lock was somewhere in the rubble below, with her purse and her identification cards. But she could slide the chain off the broken post and loop the excess up over the handlebars.

It took only a minute to free the bicycle and begin her wobbling descent toward the University of California.

Ariel expected the campus to be a pile of fallen white stones and shattered glass. But there was hardly any damage she could see. A few broken windows caught the western sun. Only the 300-foot Campanile, modeled in concrete after the bell tower in Venice, showed deep cracking.

"Score one for good seismic design," she murmured. "And a couple of million in reinforcing . . ."

As she pedaled north toward the Earth Sciences building, Ariel felt the ground begin to move with an aftershock. Above her, framed by the corner of the library, the top of the bell tower swayed and sank. She could see the puffs of cement dust before she heard the snap of rebar.

Concrete chunks and bronze carillon bells showered down onto the grass. Their clatter was almost musical.

Ariel shifted gears and pedaled harder, aching with every move. To reach Earth Sciences she had to climb Cardiac Hill. Her breath was getting raw halfway up. Then she saw her grad assistant coming down toward her.

"Where ya—going, George? Seismo—graph's back 'at way."

"I was going to find a working phone to call you." George, on foot, did a knee-popping downhill U-turn to catch her.

"Phones dead? I thought y'were off to get a Coke. Are we receiving full read-ins? Ye gods—is the *power* still on?"

"Nope, the lights went first thing."

"Well, did the backups—"

"Kicked in right away. I don't think we lost more than two seconds' worth of transmission."

"Hooray for federal funding. Who's minding the store while you're down here jawing?"

"Uhm, nobody."

"Then get your ass back up there, George. If you can't move faster than an old lady like me on a bicycle, I'll burn your Adidas." She grave him a thunk on the shoulder that sent him scrambling.

At twenty-eight Ariel was probably about four years older than George, but she had to maintain the dignity of her full professorship. She reached the basement ten seconds behind him. The damage here was mostly upset: overturned chairs, a fallen book-shelf, a rack of computer tapes spilled on the floor. But her precious machines were still clicking along.

A seismograph used to be a big, slow-turning drum covered with graph paper. When a motion sensor buried somewhere nearby felt the ground move, it sent an electric signal to a pen tracing a line around the drum. The pen would wiggle like a lie detector to show how strong the movement was at that one place. Each turn of the drum represented some cycle of time—a day, a week—and someone lowly and dedicated like George would change the graph paper faithfully.

Somewhere in this basement, Ariel was sure, they had one of the dusty old relics. One of these desks probably had a stack of the yellowing paper in a bottom drawer.

Ariel's seismograph was a computer, a dedicated mini bought with her base grant. It took readings not from one sensor but from twenty-nine located around Northern California. Because the ground movements she studied could snap telephone cables and de-align microwave dishes, she used self-powered radio beacons in the narrow XUHF band. Subsidiary readings from around the Pacific Rim were gathered by other research groups and shared by reciprocal agreement.

But Ariel Ceram wasn't studying earthquakes. She did not really care what had happened to so shake her world and almost kill her with her own house. She was studying *precursors*. She wanted to know what happened *before* it happened.

With every modification of her computer program—and they were at version fifty-three rapidly moving into version fifty-seven—she kept expecting the little "event warning" display to pop onto her screen before the klaxons announced a seismic event in progress. But it never worked that way.

"Where's the epicenter?" she asked George.

He was at a graphics terminal that built up an image of the Bay Area in green with blue read-in points.

"Somewhere on the Peninsula."

"Right. Can you be more specific? Which fault, for instance?"

"Big Daddy."

"You're kidding!"

"Nope. It's the San An'-what-am."

"Got a feel for the magnitude yet?"

"Eight point something for sure. Point eight for maybe."

"The Big One." She paused. "George, there could be a dissertation in my next question."

He glanced up from the screen. "Shoot."

"Did any of our beacons go silent along the coast."

He keyed a tabular display. "Nope, every one of them checks in."

"Rats. Then California didn't fall into the ocean."

"Sorry. Better luck next time."

It was a long day for Ariel. She didn't leave her basement until five-thirty the next morning. Three times in the night Campus Security tried to evacuate her, each time with a different story about building safety, or looters, and finally leaking gas. Each time she had mumbled something about going along and then stayed glued to her computer. Besides, she had nowhere to go.

Ariel had not paused for even a minute of newscast about the quake's death and destruction. That was all surface stuff and didn't interest her.

Her head was a mile underground.

Within four hours of the quake, the seismic readings both from California and from around the Pacific's "ring of fire" had been received and catalogued in her computer files. She now sat at a graphics terminal in the lab. Ariel Ceram was playing with waves.

First she called in and catalogued the readings taken with and after the main event, the 8.8 in California.

Ariel studied the local readings, from stations in Northern California. Their magnitudes fell off in a regular pattern, a bell curve humping at the epicenter halfway between San Mateo and Half Moon Bay. Nothing unusual there—if the strongest shock ever recorded in the state could be called usual.

Next she pulled up the Pacific Rim data. These readings, reported from some three hundred stations, were sketchy. Each foreign seismic station recorded the vibrations of the Earth, logging them against a clock running on Universal Mean Time. When a major event occurred, the reporting stations had contracted to send her half-second, computer-synthesized readings for a time bracketing the event, usually an hour before and after. Some of the Rim, however, was slow to report findings—like every six months or at convention time.

Ulan Bator, Alma-Ata, and Lhasa had all reported in. Their recordings were marred by the shallow, high-frequency waves that Ceram had come to identify as small nukes. Must be a ground war in Central Asia. She would check the news later.

She fed the data into her experimental program; it took about six seconds to load all the reference points. Then she keyed the start sequence.

The computer screen first drew a slice of the planet in blue and green, outlining the crust, mantle, outer, and inner cores. Then, at the deliberate speed that such graphics programs move, it rotated the slice into a globe and drew a box at the top labeled "epicenter" for the California quake. Next would come the P (compressional) and S (shear) waves picked out in red and yellow lines, radiating down and to the sides through the cores and the mantle, neat as the fingers of a spread hand.

Or they should have come in like that.

As she watched with widening eyes, the computer dabbed and frazzled the screen with colors. They followed the general pattern of P and S waves but overlapped. They blended into fiery oranges and purples that should not have been in the graphing program's palette. They showed nothing that Ariel could understand.

She dumped the program and ran a diagnostic on the hardware, then reloaded a fresh copy of the software and the readings and keyed in the global image.

It gave her the same buzzing colors.

When the hardware and software check out, you question the data they process. But she had, if anything, fewer reporting stations than normal—not this excess of overlapping reference points that showed on the screen.

That's odd. Could there be more than one event here?

Ceram called in the readings from before the 8.8 event. These would be her "precursors." She set the program to reconstruct and display the composite samplings at one-minute intervals. Should she show the whole preceding hour? Why not?

So the stop-jerk animation began. For two and a half hours Ariel Ceram watched the graphics screen slowly build up, display and wipe fifty-nine seismic snapshots of the planet. All showed nothing much. The Earth rumbled and mumbled to itself as it always did, appearing as stress patterns, blushes and glows on the screen. But the Pacific Rim was relatively quiet.

For the final readings she reined in her impatience and slowed the interval down to one-second snapshots. It meant another two and a half hours of crouching before the graphics terminal, squinting at blips. But it paid off.

In the last five seconds a mark appeared near the epicenter—not on or under it but perhaps a kilometer away. A pattern developed: waves tumbled outward from that first hard mark like a twist on a child's kaleidoscope.

They faded but never entirely vanished.

It wasn't a seismic event, Ceram decided. It looked more like an impact, perhaps a small meteor. Then she took note of the scale on the screen and decided it was a large meteor.

Then a second or so later—the actual event was caught between her composite samples—the San Andreas bent like a bowstring and exploded, just as the mark crossed the lithosphere and was absorbed in the mantle.

And the program went into the pattern of distorted waves she had first seen.

Ariel was going to stop it and begin a major bug hunt when something told her to let the pattern play itself out. She hiked the interval back up to one minute and watched, chin on fist, as the blurry colors chased themselves through mantle and core.

At thirty-six mintues past the event, she noticed the mark again on the screen. It was in the neighborhood of Sinkiang, in the area triangulated by Ulan Bator, Alma-Ata, and Lhasa, where her readings were thinnest. This time the mark was *rising*, coming out of the globe at an angle about thirty degress toward the east.

She stopped the action and panned back to the meteor impact on the Peninsula. That mark was likewise angled about thirty degrees off the vertical, but coming from the *west*. The two marks, thirty-six minutes apart, lopsidedly bracketed the seismic event.

Just possibly the first mark was a *precursor* to the 8.8 on the San Andreas. It was as if something punched into the Earth, then came back out again.

And the distortions? The Earth had rung like a bell, like a great bronze carillon bell tapped by a child's hammer.

The sort of impact mass needed to set off the San Andreas from a kilometer away suggested a big meteorite—big enough to punch a fair-sized crater. It would have tossed melted slag and loose stones a dozen miles, into the Bay and the Pacific at the same time.

From as far away as Berkeley she should have heard the bang and seen the flash herself—or at least a cloud of dust and smoke after the fact—as she crouched in her bedroom facing the sundeck. And she remembered seeing nothing like that before the car fell past her window.

Ceram walked slowly from the lab's computer bay into her closet of an office and looked around blindly. There were the stacks of books and computer paper, the Henry Evans botanical prints on the wall, the ceramic gargoyle she'd bought from a vendor near Notre Dame. The demon's pointed chin rested in a clawed fist—Ariel's favorite thinking pose, and perhaps that's why she had bought it. Its slitted eyes looked out, slightly downward, over an imaginary city of bustling Parisian merchants and bureaucrats and scholars. The slow grin said the creature knew how pointless all their scurrying and worrying really was. It knew where all of them would end up: in dirt and perhaps in Hell.

Something had punched through the dirt south of San Francisco. Something so . . . tiny . . . that it failed to displace any of the dirt, the bedrock, the mantle below or the jellied iron of the outer core. To it, these solids were less than soft butter to a knife, less than air to a flying bullet. It had passed right through the Earth, grazed the core, probably, and exited at China—or Russia or whatever it was called this week.

That meant the object must either be moving very fast or be very massive. She hurried back to the console and punched a few keys on the computer's calc function. The evidence denied any great speed: the thirty-six-minute lag translated into an average ten kilometers per second. That wasn't very fast in astronomical terms.

She wandered around the lab, touching papers, thinking.

So the object was very massive. How much is "very"? She didn't have suffient data to say yet, except that it seemed to have an attraction—gravity, tidal effects or whatever—that yanked the San Andreas hard enough in passing to make it slip. For that kind of pull the object might have the mass of an asteroid. In a package too small to leave an impact crater.

Intuitively, Ariel realized that her presumed object would be far denser and heavier than any normal material found on Earth or in the solar system. It might—just possibly—be a piece of a neutron star: collapsed matter, so dense that atomic nuclei nestled together like marbles in a sack.

Ariel stopped in front of the gargoyle. She grinned at the monster. He grinned back.

There were fame and fortune, Nobel laurels, unlimited grant monies for the person who identified and tamed a piece of a dead star. . . .

Ye gods! Had anyone else discovered or deduced this? Could it be all over the media and poor Ariel, stuck behind her computer, not even know it?

She had to go tune in, be sure that no one else was plowing the ground ahead of her. She said a short prayer to Poseidon, the Greek god of earthquakes (among other things), that everyone would be taking this event for the Big One, simple story, been expecting it for decades, case closed.

She was about to shut down her computer program and go find a vid, when something nagged at her. The estimated speed of the object as it went through the Earth and came back out—ten point something klicks per second—was ringing a bell in the back of her head.

Ariel Ceram was a geophysicist, not an astronomer, so she was on shaky ground here: ten klicks would be an average, wouldn't it? As the object traced its deep parabolic arc around the Earth's center, it would speed up. Slow at the surface, fast near the core, slowing again back at the surface. Unh-huh. And if it *averaged* ten-something, then it was moving a good deal slower at the breakout point.

Ariel went to the bookshelf and took out a general text on physics. She rummaged in the index until she located the fact she wanted: escape velocity at the Earth's surface, 11.2 kilometers per second. She shut the book on her finger and sat down slowly, breathing deeply.

Whatever her object was, at less than ten klicks, it was going to come back.

The Berkeley brown-shingle on the shady South Side street looked solid enough. It was probably bolted to its foundation, Ariel decided. Wes was the practical kind. The water heater was probably strapped upright, too, and maybe even hot. She began to think she might get a bath, if only with a sponge.

As she rang the bell, Ariel mind-walked through the rooms. Oak floors, bone-white plaster, natural walnut paneling, leaded glass in the bookshelves, dried flowers and Chilean textiles. For three years it had been home.

An upper window, their old bedroom, opened and Wes's sleep-tousled head came out. "Who's there?"

"Me. Ariel. Let me in."

Another head, blonde, pretty, appeared beside his.

Wes glanced at the woman, then looked down at Ariel.

"It's six in the morning, Ari. Why don't you go home?"

"Home's at the bottom of the canyon now. I've been at the lab since the quake. I need a wash and a floor to sack out on."

He looked sideways at his new woman again.

"C'mon, Wes," Ariel pleaded. "The gym's full and I haven't got coin for a hotel."

"Come in then," the blonde said, "I'm Tracy."

Ten minutes later everyone was seated around the antique butcher-block table drinking instant coffee made over a Primus and eating two-day-old poppyseed cake. Wes told Ariel that the gas was out, electric service spotty, and the water seemed okay but they had a don't-flush notice because of broken sewer lines.

Wes and Tracy were dressed in house robes, Ariel in her grass-stained jeans from the afternoon before. Everyone was either too sleepy or tired to make small talk, but Tracy was trying.

"Did you get to see your house go down the cliff?"

"No, not really."

"Where were you at the time?"

"Just getting out the door, moving the other way."

"Gee."

"Then you went right to the lab?" Wes asked.

"Yes. I'm working on something new, about seismic events like this one. So I had to check the recordings right away."

"Still the dedicated scientist." He sounded sour.

"We heard it was an eight pointer," Tracy said. "But we—uhn—slept through it." She wrinkled her nose at Wes.

"Look, can I use your vid and maybe the house terminal?" Ariel asked. "I want to catch up on the big-wide before I drift off."

"Sure." He pointed with his elbow. "They're where they always were."

After the two of them went upstairs again, Ariel tuned in on the world. She gave the vid about six key words on the quake, probing cautiously for any hints about an impact crater or meteor sighting or, please-God-no, a full report on infiltration by a piece of celestial neutronium. But all she got were damage reports and five seconds of learned professor—from Stanford yet—about the mechanism of movements on the San Andreas and, yes, this was the inevitable result of tectonic creep along the fault line.

"Have I got a surprise for you, Stanford!" she whispered to the screen.

Ariel had wanted to share first news of her discovery with someone. She had thought a gentle former lover like Wesley qualified. But now, after seeing the dipchik of a blonde he was coupling with, she had cooled on the idea.

Maybe she should call George. . . . But he was such a babbler. And besides, it was bad form to chum up to the grad students with something as important as a new discovery. Let him find out after she published—unless of course she made him write the first draft.

She turned off the vid, loosened her shoes, and pulled a quilt around her on the sofa. In her head, she was already framing the abstract of her paper. A minute later she was in a formal gown of black velvet, in Stockholm, accepting the prize with a white-gloved hand.

Ariel Ceram was not a fashionable person. It had been six years since she had taken the trouble to put on eye stencil or lip gloss. She wore any old blouse and a sweater. She even wore bluejeans, and they had gone out of fashion—for everyone except harley-bums and gentlemen pot planters—before Ariel was born.

She had lifeless brown hair cut in a layered wedge that had gone out three years ago. It was supposed to be gel-sculpted and blown, but Ariel never found time, so it floated loose around her ears.

She had what her mother called "nice eyes." They were big eyes, the color of polished walnut, with flecks of yellow-gold in the iris that took people by surprise when she looked straight at them and popped her lids.

It used to work on . . . men . . . kind of worked when she was an undergrad. But it never worked well enough. Wesley had been a lucky chance.

Instead of a femme fatale, Ariel had become a scholar and a geologist. She had dreamed of finding something important, something that would make the world remember her name. A method for predicting earthquakes seemed to be worthwhile. A piece of orbiting neutron star definitely qualified.

Three days after the 8.8 on the San Andreas, Ariel was ready to file the abstract of a paper on her seismic findings. From there it was a smooth sequence of receiving plaudits at the AmGAM convention in February and picking up her Nobel the following December.

Instead of that scholarly, stately order of affairs, Ariel's head of department, with a flair for grantsmanship, had plunged her into *video*. She was going to be today's news fad. Tomorrow she might be dead fish. Unless the Earth Sciences department and the Media Relations Office kept their promises.

"More shadow, Cindy!" The voice came from off camera, amplified. "See if you can't build up those cheekbones until she at least has a face."

They had Ariel under the lights on the set of a San Francisco midnight talkie and they weren't happy.

"That hair! Murray, if you can't do something sexy with it in three-point-five seconds you're walking over to the all-night SmartMart in the Tenderloin and buying a wig! The dogs'll be eating you for breakfast."

They weren't carping about her clothes. They had run her through wardrobe fifteen seconds after she came through the street door. The scintil-slink fabric felt strange against her naked skin. They absolutely forbade her to wear a bra.

The show host drifted over with a pre-published copy of Ariel's abstract in his hand. He wore a green bib, and two women brushed at his hair and penciled his eyes. He ignored them both.

"Now, Doctor," he began. "This is great stuff. Really great. I mean, a piece of a dead star, we're going to be scooping the *National Informer* with this."

"Uh. Thank you."

"But we've got to leave out all this stuff at the beginning about *precursors*, right? It'll only confuse people. Really."

"But that's the basis, the link explaining how I first made the observation!"

"Yeah. Well. Condense it. We'll just say you were studying the Big One because it didn't look normal, and then you found the dead star. Okay? By the way, do you know *which* star it was?"

"We—uh—don't even know for certain what the object is. Neutronium is merely one hypothesis for a massive body that seems to have impacted the Earth."

The host frowned. "Honey, you've got to keep the technical talk down to a dull roar. Not 'hypothesis,' not 'neutronium.' Okay? Just 'theory'—'dead star.' Okay?"

"But it won't be accurate!"

"Honey, this is television."

Ariel bit her lip and resigned herself to botching this interview.

At least the outline of her monograph was going to hit the Chron News Service an hour after the talkie aired. She had made her department head promise that. And the full text was going into the G-Sci data base and *DataDaily* right after that. Another promise.

Now she vowed silently that she was going to get her Nobel, or she was going to get even.

"Of course, California isn't the only place that gets quakes," the Cincinnati cabbie told his fare.

"One of the biggest they ever had in this country

was in Missouri. Back in 1811. It made the Mississippi run backwards for a couple of hours and tumbled the town of New Madrid right into the river.

"Sure, they felt it here. Where do you think those potholes come from?"

Brother Mung Xi had a very good day. By the side of the road he found a bird only partly eaten by a cat. Birds were quite rare. And cats almost never gave up their prey.

About California earthquakes, or anything else to do with the mythical land of the American round eyes, he knew nothing and cared less.

Birds were good eating, his mother had once said, remembering her childhood just after the Great Patriotic War. He was eager to try one for himself.

Chapter 3

Grace Porter: ULTRAVIOLET PLUS

The evening after her aborted flight Grace Porter, bloodied and burned, returned to her home in San Francisco's Haight. The house was a reconditioned Victorian, painted light blue with white moldings so that it looked like a classic piece of Wedgwood pottery.

As she climbed the steep front steps, Grace wondered what damage she would find from the earthquake. After seeing the battered shells and fallen roofs on her trip in from the airport, she half expected to unlock the front door and have the whole facade, bay window and all, collapse into the empty foundation, just like in a Mack Sennett comedy.

The previous owner had said something about the house being immune to earthquakes—either built on bedrock or tied to the foundation, she couldn't remember. He'd used that as a reason for keeping the price high. Back then, Grace hadn't cared. She had just wanted her own San Francisco Victorian. So she took it, paid what he asked, and never gave a thought to earthquake insurance, which she couldn't afford anyway.

But now she paused with her hand on the doorknob. She turned it gently. The front door opened on the hallway, which led to more stairs up to her narrow livingroom with the white rug, Danish leather couch, the *Ficus benjamina* she'd nursed through the indoor plant plague three years ago, and the teak cluster tables. Everything seemed to be unharmed, except the *Ficus* was on its side and the pictures were hanging by the edges of their frames.

Before straightening up, Grace went into the kitchen to make some Darjeeling. The cabinets were open and mysteriously empty. Her feet crunched on glass or sand or something, and a fine white powder was sifted onto every surface. When she looked closely, she saw porcelain slivers, some with her red wheat pattern on them. So much for a cup of tea.

Porter decided to phone her company. But when she lifted the transceiver, all she got was a strange low buzzing. She assumed the channel relays were either blocked or overloaded.

Nothing to do but wash up and go to bed. Did the plumbing still have water? Jesus, this was getting complicated. After the excitement in the plane, the details of living were too exhausting.

She finally just stripped off her clothes and lay on the covers. She was asleep in one minute.

The Monday morning commute to the financial district took more than two hours on the Muni's light rail vehicle line, but everyone agreed it was a miracle the system was running at all.

For Grace Porter the trip was an agony. A spasm of vomiting had brought her awake at midnight. It never really went away, just sort of transformed itself into a draining case of the trots. She felt weak and thirsty and feared to be more than fifteen feet from a john. But here she was in a subway tunnel creeping under the city.

Grace assumed her sickness was something to do with the water. Everyone said that earthquakes damaged the pipes and let in sewage. She tried to remember when she'd last drunk from the tap.

The LRV suffered a "service disruption" at Civic Center Station, and Grace joined the crowds parading down the center of Market Street. She had nine long blocks to go. In half a block the soles of her FootPads were cut up by the broken glass, so she leaned against a wall and changed to her office shoes. They were Italian and fancy and probably wouldn't last much longer than her commute sneakers.

A single squad of mixed police and firefighters, without riot gear, tried to head off the crowd at Third. They said something reasonable about the area being closed for fear of looters. But if any looters were hiding in the mob Grace walked with, they were disguised in Prince Henry jackets and Stallone shoes. The police let them all pass.

The elevator was out of service in her office tower, so she had thirty flights to climb—more than anyone else because, as a top executive, she had one of the prestigious upper-level offices. Right now she'd trade it for a desk in the mail room.

The stairwell, to be used only in emergencies and so lacking any ventilation at all, stank of sweat and rancid perfumes. Grace's legs started to cramp at the twentieth floor. As soon as the crowd thinned out, she took off her silly Italian shoes and went in her stockings. By twenty-five the sweat was rolling down her back and arms. She was clinging to the railing and gasping thick air that must have been a hundred and two degrees.

The atmosphere was fresher in her office because there was no glass in the windows. It was scattered over the carpet and her chair in crystals about two carats in size, the way tempered glass explodes when it breaks. It looked like someone had sown diamonds with a shovel. The hanging fern had dropped onto her desk, sprinkling dirt and moss around. The computer terminal had taken a high dive off its credenza, smashing the wafer display.

The only thing that worked was the phone. Like every other morning, it had a message for her to call the chairman's office immediately. What was unusual about today was that the phone held six messages from the chairman, each one timed ten minutes after the last.

Steven Cocci, chairman of the board of Pinocchio, Inc., had an office on the thirty-fifth floor. By the time Grace climbed those last five flights her leg cramps had returned all the way up to her fanny, her stomach was knotted, and the repair job on her makeup was slipping. She was ready to quit. One day without elevators, she decided, could spell the end of high-rise civilization.

Cocci's office, like hers, had empty window frames. A stiff breeze with a few trailing vapors of fog blew through the room.

"Jesus, girl, what happened to your face?" was the way he greeted her.

Grace touched her cheek. The burn on her right side was still tender and evidently not even a heavy layer of cremecake could mask it.

"I got sunburned, I guess."

He shook his head. "I send you and Korny to do a simple bit of sales with the LiquiSteel assembly shop and what happens? You fall asleep in the sun, he gets cut to pieces, and the quake of the century busts out every window in the city. If you didn't want to go, why not just tell me?"

He was smiling, but she heard an edge to his normally bubbling voice. Steve Cocci always reminded her of Jiminy Cricket in the Walt Disney classic. He had the same round face and high forehead, the colorful square-cut coat and vest—without the elbow holes—and the same chirping manner. Also, he was about five feet tall.

"You've heard about Kornilov?" she asked. She felt suddenly guilty about not calling in last night.

"I know he's in Bayshore Medical Center with his right hand severed and a hole bitten out of his leg. Looks like he got lunched on by a barracuda. The report I received, at midnight, said he'll live—thanks to you. But he'll spend the rest of his days punching the phone with a macrohook."

"How did you find . . . ?"

"I am a powerful man, Grace. I have unusual data services at my command, and four of them help me find people who don't keep their appointments. One logs onto the booking desk of every precinct and sheriff's office from here to Salt Lake City. The second taps the passenger manifests of any airline that doesn't carry chickens in crates. And the third reads insurance billings from every hospital and clinic that staffs an emergency entrance. Korny showed up on number three."

"What about number four?" she asked, sinking—folding rather—into a conference chair without being asked.

"County morgues. But I hate to look for my friends on that one. Now, what happened?"

"Damfino, Steve." She shook her head and then steadied herself with a hand on the table. "One minute we were taking off in the jumper to LAX and the next minute Korny just fell apart."

"Okay. That's the short form. What's the detail? What really happened?"

"He reached for his *drink* and fell apart," Grace snapped. "How do I know? Suddenly he's shooting blood into the aisle and I'm counting his fingers in my lap." She hated being the hysterical woman, but her legs, her stomach cramps, the cold wind blowing through this office . . .

Cocci moved quickly to her side. With strong hands he started massaging her shoulders, careful of the burns on her neck. "Easy, easy there," he said softly. "It's all right."

She let her shoulders sag against the massage, then straightened.

"Okay," he said again, quietly. "One at a time. What happened to the plane?"

"The plane? It was fine. Took us back down to SFO, and . . ."

Her eyes unfocused for a minute. "No wait. There was a problem. While I was tying up Korny, we were 'way out of control. Some kind of a sideslip. People were screaming. And some kind of radio problem, too."

She turned to look up at Cocci. "And before Korny got busted up, there was some kind of a flash and an explosion. I thought I saw a hole in the ceiling. Do you suppose . . . Terrorists?"

There was a glint in his eye.

"What do you know?" she demanded.

"My data service worked overtime last night. I ran a check on your flight. It's officially listed as returned to point of origin with communications problems, but the FASA has impounded the flight recorder and put the plane in quarantine."

"Quarantine? You mean something medical?"

"Sounds like it."

"It wasn't a germ that sliced up Korny."

"Hardly." Steve Cocci's brows came down. "Something else for you to ponder. You're the only one who can work out the timing, but from the early newscasts I figure that your jumper was just about over the epicenter of the quake, with the first shock just kicking off, when whatever it was hit your plane and Kornilov."

"What a coincidence," Porter said without much conviction. Her legs still hurt and she felt pale and gray, except for the bright red burn marks.

"Coincidence maybe." Cocci nodded. "You may

find, as an acceptable explanation, that your plane was shot at by a sniper, motive unknown. That it was struck by ball lightning. That some effect of the quake was at work. Even that you intercepted a space warp. Well and good, but—"

"*I'll* find?" she sat more erect.

"Yes. I'm assigning you."

"Why? What about the LiquiSteel contract? What about the rest of the load on my plate? I don't know anything about snipers or space warps or earthquakes. I can't find—"

He put up a hand. "Last to first. One, you *can* do it, because you're a good data ferret. Two, give LiquiSteel and anything else to someone in your section, the way you always do when I tap you for a special job. But wait until next Monday because I've told everyone except core staff to lock their desks and take a vacation till we can get the building back together."

"And I'm 'core staff'?"

"Of course. You stay."

"Thanks, Boss. You still haven't answered the why."

"Simple. I don't like having my people cut up," he said grimly. "And I don't like mysterious forces. All right?"

"Nuh . . ." Grace took a deep breath. "No, not good enough. I'm a high-priced executive, an expensive piece of personnel to send ferreting after UFOs and—what was it?—ball lightning."

Cocci walked over and sat on the desk edge, but he had to hike his butt up to do it. He took a pinch of skin along his jaw and rubbed gently: he was trying to look relaxed and thoughtful.

"Sometimes very profitable discoveries come from the things you don't understand, from the spidery shapes that dart beyond the corner of your eye while you're looking the other way. Where this particular mystery will lead, I don't know yet. Just my enterpreneur's intuition says to follow it up. Remind me sometime to tell you how I developed the three-point sealed joint after trying my first lobster."

"But why me and not someone else?"

"True, I could send anyone to poke this thing. But you've dealt with it, firsthand. You'll not only find an answer but be able to tell if it *feels* right, seems congruent with what you heard, saw, sensed—and remembered. All right?"

"Right, Steve." She dragged herself up from the chair, thinking about the five and thirty flights she had to walk down.

Cocci fished something out of his vest pocket and tossed it to her.

Grace caught it offhanded and winced at the movement.

"What's this?" It was a key.

He waved her away. "Operates the chairman's private elevator, which still works though it's hanging by one cable. Drop that with Security when you leave the building."

She nodded and limped out of the suite.

When Grace got back to her office, she found that Maintenance had taped a sheet of black plastic over the window. It sucked and snapped in the wind, making an erratic noise that soon drove her crazy. The lights were off on her side of the building because of trouble in the power system, so her office was a dark and noisy cave.

Grace packed up her notebooks and fled to the library. Because this space was in the building interior, it was quiet and well lit. It had only two bookshelves and both had overturned. The rest of the room was booths for on-line access terminals and microfiche readers.

Best of all, there was a women's john right outside in the corridor. Grace felt the need coming on again.

After cleaning up, she took a terminal booth and pulled the privacy hood. On the screen she began scoping a search program by listing Cocci's alternatives: "sniper, ball lightning, quake." She dismissed the space warp as undefined territory.

She gave thirty seconds' thought to other possibilities and came up dry. Those three were it. Nail one and she could go back to the LiquiSteel campaign. But first she had to weight her three alternatives by probability.

Blaming the accident on sniper fire was an attractive way out of her problem.

As a maker of industrial automata, Pinocchio, Inc. was a controversial company. The robots born at the very end of the Industrial Age had been no more than pad-mounted arms with limited functions: pick and place, spray paint, spot weld. Pinocchio's steel-collar laborers were as far advanced over those brutes as a piano sonata is over a gong solo. Their standard line featured self-actualization, full sensorium, high discretion, and a point-triple-oh-one error rate.

Some of the specialty products presented capabilities that no other designer except Nature herself had achieved: bipedal gait with three-axis balancing, stereo-optic vision with selective focusing and color perception, pattern analysis and matching of incompatible sensory inputs.

Most of the company's products were designed to perform hazardous tasks in harsh environments where humans could not or would not work: ocean-floor drilling and mining, reactor core maintenance, outer-orbit structural assembly, Antarctic heavy construction. But Grace knew a number of reactionary unions that viewed Pinocchio, Inc. as an unfair competitor in any labor market. Perhaps one of them had arranged to place a man with a rifle in the hills . . . ?

She pondered that and had to discard it. The jumpjet she and Kornilov were flying had been above

15,000 feet when it was "hit." Grace's references said three miles was too high for any commercially available rifle to shoot, even if a marksman could sight at that range. Besides, who could know that speck in the sky was the very plane that Pinocchio personnel were traveling on? Who could know which seat—and then hit it?

What about a bomb planted aboard the plane?

The damage was too selective; Grace herself would have been hurt as badly as Kornilov if it had been explosives.

What about a pre-aimed, remotely fired pistol that had been mounted below Kornilov's seat and fired upward into his leg and wrist, with the bullet then passing out through the cabin ceiling?

The damage was too small. If Grace were designing such an assassin's weapon, she would have aimed it further back in the seat, to penetrate the body cavity and possibly the spinal column. And the setup would be too easily discovered and traced, unlike a bomb, which disposes of itself.

What about . . . a mindlock on red, raving paranoia? She just couldn't make a case for malice aforethought.

Now, the accident had been somewhere over Crystal Springs Reservoir. Grace knew that a cluster of Pinocchio's Patrol Rovers was deployed there to protect the city's drinking water.

Drinking . . . Porter gulped, clutched her stomach and dashed for the hallway.

When she was finished in the stall, Grace stepped up to the sink. Hollow eyes looked out from the mirror. Even glitter and shadow couldn't make them look nice. She looked sick.

Grace took a brush to her hair and felt something give way. Every morning her brush pulled out ten or a dozen rose-gold strands; she knew because she counted each one jealously, although the magazines said it was normal. But this? She stared at a clump of hair, like something you'd pull off a horse in the spring.

Bending toward the mirror, she studied her scalp. There was a bald patch near the hairline. It wasn't bleeding, but the skin didn't look too good.

A wave of nausea hit her. She held on to the sink till it passed, then walked shakily back into the library.

The Rovers at Crystal Springs, yes. It would be ironic if one of them had malfunctioned, tracked the plane up, then fired on it with a weapon. What weapon? Grace tapped the terminal and quickly checked the armaments on the Rover series: nothing stronger than a stunner and a shot tube.

So, all in all, the assassin hypothesis looked pretty weak.

What about ball lightning? What *was* it, anyway?

Static discharge, the refnet said. Grace discovered it had been credited for decades with occasionally punching holes in fuselages. Was that a reasonable explanation of what happened? Maybe.

Ball lightning was related to Saint Elmo's fire, but involved more energy. However, every reference she could muster showed it as a relatively slow-moving phenomenon, its forces caught in some sort of equilibrium. Not the flash and bang that Grace thought she remembered.

The third alternative, quake-related activity, looked slimmer than the case for a sniper. Perhaps the San Andreas fault had shot out a fast-moving chip of rock. But even with the huge energy release of an earthquake, could flying debris touch a plane three miles up? Unlikely.

The terminal showed an intriguing cross reference to a study of energy discharges in connection with seismic stresses and earthquakes: flashes of light that might be piezoelectric in origin.

Bingo? Perhaps, although it was hard to believe

any ground-based electrical effect would reach to 15,000 feet.

Back to ball lightning . . .

Grace decided she needed a real-world orientation for all this. She wanted to see the plane again, even if it was in "quarantine."

She located it with a bit of illegal snooping in federally controlled nets. The jumpjet had been moved to a hangar at Oakland International because of the damage at SFO. All right . . . With some push-pull she'd learned at a hacker's seminar, Grace arranged an evening visit by one Angela Kelley, Federal Air Safety Advisory inspector from the Sacramento office. She hoped to find some sleepy guard who would accept a flash of her Girl Scout Peregrine card as proper identification.

A fit of the sweats overtook her, and once more Grace dashed for the john.

Angela Kelley was an older woman, Grace decided as she studied her face in the mirror two days later.

No makeup would really cover those tired eyes or brighten that gray pallor. She thought of dying her hair something mousy to match the face but was afraid that chemicals would damage it even further. Instead she chose an unfavorite wig and dyed that. Then she combed it back and did her best to make a ratty bun. With her glasses—her eyes were hurting too much for contacts anyway—the effect was perfect. She looked like death. Or fifty-five. Whichever came first.

Grace turned on the overhead light and shot three flat holos of herself against the white bathroom tiles. She scissored the print small and laminated it to her doctored Scout card. Finally she put the new identification under her heel and scrubbed it twenty times back and forth on each side. The result looked like it had been in her wallet for years.

With the Bay Bridge out and the BART tube operating on limited service only, Grace had to drive to Oakland International. It was more than a hundred miles going around the South Bay through San Jose. That made her badly late, which was good.

The guard on the closed hangar at Oakland's North Field hardly glanced at her identification. He was even less interested in her. A baggy tweed suit, flat shoes, and oversized purse and briefcase hid her figure, and she burlesqued the role of the WASP bureaudrone: sexless, efficient, and tired.

She found that the Mr. Charles who was to have shown her the jumpjet had gone home half an hour ago. So much the better. But he had left her a gray folder, stamped "Confidential," with a summary report. Excellent!

The AmAir jumpjet stood on its spindly landing gear behind a ceremonial barrier of yellow-and-black mylar tape strung between orange pylons. Every sixteen inches along the tape were the word "Caution" and the three triangles that meant radiation hazard.

Seeing those, Grace felt cold.

About half the overhead lights in the hangar were off, casting some deep shadows. The door on the jumper's port side was open, with thick cables snaking out of it. A plain tubular-steel ladder hung from door to pavement.

Porter did the prudish woman thing, ducking under the low-slung tape instead of stepping over and exposing her legs. The klutz effect was perfect. She took out a clipboard and a cheap pen and walked once around the plane, staring up at it intensely and making meaningless notes.

The plane looked fine to her.

She eyeballed the underside in the area where she and Korny had been sitting. It was in shadow, but she pulled a two-cell flash out of her purse and played it on the aluminum skin. This far back on the fuselage, AmAir's sunburst paint job was all deep reds and tans. The loops and swirls made it hard to concentrate, and Grace's head was throbbing.

Then she saw it: a puncture, about an inch across, wide as a golfball, pulling out a tatter of broken metal. Not much of a hole at all. Grace clicked off her flash, took out a holocam and strobe-shot the puncture from three different angles.

Grace went around to the open door. She climbed the ladder in a half-crouch, with both hands, trying to look just like a woman who had never climbed anything harder than stairs. The last part, getting from the top rung to the cabin, really *was* hard. She had to do a tuck roll over the door frame. Once inside she sat down, dumped the purse and briefcase on the carpeting, and pulled out the preliminary report.

It said, in guarded language, that some sort of radiation release, nature and source unknown, had burned out the plane's comm links, sensors and computers. The report also said that exposure of the passengers was likely to be within acceptable tolerances.

The language of that part was so emphatic that Grace felt worse instead of better.

The report finished with a note about an unrelated disturbance between passengers that apparently resulted in a knife attack.

Grace bit down on the discovery that life is naturally unfair.

She stuffed the folder into her case and went forward to the flight deck.

It looked like a bomb had gone off there. Half the instruments had been yanked from the panels, and some of the components were stacked on the pilots' and engineer's seats. Most of the equipment had bright red tags wired on. Grace glanced at a tag; there was just a serial number and the words "Recondition [ ] Recalibrate [ ]" with a grease-pen check in the first box. The scene went into her holocam.

Porter went back into the passenger section. Everything looked normal, except for the blood stains in the aisle carpeting and on the seats she and Korny had been using. It was now a dull brown and someone had wiped at it just once.

The carpet *under* the seats was unmarked and unstained. It looked like a new patch in the runner. The cushion on Korny's seat was cut to pieces—but it seemed to be the work of an attendant trying to remove the worst-stained fabric.

Grace looked at the overhead panel and paused. She took out her flash and studied it: no fracture. The panel also looked new.

She caught it all with half a roll of film.

Back at the doorway, Grace gathered her impedimenta and crept down the ladder. She wanted to climb on top of the plane and search for a companion to the puncture underneath, but that might attract the guard's attention.

There was a gallery running along the short wall of the hangar, near the plane. She went to the bracket ladder at its end and climbed up. Then she walked north until she could see past the tail.

Nothing.

She pretended to make a note on her clipboard, then dragged out the holocam. Grace used the long lens to study that particular area of the fusage. She was rewarded with a shadowed dimple as big as her palm. Grace's camera strobed; she walked three paces left, strobed; three paces right and strobed again.

That was all the damage she'd seen: two small holes, irregular bloodstains, and a litter of instruments yanked out of the cockpit. She looked hard at the engines, but they didn't even have the cowlings off. The wings and landing gear looked clean.

Grace climbed down, ducked under the warning tape, and walked with a knock-kneed man-stride back toward the guard. He accepted her wave with hardly a nod and let her out into the night.

It was after midnight when Grace finished writing up the notes on her secret visit to Oakland International's North Field. She was at home, and the old Victorian's nightly creaks and snaps as it settled on its foundations were an unsettling counterpoint to her keystrokes on the data terminal. To provide a light layer of distraction, she had turned on the Choosy News Channel and let it babble quietly behind her.

Out of the verbal soup, the word "quake" went ping in her subconscious. Grace looked around.

The channel was doing its real-time syntho-sampling from the vidisat. The clip was from one of those talk shows where a lion-tamer host with a picket-fence smile unleashes a studio audience of the nouveau unemployed—everyone from Ma and Pa Kettle On Welfare to the warlords of the Hayward Jaquecaderos—upon some unsuspecting victim, who was usually some frightfully earnest dolt with a silly-season product or viewpoint to sell. It's no fun unless the victim cracks: either tears or tantrums are acceptable. Watching someone be heckled to death, Grace decided, evidently had the same entertainment value as the lion feeds of Old Rome.

She gave it ten seconds—the network would give it twenty at most—to figure out where the word "quake" had come in. It wasn't obvious. The victim this time was a pretty young woman in call-girl makeup and clothing. She was trying to hold her composure against an avalanche of bitter laughs. But why would a hooker be talking about the technical side of an earthquake?

". . . indication that this was *not* a normal seismic phenomenon. Observations indicate a massive object—"

"I *objects* to your line of *bull*shit, honey!"

"You ain't never lost *your* home and all your fine things!"

"We've been through the *Big One*, baby!"

"Don't spoil it!"

The clip ended and the anchor closed the story with a polite chuckle about the latest crackpot findings from the Berkeley campus. He mumbled the windup and Grace barely caught the name: Real Saram.

Or something like that.

It was late. Grace was tired and feeling sick again. But just out of curiosity she closed off her notes file and put the terminal on line. It took about two minutes to frame a search of the science data bases for "Saram," with "seismic" and "Berkeley" as key words out of context. She backed up the search with null sorts for one and two wrong characters on "Saram."

Then she let the terminal hunt for itself while she went to bed.

In the morning, Grace's terminal had a file of abstracts from the collected works of Ariel Ceram, Ph.D. of Earth Sciences at U.C.B. The last item in the file was "An astronomical reinterpretation of the Crystal Springs event, 2014/J." It had been entered on the data base about one o'clock that morning.

If Grace had started her search an hour earlier, she would have missed it.

After parking more than a mile from the Berkeley campus—because of the stickers and the blue zones and not because of quake damage—Grace Porter found her way to the basement lab in the Earth Sciences building.

Professor Ceram was hunched in front of an elaborate data terminal. She was the same young woman from the vidshow, but now wearing a sweater and no makeup. She barely looked up at Grace, dismissed her with a head shake when Grace knocked on the open door.

"I'm Grace Porter . . . from Pinocchio, Incorporated . . . I called to ask you about the earthquake. . . ."

"You want a consultant?" Ceram didn't take her eyes off the screen in front of her. "I give advice away free. Here's your dose.

"Buy earthquake insurance. Keep paying the premiums. In a year or two you'll have paid in the total value of whatever it is you're covering—which should tell you what the insurance carriers think about living in California. One day you'll get your money back, minus a whopping deductible. On that day, stand in a doorway or crawl under a desk. You'll probably live to collect.

"I thought you'd take a hint from the raspberry I left on your answering machine. I don't do commercial consulting. Especially not now, with so much insurance litigation coming out of the woodwork. If I get dragged into 'expert testimony,' I'll never finish my research."

"It's your research I want to discuss, Professor."

Grace was tired, felt as if she had sand grating in her joints. She looked around for a chair but saw only computer terminals with tiny castored seats, all of them piled with books and papers except the one Ceram was using.

She began again, patiently. "I saw you on the vid—"

"Oh. That." The woman's face curled into a sneer.

"And I've read your abstract on the earthquake. Something about a 'massive astronomical body' . . ."

Porter sank down on the edge of a terminal stand, holding herself upright with one hand on the screen. "I want to know more about this piece of neutronium, Professor. In particular, how big you estimate it to be."

Ceram swiveled toward Grace. Her face straightened and her brown eyes grew large. "I was just polishing the calculations on that." Her voice was perceptibly warmer.

"From the way it twanged the San Andreas Fault," Ceram said, "the object has given me readings on its gravitational field strength at a distance of about a kilometer. The acceleration works out to be point-oh-oh-oh-two-six meters per second squared. Or about ten times the Moon's tidal pull at the Earth's surface."

"Oh," said Grace. She could feel her lids drooping with fatigue.

"Nothing you'd cross the street to avoid, but enough to bother land masses like the Pacific Plate."

"But how big is this object?"

"That field corresponds to a mass of about four billion metric tons."

"How much is that in terms I understand?"

"If I gave you that weight in steel—say a bunch of old Chevrolets crushed into cubes two feet on a side—they'd add up to a small mountain of blocks."

"That's too big," Grace protested. "Something like that couldn't possibly have struck the . . . ground."

"You're right. But—aha!—we're talking about something much more dense than steel. Neutronium is tightly packed neutrons. It has none of the empty space that fills the inside of normal atoms. So our object is quite a bit smaller than the mountain of Chevies."

Grace held out her hand, thumb, and finger circling a golfball-sized space. "That big?"

The professor looked at the hand for a long minute. "Could be . . ." Then she shook her head. "Probably bigger, like a softball."

"*That's* no good!" Grace sagged against the terminal screen with a sigh.

"You're looking for something specific, aren't you? What?"

Slowly, trying not to juggle the facts, Grace told about the jumpjet, about her fight to put tourniquets on Kornilov, about her examination of the fuselage at Oakland International. She fished out the holostrips she'd taken in the hangar as proof.

Ceram absorbed it all. Halfway through, she started nodding. There was a wicked gleam in her eyes.

"What a remarkable piece of luck," the professor said when Grace had finished. "The first person to walk in the door and you're my corroboration."

Grace looked blank. "But it doesn't work! Nothing as big as a softball tore through that plane. Here are the holes."

"So? If the theory doesn't fit the facts, change the theory."

"To what?"

"Slow down. You just brought in some new facts. I'm not a sausage machine, you know, peddling baloney by the yard."

"Maybe I'm not *your* set of facts. This could all be just a coincidence."

"Yeah. Sure. I'd believe that, probably, if your jumpjet was five miles from my observed exit point and the holes through it lined up *side*ways. But— naw!—it's not common sense to look for two separate and unexplained events going on in the same place at the same time. Occam's razor hacks that kind of thinking right to pieces."

"We thought the damage—to the plane and to Korny—might be from a sniper."

Ceram wrinkled her nose. "At fifteen thousand feet? You must be desperate for alternatives. No, let me show you the path of this thing."

The professor swiveled to another computer screen and typed some commands. While Grace watched, the screen built up a globe in brilliant, frazzled colors. Ceram pointed to a faint line in the sequence that she was sure meant something. Grace didn't know what to believe. Maybe the fizzy colors were the sign of deep vibrations from a heavy object. Maybe the screen just needed tuning.

"Make you a deal," the professor said. "Let me take your holopix for a day or two and try to triangulate some measurements off them."

Grace hesitated.

"It would be useful to both of us."

Grace reached across with the strips and had to rise from her perch on the terminal table. Her foot slipped and she sat back down hard. Ceram was at her side quickly, supporting her to the chair the professor had just left.

"You're obviously ill. What is it?"

"Bad water. I've had some lower intestinal cramps."

"You look worse than that. Tired all the time?"

"The last few days."

"You're losing hair. Vomiting too?"

Grace nodded.

"And some kind of burn. But only on one side. Where'd you get that?"

"On the jumpjet."

"If I had any doubts about the connection between my discovery and your plane accident," Ceram said, "your condition would nail them."

"My cond . . . What condition?"

"I can't tell until we get you to a doctor for proper tests. But I'd say you've had one hell of a dose of ionizing radiation. Almost certainly from our pile of crushed-up Chevies, or whatever it is."

Grace was suddenly cold. "Am I going to get cancer?"

Ceram looked bleak. "It's a possibility—if you don't die in the next week."

Grace leaned forward and threw up on the floor.

Chapter 4

Eldon Richardson: PILLAR OF FIRE

After six years on the Farm Report, Eldon Richardson had learned that hog farms were the worst. If it wasn't the smell, it was the liquid mud. And all hog farmers were slightly crazy. It was probably the smell and the mud.

Jesse Rebstock was probably the craziest of them all. And mean, too, if Richardson was any judge of such men.

Rebstock trotted Eldon and his vid operator all over the farm. Showed him where the great-grandfather had run a still. Showed him where the second cousin had been mobbed and eaten by hogs at a birthday party. And showed him where the pillar of fire had come out of the ground and risen into Heaven last Tuesday night.

Out of a mud hole that looked about twenty feet deep. Through a corner of the feed shed with a bite about eighteen inches across. Not smooth but ragged, like a pair of teeth had chewed and pulled on the galvanized metal.

"Went up like a shooting star," said Rebstock. And Emma Mae, Mrs. Rebstock, nodded like gospel.

Eldon used a hand signal to move the vid operator in on Rebstock. "Will you show me?"

53

The hog farmer crouched down over the hole, wrapped his brown hands around an imaginary column and threw them skyward, bouncing up on his tiptoes.

"Went up like a Independence Day rocket, with a bang and a swoosh and a sizzle. Looked like the public fountain in Colwich, all white and frothy and burning bright. Hurt my eyes to look at her."

"It came *down*, you mean," Richardson said with a straight face, testing.

"No sir! What have I been telling you? It came *up*. Out of the ground." Rebstock pointed down the hole. "There!"

"Did anyone else see this, besides you and Mrs. Rebstock?"

A glint came into Rebstock's eye. "Only about two hundred prize razorbacks. It damn near served up General Stuart there before his time."

Eldon motioned the vid to get a closeup of the jostling hogs.

"Any ideas about what it was?" he asked Rebstock.

"Well! I do believe it was a sign."

"From Heaven?"

"Or from that other place. We are at the millennium, sir. The power of darkness has grown fearful strong. Strong enough, perhaps, to make war on Heaven with Heaven's own weapons."

"Ay-men," Emma Mae said harshly.

"How do you feel, Mr. Rebstock, about the power of darkness using your farm for a battleground?"

"Proud to be singled out. And afraid. But gladder that it should happen here than in some schoolyard, full of young 'uns."

"That's a noble thought, Mr. Rebstock." Eldon rolled his eyes at the vid man.

"Of course," the farmer went on, "they'll soon be growing up right quick. No time for childhood. Not with the end so near." There was a crazy light in the farmer's face.

Eldon nodded. "That's a wrap," he said quietly to the vid operator.

"Crap, sir? Do you dispute me?" The light shone brightly in Rebstock's eyes now.

"Uh-no. I said 'wrap.' That's technical talk for—for we've run out of film."

"I see." The bristles came down on his neck. "Well, you have your story. Best you go and tell it to the world. The end is near."

The KSAS Farm Team waded through the black mud to their truck. They passed close to the hog that Rebstock had identified as General Stuart. If Eldon Richardson had ever seen a sick pig, this was it. Only the labored breathing showed it was still alive. From the glazed eye and the sores, it might have been dead already.

Later that afternoon the KSAS news producer sat for about thirty-three seconds of the sequence, then told them to deadfile it.

"There's no way to play it, El," she said. "The guy dug that hole himself and tore up his roof with tin snips. Or his neighbors did for a joke."

"I don't know," Richardson said, undecided. "The hole looked pretty deep. Too deep and too messy for a joke."

"That's beside the point. What's our editorial slant on this one? If we synch you in for a grinning disbeliever and play it for yucks, then we'll have half the Revelationists in the state howling through the studio, looking for your blood.

"And if we synch you as straight, maybe a little sympatico, then we get the same horde of crazies. And they'll have everything from double-yolked eggs to jars of well water soured by lightning as a sign that the end of the world is at hand.

"Now you can go ahead and watch the parade, or you can UV the sequence. The choice is yours."

Richardson reached behind him and stuck the tape wafer in the cooker.

"But I still say the hole was too deep."

Andros 'Aitopoulos was the biggest used-car dealer in the Peloponnese. His great-grandfather had been the country's biggest trader in horses. The legend, no doubt put about by unfriendly competitors, was that not all of the grandfather's horseflesh had its registration papers in order, either. So 'Aitopoulos was carrying on a family tradition.

He preferred to think of himself as a financier and transportation magnate, just like Onassis. Except that his trade was for the road, not the sea. It was all a matter of scale and opportunity.

But 'Aitopoulos knew the opinions of his competitors. He also knew their petty ways. They came immediately to mind when the manager of his lot in Argos, second biggest of his properties, told him about the antique Fiat Strada.

It seemed that the hard Greek sun had risen that morning to shine on row after row of dusty bonnets and smeared windscreens. All except for the Strada thirteenth from the end in the fifth row.

The car was a burned-out hulk. Four charred wheels and some scrap metal. The unit body was caved in, the roof destroyed, the side panels sucked in like a sun-dried fish skin. The manager couldn't even find the engine block. And the cars on all sides around it had smoke damage and paint blisters.

"So what did the night watchman see?" 'Aitopoulos asked into the phone.

"Nothing."

"Drunk or paid off?"

"He admits to being in the toilet. He heard nothing. Perhaps he dozed off."

"Convenient. But why should they have blown up only the one car? And in the middle of the lot? And such a useless one? Why not something expensive and Japanese?"

"I don't know, Kyros. Shall I ask these questions of the police?"

"You will ask the police *nothing*! If you have been enough of a fool to call them, send them away. Say that the battery shorted out and the petrol tank exploded."

"Yes, yes, of course."

"The police have been trying to sneak onto my lot for years. And the first thing they would want to see are *records*. You understand? After that come impounds. Then court inquiries. Then bankruptcies. You understand, you spawn of a goat!"

"Yes, Kyros."

"And if I must walk that path, then you will walk it before me!"

"Yes, Kyros."

"Good. See that the matter is handled discreetly. And see to it yourself that our friends do not go unrewarded. Tonight. Two cars, this time."

'Aitopoulos put down the phone. It would be weakness to let such a joke go too long unappreciated. Or to remain the butt of it.

Chapter 5

Ariel Ceram: NIBBLE, NIBBLE

Ariel Ceram took the Porter woman to Alta Bates Hospital Annex and stayed with her through Admitting. She explained to the Emergency resident that Grace was suffering from radiation sickness. The interns moved quickly then, slapping on a glucose IV, taking blood and urine samples. The resident bit his lip for two minutes and then ordered a complete blood replacement. They swabbed, scanned, thumped, and probed. They wrung her out and filled her up.

Through it all, Ariel sat against the wall and watched. Her mind kept chewing on Grace's story.

Porter was the center of attention in the emergency room, and she looked like death: thin and gray like an old bedsheet. One side of her face and neck was glazed and leathery from the radiation burn. She was taken to a semi-private room shared with three quake victims, mostly lacerations.

At eight that evening a short, bald man with a round face, dressed in a fashionable square-cut business suit, walked out of the gloom by the foot of Grace's bed. He peered at her with a hard frown, reached down without looking, and put a hand on her wrist.

"No pulse, if that's what you're feeling for, Steve." Grace said from the pillow.

"A comedienne. You feel cold."

"It comes in flashes. Sometimes like I'm baking, sometimes the deep freeze."

"We called Bayshore Med Center as soon as we heard. Kornilov has the same symptoms. Now they're treating him for quote radiation sickness unquote, too. Whatever that means . . ."

"Poisoning." Ariel said, still against the wall in her straight chair.

He turned to stare at her.

"Hard radiation," she continued, "like stray neutrons, will knock atoms and molecules apart inside the body. They become new elements, new substances. The more radiation you get, the more changed molecules. Some of them are poisons; all of them are the wrong thing in the wrong place. So cells die. Enough radiation and you don't survive."

"Do they know how much I got?" Grace asked.

Ceram shook her head. "You measure exposure while it's going on, with a film badge or a geiger counter. After the fact, all you can do is look at how sick the patient is, then make a guess."

"Have they . . . the doctors made a guess about me?"

"When you stop getting worse, when you start getting better, then they'll guess."

"Humph!" said the man.

"Exactly," Ariel agreed.

"What about cancer and . . . birth defects?" Grace asked.

"The radiation also knocks around the chromosomes, both in your own cells and in the eggs you carry. Enough radiation, and some of those cells will go bad, go to cancer.

"Some of your eggs are also certainly damaged. But that happens to everyone through cosmic rays, background radiation, chemicals. You just have a higher percentage of bad chances. For you it will be monthly roulette with a lot more red on the table than black."

"Grace, is this your doctor?" the man asked stiffly.

"No. Professor Ceram is the seismic expert I went to see about our 'mystery.' Ariel—may I call you that?"

Ceram nodded.

"Ariel, this is my boss, Steve Cocci, chairman of Pinocchio, Inc."

Cocci dipped his head in Ariel's direction, then turned back to Porter. "Do you, or she, have any idea how you got exposed?"

"On the plane," Grace said. "Somehow."

"Were they carrying isotopes? Was there a leak of some kind?"

"Nothing like that. I got a look at the jumpjet in Oakland. The 'quarantine' has something to do with radiation, origin unknown. And I found marks where a small object punched through the fuselage. In the top and out the bottom. Right about where Korny and I were sitting."

"A bullet?"

"No, it was . . ." Grace looked over at Ariel. "Something came out of the sky. It was big enough that Professor Ceram's computer could see it shaking the Earth."

"What was it?"

"We're dealing with an object," Ariel interrupted quietly, "that is physically small and yet massive. Massive enough to have its own measurable gravity well.

"I thought at first we were dealing with a *goblin*— Zwicky's name for a tiny fragment of a neutron star. But, from the punctures Grace describes in the jumpjet, I now believe we're dealing with something smaller and even more malevolent."

"Goblin," Cocci repeated softly.

"Ever since I heard her story this afternoon, I've been thinking about the emissions. Ultraviolet plus ionizing radiation plus a lot probably in between— they're the giveaway. A particle of neutronium probably wouldn't radiate at a bunch of frequencies like this. Neutron stars are like beacons, focused on one frequency. Hell, a lump of neutronium that's less than stellar mass couldn't exist, because it would need tremendous outside pressures even to hold together.

"My guess now is that our object is a black hole."

Cocci wrinkled his brow. "A black . . . I thought those were huge things, collapsed stars or galaxies or something."

"A *micro* black hole," Ariel corrected herself. "They've just been theory since British cosmologist Stephen Hawking first proposed them in the '70s. Micro black holes are supposed to be knots of superdense matter left over from the disruptions of the Big Bang. But no one has ever detected such an object."

"Then why should you think we have one here?" Cocci asked.

"Nothing else fits our facts."

"This thing is radioactive?"

Ariel shifted in her chair. "Not by itself, no.

"Alone, hanging in a vacuum, it's a high-grade form of nothing. A focus point of gravity. A 'singularity' . . . The black hole is matter so compressed that it takes itself right out of the normal time-space continuum. So compressed that not even light moves fast enough to rise out of its gravity well.

"It cannot radiate anything—not light on any wavelength, not atomic particles, nothing. But its gravitational field attracts other matter, pulling it down— hard!—at very high speeds. Air molecules, dust, bits of earth, pieces of the plane and your friend Mr.

Kornilov. These things begin a long slide down to the center of the black hole. As they go, they move faster and faster, approaching the speed of light. The speed pulls this material apart into a paste of sub-atomic particles. These form an 'accretion disk' in their jostling to get into the hole.

"That atomic disintegration is what causes the radiation," Ariel went on, warming to her subject as a lecturer. It was an antisocial habit, she reminded herself.

"Judging from Grace's sunburn and the fact that no one reported an intense burst of visible light, I'd say that ultraviolet light was the largest part of the emission. And it's a lucky thing that neither you, Grace, nor Kornilov were looking directly toward the path of the object. Or else you'd probably have been blinded."

"What about the radiation sickness?" Cocci asked. "Did ultraviolet cause that?"

"No. Maybe x rays. Gamma rays. Neutrons from dying nuclei. It's anybody's guess what will come out of the soup of a black hole's accretion disk. None of it is friendly to human life. Nor, from what Grace told me about that jumpjet's instruments, to electronics."

"If we knew what the radiation was," Cocci asked slowly, "could it help Grace get better?"

Ariel shrugged. "It's not a virus or bacterium we're dealing with, or even a specific kind of poisoning. There's no serum or antidote we can offer her. She has a general toxic condition that can only be treated as the doctors are doing. Flush her out and watch her.

"Besides, the emissions of the black hole's accretion disk depend on its diet—on the dynamics of its environment. It would change if we tried to isolate and study the object. The disk will probably be radically recomposed by the time it comes back again."

"Comes back?" Grace whispered from the bed.

"Yes, something else I found. The object's speed puts it well below the Earth's escape velocity. It's now in orbit around and probably through the planet."

Grace sank back against the pillows, paler than ever.

Cocci was staring at Ariel thoughtfully.

In two days' time Ariel got a call from Mr. Steven Cocci's secretary inviting her to lunch at the New Poodle Dog at the Galleria. Ariel guessed that it wasn't because he was fascinated with her body.

The glass arcade of the Old Galleria had suffered badly in the quake. Plyboard now filled in the frames, leaving a gloom that was only made worse by the two or three dozen panes still letting in sunlight.

As befitted a restaurant claiming a heritage from Gold Rush days, the Poodle Dog was struggling along bravely when most others were closed for repairs. However, Ariel's water came in a glass with a chip out of the base, and her butter plate was cracked.

Cocci's approach wasn't much of a wooing. Half-way through the salad he said that Pinocchio, Inc. wanted to hire her as a consultant to study the micro black hole. He named a per diem figure that, compared to Ariel's university salary, sounded like a per monthem.

She put down her fork slowly, thinking hard.

"Most high-tech companies," she said, "have a standard clause in their employment contracts about the rights to patents, processes, discoveries and so on. Usually it reserves those rights for the company, not the employee or the consultant. Is that, um, how it is with your contract?"

He speared a cherry tomato and popped it into his mouth. "Yes, I suppose so. Though I haven't read it in years, really."

"I'd have to think about that."

Ariel knew that the Nobels didn't go to the first

scientist who described an unusual condition like her seismic trace. She already had that hammerlocked with her technical abstract filed in the data bases. No, the prizes—and the fame, glory and future grants—went to the one who showed what it meant. By publishing early, she had become vulnerable: her findings were now public property for others to build on.

Besides, her paper had proudly—and now wrongly —guessed that the object was a goblin of neutronium. The physical reality of the object and her new black hole theory were waiting out there for anyone to find and proclaim. Probably someone with a lot more theoretical astronomy under the belt than she had.

The only new data Ariel had to work with were the memories of and holopix taken by Grace Porter, a loyal Pinocchio employee. The airline had never publicly acknowledged the jumpjet accident. All this was tricky enough. Ariel didn't want to be axed at the last minute by some finicky legal clause that was originally designed to protect trade secrets like robot elbow joints or eyeball control circuits.

". . . the offer won't stand forever," Cocci was saying. "Of course, the sum I mentioned is subject to a certain amount of revision."

"I simply want to protect my interests," Ariel said.

Cocci grunted. "It has occurred to me that for studying a celestial object like this we probably need an astronomer, not a geologist."

Ariel's heart clutched but she kept her cool. "Just a minute, please. *I'm* the one who found it."

"You've told us about an interesting theory concerning our accident, Professor," he said breezily. "That's all."

"But it was my equipment that traced the object!"

"And it was the experiences—not to mention the pain and suffering—of my two employees that confirmed it for you."

"You won't be able to claim credit for the discovery. You haven't the hard data."

"We can get it. Probably for a good deal less money than you're willing to accept."

"The money isn't the problem."

"I'm sure it isn't," he said with a straight face.

"The first person who proves the existence of a black hole, why, that person will be famous forever."

"Really? I thought they were all over the sky. In the center of our galaxy. Just everywhere."

"There are unexplained phenomena," she said cautiously, "which the black hole hypothesis seems to fit. But . . ."

"That's all we have here then." He dabbed his lips with a napkin. "An unexplained phenomenon."

"But this is right here on Earth, you ninny!" Ariel's voice, pitched low through gritted teeth, stopped conversation at the next table. "It's moving *through* the Earth. We can capture this little sucker and take it apart."

"Now *that's* an interesting thought," he said, as if surprised.

"It's the only thought worth thinking right now."

"My company would be able to put a good deal of resources toward that effort. If only you and I could agree to a sum . . ."

"Hang the filthy money!" Heads were definitely turning at three different tables. "I just want to be recognized as the person who discovered the first verifiable black hole."

"Well, if that's the only problem, I'm sure we could arrange to get you into the history books. . . ."

"Thank you!" Ariel snorted.

It was all settled by the time the pasta arrived.

Cocci's first request of Ceram had been that she refine her numbers and then brief his staff. He wanted everything she knew or could determine about the black hole.

"But I wouldn't waste any time contacting outside sources just yet," he'd said.

He could bet his life she wouldn't. Ariel was not about to share any more of the story, until she had to. And she didn't need him to tell her to sharpen the numbers. She'd been at work on that since she left Grace in the hospital.

A few days later she met with the Pinocchio people in a closed conference room that contained a long table, sixteen plastic armchairs in a rainbow of colors, and two pale-green chalkboards. The rest of the room was stark white walls and shaved beige carpeting.

Cocci, looking cool as ever, was there with another man. A white-suited attendant brought in Grace Porter in a wheelchair. She looked terrible.

The right side of Porter's face was peeling in big gray tatters. Underneath was a moist pink and looked tender. A blue bandanna really didn't hide the fact that most of her hair was gone.

"How are you feeling, Grace?" Ariel asked.

Porter shrugged stiffly. "I stopped getting worse, so the doctors say I'm getting better. They thought this little excursion would help."

Ariel nodded and turned her attention to the third member of the Pinocchio team.

Cocci had introduced him as their chief programmer-slash-psychiatrist, Jason Bathespeake. Ariel had never met a cyber before.

He was a tall man, as thin and angular as something assembled from pipes. Over his eyes were a pair of goggles with heavy lenses. When he looked at Ariel, she could see the lenses counter-rotate to focus on her face. They made a slight *whirr*. He spoke not with his mouth but with a voder attached around his neck.

"I'm pleased to meet you, Professor. You've handed

us quite a puzzle." The speech sounds were good but scratchy and whispery, like listening to the BBC on short wave. He actually said "plessed" and "pussle."

Ariel thought about giving up her brain's optic centers and speech strip in order to communicate directly with a computer's input/output circuits. It wasn't a sacrifice she would be willing to make.

Cocci called the little group to order and waved a hand at Ariel. "Why don't you begin, Professor. Grace and I've briefed Jason on the background of our— visitor."

Ariel stood uncertainly and then went over to the nearside chalkboard. She picked up a piece of yellow chalk and twisted it in her fingers.

"I've used the observations from our seismic stations," she said, "to draw some conclusions about the object we are tentatively calling a black hole.

"It's in a wildly elliptical orbit. The perigee— although that's not the right word, because it actually occurs *inside* the Earth—is about 2,600 kilometers, or 1,600 miles, from the planet's center. That puts it somewhere in the semi-liquid outer core.

"Apogee is about 88,000 kilometers, or 55,000 miles, above the surface. That's awfully low, less than a quarter of the distance to the Moon."

"What iss the object'ss period?" Bathespeake asked.

"Nine hours, forty-two minutes and twelve seconds, approximately."

"I will want to confer with your program to verify thesse numbers."

"Of course."

Cocci looked puzzled. "What's a period?"

"Excusse the jargon, plesse, Steve," Bathespeake whispered. "That'ss the time it takes the object to complete one orbit."

Cocci nodded.

"Is it still going in here at California and coming out in China?" Grace asked.

"Not at all," Ariel said. "The black hole spends more than nine hours of its orbit outside the Earth. In that time the planet is turning. So the next punch-in is about 135 degrees of longitude east of the previous entry point."

"So!" the cyber whistled. "The paired impact and ex-ssit pointss are walking around the planet, alwayss at a spread of 145 degrees . . . ?"

"Yes, like a sewing machine making stitches in a baseball cover." Ariel sketched a sphere on the board and looped the object's path into and out of it.

"Except," she went on, "the points don't follow a great circle around the globe. The orbit is inclined just over thirty-seven degrees north of the equator. Because the southern portion of the orbit occurs inside the planet, the 'stitches' are always along latitude thirty-seven degrees, thirty minutes."

"We're right under it, then, aren't we? All the time," Grace said. "It'll always be coming down right on our heads."

"Or coming up under our feet," Ariel agreed.

"If it were a knife, it would cut the top off the world," Cocci said. "How dangerous is this object?"

"In terms of impact?" Ariel asked. "Fortunately, most of the real estate along this latitude is either desert or ocean.

"West from San Francisco is a whole lot of empty Pacific. Then you come to northern Japan, China and a near miss at Beijing, then rural nothing spots in Central Asia, Iran, and Turkey. The line runs just south of Athens, across the Mediterranean, through Sicily and Spain. Then you have the Atlantic and a string of little towns in the U.S., the biggest of which is Wichita, Kansas. Then back to us.

"So not a lot of population is in danger, except in Japan and China," Ariel concluded. "But there are several active fault systems—Japan's, southern Italy's, and ours. They could be the real problem."

"How much of a problem?" Cocci asked. "Could we count on earthquakes every pass?"

"Oh, no! This object has a very concentrated gravity field. At close range, it's quite powerful—the shearing force, for example, that cut Mr. Kornilov's hand off when he reached across its path. But beyond a mile or so it has only a weak attraction—no more noticeable than, say, the Moon's here on Earth."

"That's too bad," Cocci muttered.

"Has anyone else reported a hit?" Grace asked.

"Nothing I've been able to find. But then, this is a very small object. Unless it goes in right on top of you—as it did for you and Mr. Kornilov—you wouldn't notice it much. Just a flash of radiation and a yank from its gravity field.

"When it comes out," she said thoughtfully, "it's pushing a fireball of collapsing matter that the black hole has absorbed from the Earth. But, again, unless it came up in your neighborhood, you might miss it."

"Iss your computer program still getting seismic signals from the object?" Bathespeake asked.

"Only when it punches in or out near one of our recording stations. But then, yes, very distinctly."

"I wonder how long it's been in orbit and nobody noticed?" Grace mused. "Why did you say, Steve, it's 'too bad' when the target spots are isolated desert or ocean?"

"Because even if we can get them to believe our evidence, they are not going to care about it much unless this—well, this new moon of ours—presents a clear danger."

"*Who* isn't going to care?"

Cocci shrugged. "The Feds . . . The American Academy . . . The U.N. . . . Whoever is going to bankroll the effort to catch and study this thing."

"Catch . . . ?" Grace stared at him. The whites of her eyes were showing all the way around.

Through the quiet that had settled in the room, Bathespeake asked, "How big iss the object?"

"Just a bit less than four billion metric tonness."

"Very small," whispered the cyber. He suddenly jerked straight up. "Too small!"

"Why?" Ariel asked.

"If this iss a black hole as Hawking originally proposed—a fossil from the Big Bang—then it must be larger than four billion tonnes. Otherwise it would have evaporated by now."

"Evaporate?" Grace shook her head tiredly. "But I thought black holes *absorbed* material."

"They do. Ex-ss-cept when they are below a certain size," Bathespeake said. "It's just a theory, but the . . . well . . . spontaneous generation and recombination of photon and antiphoton pairs—which iss going on everywhere in the cosmos, if you believe in quantum mechanics—would be disrupted in the neighborhood of a tiny black hole. At any instant, the hole could swallow only half the pair.

"If that half wass the photon, then the antiphoton would not be able to recombine. Rather than exist in isolation in our universe, the antiphoton would force the black hole to give up energy. The black hole would lose some of its mass.

"And unless it had originally massed more than a certain size, around four billion tonnes, the black hole would by this time have expelled *all* of its mass.

"Or that's the theory," Bathespeake concluded. "Small black holes are *hot*."

"How hot?" Ariel asked quickly.

"A billion degrees Kelvin." The cyber said. "In that range."

"Is that what burned Korny and me?" Grace asked.

"Possibly," Ariel cut in. "But it's more likely you caught the radiation flash from the accretion disk. This object isn't evaporating. Every orbit that I can trace, it checks in with the same seismic trace. It's *not* getting any smaller. If anything, a little larger each pass."

"Would I be able to see the black hole?" Grace asked.

"No. The hole has no physical presence in our universe," Ariel said. "Even its event horizon, the last point at which any material falling into it can be detected, is very tiny. About a hundred-billionth of a millimeter across. That's about one ten-thousandth of the radius of a typical atom."

"For a bottomless hole, it has a tiny mouth," the cyber observed. "A pinhole."

The room was quiet for three heartbeats. Then Grace asked: "But if that's so, how did it make an inch-wide hole in the jumpjet? And a bigger one in Korny?"

Ariel thought for a moment. "The black hole is a focus of gravity. Its field is going to attract and pull apart the material around it, depending on the strength of that material. The plane's aluminum skin and Mr. Kornilov's flesh have different tensile strengths, so the black hole takes odd-shaped bites."

"Inside the Earth, it iss different, yes?" Bathespeake prompted.

"Yes. There the accretion disk becomes almost solid. It sweeps everything in its path into the hole."

Cocci shifted uneasily. "Well, how much of the Earth *is* it absorbing?"

"Not very much," Ariel answered. "As the object passes through the planet, its speed increases. So the surrounding matter becomes relatively—um—stickier, less inclined to be dragged along. Thus, the accretion disk contracts.

"At the average speed of the hole through the Earth, the disk is . . ." Ariel consulted her notes. ". . . half a meter, say eighteen inches, across. If it absorbs everything—soil, rock, and liquid iron—in a path that wide, it's still collecting only about three million cubic meters of material on each pass. Or twenty billion kilograms."

"So the world is being eaten up," Cocci said. "Is it going to collapse? Soon?"

"Hardly. At that rate, maybe in three hundred billion years," Ariel answered. "And in a fraction of that time—say six billion years—the sun is supposed to go nova. Personally, I'm not worried."

Cocci shook his head in frustration. "None of this does us any good. Something so tiny you can't even see it. Something you wouldn't much notice unless it went past within a couple of feet of you. All it's doing is digging holes in godforsaken Kansas and Central Asia. Grace and Korny's encounter was, I gather, a trillion to one chance, right?"

Ariel nodded.

"The thing does us no good if it's so . . . damned . . . insignificant," he said.

"What 'good' would you expect from it, Steve?" Grace asked.

"If it was a big, roaring monster, knocking down cities, scaring people—"

"It did that all right on the first pass," Grace said.

"Yeah, sure. But since then? Nothing. How are we going to get a project team behind stopping and catching this thing, if it's all so theoretical?"

"It is still a scientific marvel," Ariel said.

"Of course," Cocci replied. "But would you pay a few hundred megabucks to put it under a microscope?"

"Yes!"

"Do *you* have that kind of money?"

"You do!" Ariel said.

Cocci laughed at her. "Oh no, lady. We won't *pay* to fiddle with this problem. We'll *get* paid to. That's the essence of our business."

"Why should we—Pinocchio—get involved in this?" Grace asked.

"We happen to be the ones with the information. It gives us certain—ah—leverage."

"Then you *do* smell a buck?"

Cocci nodded slowly.

"A market?"

He shrugged. "Not sure yet. But I do know space isn't all it was promised to be. Not for our automata. There are the solar power stations and the manned platform, which need our Fixits, but that's a pretty mature market. The Farside Observatory has our Mules and a team of Miners adapted for vacuum and radiation shielding. But that's practically a charity account for us. Good will.

"The exotic materials? Space factories making null-gee steels and pure crystals? Everyone hems and haws and says they haven't the budget. Not this year, not next, maybe in another five."

"There was LiquiSteel," Grace suggested.

"They wanted a bunch of free engineering. We would have put five figures into conceptuals for an automated factory—and then they'd have backed off. Your campaign was scoping out to be a replay of six years ago. Lots of nice music and a long ride on a painted horse, but no brass ring."

"And you think our little visitor will change all that?"

"I'll know when you all, as a team, have played the angles. Get in touch with Korny. He's our best man on the space market. Pick his brains. It will give him something to occupy his mind while he's taking hydrobaths and squeezing little rubber balls with his new hook."

Grace made a face. "Then what?" she asked.

"Then give me a way to capture the hole. Preferably using the maximum number and types of Pinocchios you can imagine."

"That's a tall order, Steve. Black holes—even microscopic ones—aren't exactly something you can pick up with a manipulator."

"I know."

"It's a pity they don't have an electric charge," Bathespeake said glumly.

Ariel opened her mouth, but before she could ask why, the cyber put up a warning hand.

"Something, some signal iss interfering with my inputs. It's very annoying . . ."

Bathespeake looked around the room, stood up, went over to the chalkboard behind Ceram. He ran his fingers down the left edge, paused, rubbed a spot. His "eyes" rotated into sharp focus.

"There's a bug here," he whispered, his hand shielding the voder.

Cocci came over and took out a penknife. He probed at the spot Bathespeake had indicated, coming up with a sliver of metal. They walked it back to the table and set it in the ashtray.

The chairman brought up a butane lighter.

"Perhaps you'd better leave the room, Jason."

The cyber shook his head and pointed at the bug. Cocci played flame on it until the casing cracked, sputtered and turned to slag. During the process, Bathespeake winced.

"It iss dead," he announced.

Grace let out an audible sigh. "Whose was it?"

"No telling," Cocci said grimly. "Odds are it was some competitor's. Could be the government's. We have friends all over. Professor, you were saying . . . ?"

"An electric charge . . ." Ariel began. "Why is it a pity that black holes don't have one, Jason?"

"Because we could have used it to trap the beast in a linear accelerator."

Cocci grunted. "Well, that's one idea down . . . Keep working. I'm sure you'll think of something." It was a definite dismissal.

As Ariel and the others left the room, Cocci was idly jiggling the ashtray with one hand, staring into it as the melted bug danced across the bottom.

"Did you hear about the UFO in Portugal?" the Cincinnati cabbie asked.

"Yes, right up out of the river. Over fifteen hundred people saw it. They even signed a paper about it. A couple of them got pictures. Only, nobody thought to snap it until the UFO was real high, then they just got a white dot with some sparkles. . . . But all the pictures show the same thing.

"So there goes your 'mass hypnosis' theory into a cocked hat, huh?"

Chapter 6

Jason Bathespeake: GULP

As a professional cyber, Jason Bathespeake knew exactly the frustrations behind the expression "explaining color to a blind man." But it wasn't because of his own dead eyes. His mechanical photoreceptors could pick up the entire visible band and shift at will down into the sub-infrared of radio and radar waves.

No, he knew the expression because people always had a hard time understanding exactly what it was he "saw" when he tied into a computer sysnet. It wasn't letters and numbers, such as a normal programmer saw on a terminal screen. It wasn't pictures, either, although color graphics were far closer to his reality than symbolic words.

Jason saw the flow of information. It was a pattern, a set of values and contrasts that aligned themselves and reiterated with the program's loops and branches. He identified sequence with pattern. He identified values with color harmonics. He could spot a programming bug as a distortion in the pattern, a discord that scraped across his nerves.

Bathespeake had come to Ariel Ceram's Earth Sciences lab at Berkeley with his "black box," the sensorium interface. He planned to spend the morning in an interview with her minicomputer, learning and verifying her program that analyzed and graphed seismic waves. He hoped to use the program to pinpoint the black hole in space and time.

He could tell that his appearance unnerved Ariel. It often had that effect on people who used computers regularly. They were so accustomed to the machine's being something *outside* themselves. They might find it seductive enough to play thinker games with words on a screen, but to have the information appear inside your head must seem the ultimate violation of the soul.

Jason could never explain to the young professor just when he had chosen to be a cyber. Machines had always been real to him, closer than most people. His first toy was a pet turtle with four-wheel drive, 256K of on-board memory, and five sonic sensors. He had played pounce with that robot before he could walk, until he pried off the cover and shorted it out. Just curious . . .

As a student, he had learned more from data terminals and mentoroids than from human teachers. So when he graduated from the lycee, his decision to major in industrial psychology with the artificial intelligence option had seemed natural. Cyber surgery was just an extension of that decision.

"Do you need any special, unh, connections?" she asked.

"A standard communications port will do. A high-speed modem would be perfect. I could do this over the phone, but 9,600 baud is so slow it's an irritation."

"Yes . . . of course." She twisted her mouth.

The modem port was tied into her data-gathering net. Bathespeake temporarily spooled the net over onto a bulk recorder and connected his black box to the empty port. The flex lead from the interface went into a contact patch at his right mastoid, where the goggles usually connected. He could hear the professor move away quickly.

Jason turned his now-blind eyes toward her.

"This won't take long. About twenty minutes." He smiled in her direction.

"Should I, um, boot the program for you?"

"I've already asked the system for it. I assume it's the one named 'SPLICE.' That's the only file that seems to be the right . . . shape."

"That's it. I think I'll just wait outside. You can buzz on the phone if you have any questions. Okay?"

He smiled and put out a hand to reassure her. But she had moved out of range. The door slammed shut a second later.

Jason sighed and, before running the program, paused to scan through it, examining the flow of control and the data-entry points. For a programmer working through a vid screen, analyzing another person's code was a nightmare of tracking control loops and counting variables. For a cyber, it was as easy as tracing the pattern in an oriental carpet with his finger.

Dr. Ceram's code seemed to be a simple bubble sort in three dimensions, with a contouring factor. The graphic DRAW routine was the most complex part of it, but it was still too simple to get itself into much trouble.

He told the system to run the program, taking the data points from a SAMPLE.DAT she had left in the disk directory.

The pattern was clean: the seismic records sorted themselves out by time, strength, and distance. A check routine compared signal strength with reporting station so that the program didn't confuse a weak signal at a close station with a strong one from a distant station. The simple colors from DRAW tumbled through his optic centers.

Jason then loaded and ran the data that tracked their black hole. He verified the hard marks of impact and exit, the scrambled colors from the Earth's tertiary and quaternary vibrations. The disturbances threatened to give him a headache.

Ariel's original discovery, the seismic track through the Earth, could be accepted as accurate. What standard of precision her data represented, however, would depend on the quality of instruments at her reporting stations. That was something only site visits around California and the Pacific Rim could verify. Jason would let those go for later.

The picture was generally accurate, but hardly detailed. Ariel's equipment could only place the entry and exit points on the Earth's surface within target areas two kilometers across. For an object smaller than an atom, dragging with it a fireball only about eighteen inches in diameter, two kilometers was an ocean of room.

From the scattered reporting stations in Asia, the precision was much worse. The slip factor was in the tens of kilometers.

Far from being able to catch the black hole, Jason could hardly tell where it was. He could not plot even a planet's orbit accurately with only two points. And this was a tight, fast ellipse cutting through the varied densities of the Earth, moving through the perturbations of the Moon and Sun, with only a seismic snapshot to estimate its speed, and that not even accurate to the millisecond. . . . He might be able to know how fast the object was moving, but he couldn't locate it exactly.

He was reminded of the Heisenberg conundrum of quantum physics: it is possible to know a particle's position or its momentum, but not both at the same time. The act of observing one changes the other.

Jason could, however, examine at his leisure Ariel's rough estimates of the black hole's mass and dimensions. Those were simple mathematics.

He interrupted the seismic program and closed it

down. He put the data net back on line and spooled in the lagged information. Then he buzzed for Ariel.

There was no answer for more than a minute. A young man's voice finally came on the phone and said the professor had gone to lunch.

That was odd, because it was only ten-thirty.

Jason refitted his goggles and let himself out of the lab.

Bathespeake returned to his office in the third subbasement of the Pinocchio, Inc. high rise.

It was a cool, windowless room with few furnishings except for an elaborate array of terminals and—since pieces of the Sausalito Dome had sliced both the front and back porches off his condo—a seven-foot-long couch and a carpetbag with shaving kit and change of clothes. There were no pictures on the office walls, and if the light switch had broken Jason might not have reported it for weeks. He seldom used any sense but infrared in this most private of spaces.

He lay at full length on the couch, letting the frayed brocade tickle his neck, and began playing solo handball. Or what he thought of as handball—for the mind, as other men played for the body.

Bathespeake fully believed they were dealing with a micro black hole, as described first in the 1970s.

The black hole is an object of immense mass but no dimension, a perfect "point" in space that Euclid would have been proud of. The matter of a black hole—whether a large one of stellar mass or a small one of a few billion tons—is so crushed together that it takes itself outside the normal fabric of space. Like a pinhole in a piece of paper it is there, but not there.

The force of gravity in any black hole is so strong that, near the hole, no particle or wave can travel fast enough to reach escape velocity and break free of it—not even light, which is the fastest "wavicle" or "parve" in Mr. Einstein's universe. That is why it's called a *black* hole: no light reflects from or shines out of it.

How far out from the hole a passing photon must be before it can escape the gravity well depends entirely on how much mass exists inside the hole. This distance at which light can break free is called the "event horizon," because it is the closest limit at which human senses and instruments can detect the hole. This limit, which actually applies to any massive object, was described by Karl Schwarzschild about a half-century before Hawking proposed the micro black holes. Even the Earth has a Schwarzschild limit, although most of the planet's mass lies outside it. The Earth's event horizon is deep inside, just inches from the center of the core.

A stellar-mass black hole might have an event horizon three or four miles across. The tiny black hole Jason and Ariel were dealing with—which weighed as much as a mountain—had an event horizon smaller than an atomic particle.

Of all the objects in the Solar System, this little lump of nothing was the strangest. Where it came from was a mystery: no collapsing star would shed so tiny a piece of itself. It might truly be a fossil knot in the superdense matter that preceded the Big Bang: instead of expanding smoothly into a star or a galaxy, it had constricted into this minute focus of gravity. If so, it was also the oldest object in the cosmos.

Of course, Jason reminded himself, the Big Bang is the graveyard of busted cosmic theories. It explains everything. You might as well say that God shat out these little black holes and be done with it.

Jason compressed his sense of self to visualize their orbiting visitor at that level.

His awareness shrank past floating dust motes; past large molecules, where atoms chain themselves like flashing diamond points in a necklace; past individual atoms, where knots of protons and neutrons huddle under the rigid shells of electron orbits. Between nucleus and electron, an atom is pure space without gas or dust intervening. Jason's awareness lingers. The protons, neutrons and electrons are almost resolvable into clumps of bright energy, each a mosaic of subatomic particles.

Into the space of the atom drifts a different kind of a particle, the dull, null-colored event horizon of a micro black hole, one ten-thousandth the size of this atom. Where the atomic particles flash and glow, this object remains sullen and dark. It drifts through the electron shells, through the empty space, past the nucleus. A silent, unwanted intruder.

But wait . . . That was too static an image. Like a movie projector, Bathespeake's imagination added action to the scene.

The hole does not drift silently, enigmatically through the atomic space. With a force far stronger at this close range than any subatomic bond, it rips electrons from their shells like gnats from the still air and pulls them toward the event horizon. It plucks the protons and neutrons from the nucleus like grapes from a bunch and swallows them.

Nearby atoms, seemingly light years away on the scale of Jason's awareness, stretch and distort toward the dull particle. Then they too split apart and rush toward it.

Every object that approaches the event horizon accelerates until it is traveling at a fraction of light speed as it crosses the horizon—at which point it is beyond human knowledge. Just short of the horizon, objects are reduced to their least components: subatomic particles and, ultimately, energy.

The black hole becomes the center of its own whirlpool. In the jostling of atoms, atom-pieces, and energy smears around it, a near-solid mass forms.

The matter flowing in collides with that which went before. Some is deflected from its inward flight, to fly off in fountains of radiation and high-speed particles.

With time and a thinly spaced environment, the whirlpool would form a flattened disk. The expelled particles would form two jets of plasma at right angles to the disk. It would look like a glowing platter stuck on a feathery-fiery spindle, clearly visible to the human eye without a microscope—until radiation burned out the eye's retina.

That was the picture of the beast they sought, except that their micro black hole was not stationary. It followed an elliptical orbit around the Earth, sometimes cutting fast through the planet, sometimes cruising slowly above the atmosphere, digesting its catch.

As the hole traveled through the planet, it did not have the luxury of open space. The accretion disk would become a solid knot of fire as cubic meters of liquid rock and nickel-iron were gathered by the object's gravity well.

Now Bathespeake realized that both he and Ariel Ceram had missed something.

She had said that the black hole would eventually absorb the Earth—in a comfortable thirty-three billion years. But what was she basing that on? Obviously an arithmetical sequence, taking the amount absorbed on each pass and adding it until the whole equalled the Earth's huge mass. And was that accurate?

As the hole absorbed matter, its own mass increased, which increased its gravity field, so it would absorb more material, which increased . . . The process was exponential, not arithmetical!

Jason was off the couch in a second and groping for his terminal. A simple calc function told him the answer quickly.

At the rate the hole was gulping down iron and

growing, its mass would equal the Earth's in just over seven years.

Of course, it wouldn't be obvious for a while—most of the hole's growth would come in the last year or two. And by that time the planet might be so shattered that the absorption rate would have slowed a bit. But Jason didn't think he would be around to care.

"Grace? Grace!" Jason found her nodding, barely awake, at the desk in her newly patched office.

"Whatzit? Jason, it's you." Her head came up quickly. She looked better than she had two days ago but still sick.

"I've just figured out something about our—friend."

"Our—oh." She looked around the room, her eyes more in focus now. "Why don't you wheel me out by the Stone Fountain. That's a good place to discuss—him."

Jason helped her with the chair. In the elevator going down to the plaza, he tried to tell her the terrible secret, but she hushed him and just said something about needing light and air.

He pushed her over to the fountain, a ring of hewn rose-granite with water welling over its lip. The wind from the Bay randomly curled the sheet of falling water and sent it off in spray and droplets across the flagstones. The fountain was, Jason knew, part of the building's heat sink.

"Why don't you listen and tell me what you hear," she said.

He paused. "A tinkling sound. Like glass. Perhaps some left over from the quake is caught in the pumps."

"Anything else? Any—insects?"

He listened with his other senses. "No electronics."

She motioned him to a bench near her wheelchair, shoved her hands at the tires to bring herself closer.

"Now. What have you found?" Grace asked in a throaty whisper.

"Dr. Ceram was far wrong in her estimate of the danger. She forgot to account for the absorption of mass into the black hole itself. It's growing with each pass, getting stronger."

Grace nodded. "What does it mean?"

"The Earth will collapse in less than seven years."

"Collapse." Grace was still whispering and seemed calm. The midafternoon sun threw shadows on her face, but Jason could see that her skin had gone white around the mouth and eyes.

"You mean sinkholes, cave-ins, that sort of thing?" she asked after a minute of thinking.

"No. Fire raining from the sky, subsiding land masses, molten asteroids. *That* sort of thing."

Grace looked at him for a minute more. She was unconsciously chewing her lower lip.

"Have you told anyone else about this?"

"You're the first, Grace."

"Is there any way to stop it?"

"I thought we had all pretty much drawn blanks at our last meeting. This new scenario doesn't help anything."

Grace went on chewing until there was blood. She swallowed some.

"Keep this quiet until I get a chance to talk with Steve."

"Of course."

"What are you going to do?" Her voice was shaky.

"I've always wanted to see Delphi and the Aegean," Jason said softly. "Perhaps I'll take time for that now."

She studied him for another ten seconds.

"Don't count on that," Grace said finally. She turned and began wheeling herself toward the building.

*   *   *

The next day Cocci called a lunchtime meeting, again at the Stone Fountain.

He had a brown bag with tunafish catered from a south-of-Mission lunch counter. Grace had soup in a styrofoam cup. Ariel was eating fruit.

Jason didn't know he was supposed to bring anything. He sat there feeling hungry until Ariel slipped him half an apple. He smiled his thanks at her, but she still wouldn't look directly at his goggled eyes.

"Seven years, Jason?" Cocci began. "Are you sure?"

Bathespeake explained his calculations. Beside him, Ariel started to object. Then she understood and was quiet.

"You couldn't be wrong, I hope?" Cocci said.

"Oh, wrong by a year or two, perhaps. But by millions of years? No, Steve."

Cocci chewed his tuna as if it was sour. "Ariel? You were starting to say . . . ?"

"Nothing." She looked small and cold.

"Grace? Suggestions?"

Porter stirred her soup thoughtfully. "We could emigrate to the Moon."

They all considered that for three beats.

"When the Earth fragments," Jason said at last, "it will do interesting things to the Moon's orbit. Few of them will be healthy for people living there."

"Mars?" Ariel suggested.

"Safer," Jason agreed. "But I wouldn't expect a colony to survive long without materials and technical support from Earth. Mars has little that humans need or want."

"We wouldn't live long, period," Cocci said. "Imagine life—an indefinite forever—under pressure domes, breathing canned or recycled air, watching gauges and hoarding food supplies."

He shook his head. "We're not a gentle species. One good drunken Saturday night, and someone would blow a gasket—literally—that'd end the whole colony. Puff. Snuff . . . No, evacuation isn't the answer."

"Then we have to fight this thing," from Grace.

"Looks like it," Ariel agreed.

Jason simply nodded.

"Right," Cocci sealed the convenant.

It was that simple.

"And we'll stick to the original game plan," Cocci went on. "You three and Kornilov are now the—um—executive steering committee of the Black Hole Task Force."

"The Un-Holey Four," Jason murmured.

"You're to be relieved of all other duties," Cocci rolled on, "except for finding a way to stop, capture, or destroy the black hole."

"Shouldn't we be telling someone about this?" Grace asked. "The government, maybe, or the—"

"Who, exactly, in 'the government' would you tell?" Cocci asked, with a sweet and reasonable smile. "The Environmental Protection Agency? Or the Federal Emergency Management Agency? How about the Red Cross? They all clean up after the fact . . . Or do you want to tell the *military* about it?

"And you can't just *tell* them. They'll want a document, a report, that they can pass from out-basket to in-basket while they try to figure out if the end of the world is in their own department's best interest. Finally someone will decide that it's ridiculous, hysterical—and deniable. We'd get a polite letter of refusal . . . two years from now.

"No," Cocci said decisively. "We'll get only one chance to cry wolf on this thing. I don't care how much hot tar you think the world is sinking into. We still have only some conjectural seismologic readings and a funny incident aboard an airplane. I want the lid kept on until we have a second confirmed sighting—and a plan. When we have a plan of action, then we tell the 'appropriate authorities.' Not before. Right? And that goes for you, too, Ariel. Right?"

Ariel nodded, stunned at being singled out.

"Right. So let's get to work."

Cocci balled up his lunchbag and stood. As he turned to go back in the building, he tossed the ball into the welling pool on top of the fountain. Smooth ripples from the splash soon made a rhythmic stutter in the falling water.

The sequence momentarily hypnotized Jason while another part of his mind speculated about what Steve Cocci had up his sleeve.

Chapter 7

Eldon Richardson: LOOSE TALK

At the Honda Fusion test plant near Haramachi, the new Kyoryoku reactor design—under joint development with the People's Republic of China—was being tested at fifty-percent power. The operators adjusted the magnetic flux of the cryomagnets and occasionally peered out to study the toroid. Three feet of beryllium glass shielded them from the test chamber. It almost saved them.

At first, the techno-sans who were assigned to evaluate the accident thought it was due to defective materials. They were primarily studying backup videotapes which had been telemetered to a remote recorder. The tapes showed a section of the toroid exploding in a flare of light, then the whole ring coming apart. Plasma at 70,000 atmospheres and almost a billion degrees filled the chamber in a rush. Then the tapes went blank as the pickups melted.

Pieces of the building's roof were discovered over a thirty-square-kilometer area.

The Honda technical squad was thorough. Before they would admit to faulty construction or design, they went over the rubbled crater at the test site with shovels and brushes. It took them four nonstop days, wearing moonsuits and rotating in every techno-san on the watch list, but their thoroughness paid off.

It was not a fault of the reactor. Below the calculated point of failure in the toroid, but offset at an angle of thirty-two degrees, they discovered a neat hole sixty-one centimeters across. When they probed with a rod, they could find no bottom. The hole evidently extended far below the building's foundation into the site's bedrock.

They redoubled the search, looking for other evidence of pitting or impact that would create similar holes in the concrete. But they found nothing more.

The story, as it reached the world, was that a strange object had risen from the Earth and punctured the toroid.

Eldon Richardson was on the Kay-Sass news board when UPLink sent over the story of Haramachi, complete with vids of broken concrete, twisted rebar, and the last two seconds of light in the telemetered tapes. He watched the men in moonsuits put a probe down the hole, a foot and a half wide, that they claimed lay under the point of catastrophic failure. The probe—all forty feet of spring steel and yellow mylar pennants—slipped from sight.

In his mind's eye, Richardson saw a pig farmer framing a hole under the eaves of his feed shed and then flinging his body to the sky.

The holes looked about the same.

Richardson was punching terminal keys before he even thought about it. Those keys signed out the six days of vacation he had coming for the rest of the year; drew travel expenses on the station's budget, denominated in yen, for himself and a vid-tech; and booked a polar midnight special from Dallas to Tokyo. He had fifty-two minutes to get to Dallas. He could leave word for the vid man to fly out the next night.

* * *

The assigned guide from Japanese Television's *Omoshiroi* program knew less about the Honda Fusion accident than Richardson did. But then, he had been studying the technical analysis since he'd crossed 89 degrees latitude, while she had probably picked up her sheet about four hours ago.

The Haramachi crater was a desolate scene, viewed from spotter scopes half a mile away. When he suggested they suit up and visit the site, she smiled shyly and explained, *gomen nasai*, so sorry, in a sudden, embarrassed Japanese-slanglish he could hardly follow, that it was impossible.

"Over there," he insisted.

She smiled, nodded that she understood, then shook her head.

Her one word that he understood was "radiation."

Japanese Television courteously allowed him and the vid man fifteen minutes' uninterrupted taping on the Ginza for local color and then, for a huge fee, granted him two hours' use of an old-style editing board.

Richardson wondered if it was because of his credentials. When the JT flack had asked for his cards, he said he was freelancing it. The word meant nothing to the man, so Richardson used the word he thought matched the idea in Japanese *ronin*. The flack became noticeably stiffer, nodded once, and proceeded to treat Richardson and his sidekick like used cat litter.

Evidently corporate loyalty still mattered in the Land of the Rising Red Flag. It sure as hell still mattered in Kansas. After two days Kay-Sass had sent him a satelgram ending his employment. The vid man got a similar note but offering amnesty if he caught the next flight back—using his own credit, of course.

By that time it didn't matter. Richardson had spliced together the early Haramachi scenes from UPLink, a copy of the raw frames he'd shot on Rebstock's hog farm and deftly retrieved from the cooker at KSAS, and his own latest narrative shot on the Ginza. Altogether it ran 150 seconds and told a story he could peddle to the independents—maybe to the syndicates.

One last pass-through on the JT board let Richardson listen for and re-syntho any garbled words.

". . . So what we have is a mystery, ladies and gentlemen. Two events, separated by half the globe and more than a week in time. Did something, indeed, rise out of the Earth, as claimed by both Japanese scientists and a Kansas farmer—unlikely as that may seem?

"Or did something *strike down* from the sky?

"Could it be a new energy weapon—some beam of incredible power—that the superpowers are testing? Or is it a rogue transmission from the solar power stations—an accident no one will admit to?

"I only know—" Pause. Look up to the flashing neon of the Ginza roofline. "The sky seems not so friendly tonight.

"This is Eldon Richardson, reporting from Tokyo."

He dictated a cover and blip-squeaked the finished report via satellite.

Coming back through customs at Dallas–Ft. Worth, Richardson wondered who had hung the kick-me sign on his back. The blue-suit boys saw him coming and hefted their beefy backsides off the stools. Like hound dogs scenting a coon.

They went through his bag with fingers, needles, and a hard-radiation fluoroscope, then gave it to the German shepherd to play with. They tried to scope his tape container and, when that didn't work, opened it up and *then* scoped it. That effectively bulk-cooked forty-eight hours of blank footage.

Richardson couldn't help but smile, and it was his undoing.

By this time the blue-suits had been joined by a pair of button-across types in dark glasses. State Department or FBI. They made finger talk with the customs men and Richardson found himself in a closed room undergoing a full-body search including cavity probes—without benefit of Vaseline.

They took his passport and his driving license, thought about the credit cards, then left him one.

Two hours later they turned him loose on the taxi curb without even a receipt.

Somehow he had a feeling that, when he got to his apartment—if it hadn't been rolled up into the wall—he would find it ransacked. And probably bugged.

But what had he *done*?

Weird Willie Wilson, the toker's friend, was feeling as persecuted as Eldon Richardson. During the night the Feds, the narcs, or the competition had firebombed two acres of prime—um—alfalfa on his farm west of New Harmony in southern Utah.

Restate that. They must have hit it with a mortar round or maybe an Army-surplus Sidewinder missile. There was a hole in the field that no gopher ever saw the bottom of.

It being the end of summer, the weed was stalk-dried and ready to shake out. So it went up in the biggest waste of smoke this part of the state had ever smelled.

There went the tourist trade next summer.

"Do I think we have too much government?" repeated the Cincinnati cabbie.

"Let me ask you a question. When was the last

time you heard of anybody getting in trouble that the cops weren't dishing it out?

"Sting operations, snooping, SWAT teams and commando raids. They gave up trying to *catch* criminals. Now they just run 'em out of the market."

Chapter 8

Jason Bathespeake:
FIRST RIGHT ANSWER

When Bathespeake walked into Kornilov's hospital room, the Mad Russian was sitting up in bed.

He looked like one of those Easter Island statues: the long face with its straight nose and pointed chin, the overhanging brows, the high square forehead, even the rough skin, legacy of a childhood acne. Kornilov's having lost his hair to radiation sickness enhanced the likeness. Normally it was curly and blond with only faint gray wisps at his temples.

"You've finally gotten your way with me, Jason."

Kornilov held up the stump of his right wrist. Two stainless steel bars, three-quarters of an inch thick and anchored in bone, emerged from the pink skin. The tips were rounded and tapped with a hex connection. Beneath the bars was a ribbon of twenty-strand flex with a flat D plug.

Jason examined the skin around these artifacts. The healing was clean.

"How's the wrist action?"

Kornilov wagged his forearm and the two bars flip-flopped. "They've built in some kind of universal joint, I swear it. The wrist should be locked solid, but . . ."

"But you have control. That's good."

"Yeah, and while I was out they put wires in my skull. You told them to, didn't you?"

"Merely a suggestion," Jason admitted.

"What kind of a freak does that plug turn me into?"

"They haven't fitted you with a hand yet, I see."

"No . . . Do I get a *normal* hand?"

"I should hope not. We plan to fit you with a Pinocchio Max-Flex. You'll have separate control of each of three finger joints and two thumb joints. You'll have heat and cold sensation—they'll register as reddish or bluish tinges in your right vision field. You'll sense position, touch, and texture through a matrix of small gyros. You'll also tie into an on-board status checker; if the hand malfunctions, it'll feel like pain."

"Gee, thanks." Kornilov stared at the steel bars. "What's the power supply? A battery pack around my waist?"

"Nothing so crude. We tinkered with your stomach and tapped into one of the hydrochloric acid glands. It now services a bio battery with a fifteen-year replacement cycle on the plates. The power comes out on pins eight and twenty in the plug."

"All that for just a hand?"

"More than a hand. That D plug is standard for most manipulators, as I'm sure you've noticed."

"Yes. So?"

"Your new hand will have standard manipulator circuits. When you need fine control in the field, just plug into the Pinocchio or its remote, and the unit will become part of your arm."

"Can you adapt a Fixit paw to the sleeve of a pressure suit?"

"I don't see why not. That's what the hex fittings are for."

"A fistful of wrenches and pliers would put me about five jumps ahead of the average human in space," Kornilov said thoughtfully. "Unless the medics ground me."

"I guarantee they can be persuaded to let you fly."

Alex leaned back into the pillows. His eyes closed for a minute. A smile crept across his face.

Now for the bad news. Jason took a long mental breath and asked: "Did you see any of Grace's early reports?"

Kornilov nodded. "It seems that I am the first human being to make personal contact with an authentic piece of the Big Bang. The honor escapes me."

"Let's hope you're the last. I imagine that if I had been in your place—and remember I was originally assigned to the LiquiSteel campaign—the electronic interference probably would have blown out the side of my head."

"Instead I lost my hand. If Gracie had only found it, I'd have my flesh-and-blood back, not this gizmo you're cooking up for me. This is a national tragedy, Jason! That hand had brought more women to heaven than you'll ever know."

"Sure," Bathespeake made a noise that, from the voder, would sound like a lascivious male chuckle. "But it was your own filthy habits that caught up with you. If you hadn't been reaching for a drink, you'd only have that hole in your leg. Don't you blame Grace. If she had done any differently, they would have delivered you in a set of plastic pajamas without sleeves."

"Right. She did save my life." Korny smiled. "Do you suppose that means she likes me, just a little? Has she been asking about me?"

Jason could feel his own mechanical goggles rotate into a harder focus.

"Yes she likes you, and yes she asked, but not in the way you mean, you fool."

Korny's smile grew for a moment. Then he changed the subject. "So, while I've been lying here on my backside, what has everyone in the shop been up to?"

Now was the time to let him have it, Jason decided.

"That black hole is more than just an astronomic oddity, you know. It's truly bottomless. Everything that falls in, stays forever and adds to its strength. And for half an hour out of every ten, it's inside the Earth. . . ." He waited for Korny to finish the thought.

"How much has it absorbed—so far?"

"About seven hundred million tons. I only have exact figures as of midnight. In another two months, the hole will have doubled its mass."

"And the second doubling after that will be faster."

"Yes."

"Soon it will outmass the planet." Korny took a grip on the bedsheet with his good hand, the bars in his other wrist twisted in sympathy. "How long do we have?"

"Seven years. But things won't get too bad till right near the end."

"Yippee . . . What are we doing about it?"

"Cocci's reassigned us—Grace, you, me, and the professor who discovered the object—to a task force. Very secret. We're in high gear now to find a way to capture the black hole. Put it under a microscope, if we can. Maybe, when we're done with it, we'll donate it to the Smithsonian. If not, we're to destroy it."

"Don't we tell the government or somebody?"

"Steve seems opposed to the idea. Forcefully. I don't know why. Yet."

"Hmmm. 'Don't poke the bear in his lair,' yes. . . . Who's heading up the project?"

"Grace. But there's definitely an important place on the team for you."

"Don't want one. I've got a full plate with that orbiting mini-mill."

"That's shelved for now. Besides, Cocci thinks you would go after the hole for personal reasons."

Korny squinted at him. "Personal?"

"Revenge—for your lost hand."

"That's silly. An accident is all it was, like losing

your finger to a power arc or vacuum bite. The thing's just a rock."

"A black hole. It's a very spooky object."

"Yes. Well. Still, it's just a piece of nature. Revenge would be stupid." Korny grinned. "But for *sport* now . . ."

Jason nodded. "We have a fascinating and impossible riddle to solve: touching a hole that has no bottom, holding a thing that cannot be held."

"Do we have any ideas so far?"

"Yes, a lead-lined catcher's mitt," Jason laughed. "Mounted on a Steel Boss dressed in a Giant's uniform. Perez at third base. You get to drive the doppelganger."

"Huh-whamm!" Korny started to pantomime slamming his right fist into his left hand but was jerked to a stop by the clicking of steel bars at the end of his wrist.

How to catch the black hole? That was Jason's problem.

He talked it over separately and together with Korny, with Grace, with Ariel Ceram. And he obeyed Cocci's strict order to discuss the hole—which they had tentatively christened Hawking-1—with no one else.

In the hospital, at lunch, in the seismology lab, the four of them had argued and proposed, theorized and debunked. And still they had nothing.

They had fantasized about dense materials—Bathespeake's "catcher's mitt." But if more than 13,000 miles of rock and iron from the Earth's interior couldn't even slow the object down, what human-made material would block it? The hole had no physical presence in their universe.

They had wished a magnetic field or an electric charge on it, so that they could imagine powerful coils that would snare and tame the black hole. But it had only the attributes of mass and spin.

Grace, who was elbow-deep in books on the subject both serious and fanciful, had read that a spinning black hole created an opportunity for time travel. Because it was no more than a dimensionless point, the hole could not turn around itself and would therefore have to move in a tiny circle. If a rocketship could dive *through* that circle, down the sides of the hole while missing the hole itself, it would skim past eternity and move through time and space to distant parts of the galaxy. Wasn't that exciting?

Bathespeake gently pointed out to her that no rocket could drive through a geometric point that was spinning around itself. If it tried, it would only send a gram or so of its nose cone, at most, through the black hole. The rest would pass around the event horizon. Perhaps, he said, a fragment of Kornilov's wrist bone had traveled to faraway places, far-off times. The rest of him remained in the here and now.

Grace had pouted and said Jason had no poetry. He thought she'd meant to say no *soul* but her tongue caught it in time.

And so they were left with the problem. How does one pick up an object that is without electric charge or even physical presence? No manipulator could touch it. No material, however dense, could stop it. No magnetic bottle could hold it.

And yet Hawking-1 itself picked up objects—dust, gases, pieces of an AmAir jumpjet and a Pinocchio engineer. How did it manipulate them?

With gravity. It had the universal attraction of mass for mass, a force still unexplained by even the most abstruse of theoretical physicists.

And the Earth, while not stopping the hole dead, had captured it in an endless orbit.

How?

With gravity.

Jason held that thought in the front of his mind

while he slipped off his goggles and turned to the computer interface in his office.

When he "spoke" to the computer, he used his brain's speech centers. It wasn't actually like speaking words. It was more like singing a song. Pattern, rhythm, harmonics, and pitch all played their part in the symbology he ran through his head.

He began setting up relationships, starting with a mass of four billion tons, the size of Hawking-1. As he fed in more data points, the hole's gravity well became a mere grace note among the whole notes of the masses representing the Earth and the Moon.

The Earth's mass had forced the object to curve its trajectory, presumably from a straight line, into the closed ellipse of its present orbit. Could another body of sufficient mass, by intersecting that orbit at the precise instant, steal the hole from the Earth? Could it be guided into a more controlled orbit around—or even to find rest at the center of—that other mass?

Jason specified a range of planetary masses and compared their escape velocities at various radii from their cores with the speed of Hawking-1 at its apogee: about 880 meters per second. If the escape velocity was greater than the hole's apogee speed, it fell in and stayed.

He found that any one of the masses could capture the black hole. But with a smaller mass the margin for error decreased. That margin was the dimension of the globed space the object would have to hit if it were to be captured from its present Earth orbit.

A small asteroid like Mnemosyne, with a diameter of 109 kilometers, would have a "sweet spot" less than 800 meters across at its core. The largest planetoid, Ceres, with a diameter of more than 1,000 kilometers, had a sweet spot of about 4,800 kilometers, or more than four times the Earth's own diameter. Ceres could easily steal Hawking-1 from Earth.

These planetoids, however, were large bodies and far away. Driving them from their stable orbits beyond Mars would probably require energies beyond current human technology.

What about nearer objects?

The Moon could also capture the hole easily. But the Moon's large mass and broad diameter would never survive the tidal forces in the near orbit needed to match the black hole's apogee point.

One of the moons of Mars might be moved close to Earth. Phobos, the inner and bigger moon, was an irregular ellipsoid object with an average diameter of twenty-two kilometers. It was a small body that might conceivably be moved—at great expense. Its calculated sweet spot, however, was slightly more than three meters. Or about ten feet. It would take a delicate hand to move Phobos into the right Earth orbit at the right time to snag the black hole.

There were the "close approach" asteroids, the Amors and Apollos, whose orbits grazed or crossed Earth's. Most were far smaller than Phobos, but a few were bigger. Well, somewhat bigger: the largest, Ganymede, was thirty-five kilometers in diameter. Still, if any of those happened to be near Earth in orbit . . .

"Oh, hell!" Jason's snarl jarred the shapes of his program.

It was impossible anyway, he decided. If they did not know Hawking-1's true location within two kilometers, it was absurd to think about moving a moonlet to place its center within *ten feet* of the object.

His data had too many gaps! It was pointless!

Bathespeake closed down his program with a feeling of deep frustration.

Seven years. And counting.

Jason was in a closed meeting with Steven Cocci and Grace Porter to explain his idea for catching the subatomic-sized black hole. He felt absurd when he got to the part about moving an entire asteroid to a close orbit around the Earth. It was like stealing one of Barnum & Bailey's elephants to step on a flea.

Cocci didn't bat an eye. Instead he asked how Jason proposed to move a stone tens or hundreds of kilometers in diameter.

"With a fusion engine, I suppose. We could bore out a chamber and line it with magnets. Then compress a reaction mass—"

"What mass?"

Jason considered. "There are atmospheres in the outer solar system . . . Jupiter has mostly hydrogen and a large fraction of helium. The hydrogen should contain a suitable proportion of deuterium."

"The reaction chamber—it would be large?" Cocci asked.

"Oh yes. A deep cavern in the asteroid body. Maybe a hundred meters in cross section."

"It would take a lot of our Miners to dig such a pit."

"Yes," Jason agreed. "Miners. Artificers, Fixits, a whole platoon of Pinocchios could be kept at work on such a project."

"If we used Phobos as the entrapping vehicle," Cocci mused, "we could establish a base on Mars, a dome city. We could even set up an autofactory there to support the work."

"Possibly. But as I said, Phobos is too small a mass. The margin for error is unbelievably tight. We might not be able to locate Hawking-1 closely enough to steer Phobos to a rendezvous using a reaction drive."

"Yes, but Phobos is closer. We can get her more easily. Faster. And that seems to be . . ."

At that moment a junior tech came bursting in through the door. The three of them turned, but the the tech went to Grace. He spent half a minute whispering in her ear and then ran out of the room. Bathespeake and Cocci turned toward her, impatient while she digested what she'd heard.

"A late report from Haramachi," Grace said finally.

"Hara—" Jason started to ask. Oh yes, the experimental fusion reactor in Japan. He'd heard about it somewhere.

"They found a hole sixty-one centimeters across under the toroid's foundation," Grace continued. "Angled at thirty-two degrees. The press is now linking it to strange events in Kansas, Portugal—all along our thirty-seven thirty line."

"Outgoing or incoming?" Jason asked.

"Disputed. The Japanese say punching out at Haramachi. Someone from Kansas disagrees. Other reports have no firm data."

"But they have an exact time and place in Japan . . ." Jason persisted.

"Of course."

"What does this mean?" Cocci's brows were coming together.

"We have our second sighting, Steve," said Jason. "And a timing mark. We can tell exactly where the black hole was and when. That is, if the Honda people will cooperate."

"They will. They'll honor our exchange agreements, or they've bought their last batch of photo membrane," the chairman said darkly.

"Then we can take the black hole," Jason affirmed.

"Good. We'll use Phobos."

"I'd prefer a larger mass, Steve. More room for error."

Cocci frowned. "That means going to the Asteroid Belt, farther than any space expedition has gone. It would inject a lot of imponderables into your scheme."

"I would still prefer a larger mass," Jason said carefully.

"Ah, but Phobos is in our reach, don't you see.

We would use a good number of Pinochs to get it. And you never know, we might even catch the hole with it."

"I see," Jason said after a pause. He felt his eyes twirling out of focus so that he would not see Cocci's grin at that last remark.

Like an abscess in soft tissue, the weakness described by Jason's computer calculations spread through the semi-solid iron. There was no cavitation, just a steady draining. As Bathespeake watched this on the "front screen" of his optic centers, he was reminded of a needle drawing the yolk out of an egg.

"Jason! Is it true?" The voice was Ariel Ceram's. She sounded frightened. Something would have to be very wrong for her to overcome her distaste and enter Jason's gloomy basement room.

He turned his head toward her voice in the doorway. "Is *what* true?"

"That Cocci wants to use *Phobos?* Didn't you tell him the margin for error? I knew he was crazy but I didn't—"

"I told him."

"And he wants to go ahead anyway? You've got to stop him!"

"Steve Cocci is not a man who enjoys arguments— not from the people he pays to solve his problems."

"You know what happens if we don't intersect the black hole's orbit with the *exact* center of Phobos."

"Actually five feet either way . . . But yes, we slow down the hole. It stops orbiting the Earth and falls into the planet. I've already calculated the absorption rate."

"How long?"

"Positing Hawking-1 at rest in the central core— not just passing through every nine hours and forty-odd minutes—and assuming continuous pressure from the semi-liquid material, then the process completes itself in just over six million seconds."

"What about back-pressure from the accretion disk? That should slow the absorption down some."

"Some. Not enough." Jason disconnected the mastoid plug and reached for his goggles. "The pressures at the Earth's core would snuff the disk like a candle flame."

"Six million . . ." Her lips silently worked on the number. "What's that in years?"

"Ten weeks. Less than that, actually. I was just working out the structural calculations."

"Structural?"

"Yes. The planet can probably withstand a loss of up to ten percent of internal mass. At that point, the surface will be in almost continuous seismic activity, but it will maintain its integrity. Beyond fifteen percent losses, however, the mantle and crust collapse. It's not a smooth process of shrinkage."

"Fifteen percent . . ." Ariel's eyes were closing. She was slumped against the wall.

"Something like seven weeks. Counting from the minute we fumble with the black hole."

Jason caught her as she folded toward the floor. He carried Ariel over to the couch, set her with head between knees and began rubbing the back of her neck.

Chapter 9

Steven Cocci: POSITIVE PRESSURE

Steven Cocci was tired of selling his soul in pieces.

He stood in front of the cracked marble of the walk-in Mediterranean fireplace, trying to decide if he wanted to set and light a fire. The fog was running through the pines of the San Francisco Presidio and walking down around the boarded windows of Cocci's Pacific Heights house. It was cold in here.

Cocci would have preferred to keep tonight's appointment at the ranch in Napa, where he had moved more or less permanently after the big quake, but the visitor insisted there was only time to meet in the city. Such as it was.

A junior Mephistopheles from the State Department was coming "on urgent business." His masters would have another favor to ask. It was always either State or Commerce or Defense, with a bill to pass, a cause to fund, a Third-World country to develop a plantsite in—or to keep out of. And Cocci, because Pinocchio, Inc.'s profit margin sometimes survived on shaky foreign economies and a strong U.S. foreign policy, gave them what they wanted.

When the doorbell rang, he answered it himself.

The visitor was a young man Cocci had met perhaps once before, in Washington. He wore a gray suit, gray tie, carried a gray fiberglass attaché, had parked his gray government Chevy in the gray fog on the street. Even his hair had a patina of young gray.

But his eyes were green, and flashed with a smile of recognition.

"Good evening, sir. I'm glad you could make time for me this evening."

That was a polite lie, the currency of the diplomat. The man's name was Barry Something. Or Something Barry.

"Evening, Barry. Always have time to meet with the State Department . . . Come in."

Barry gave a long look over his shoulder, up and down the street, then moved past Cocci.

In the living room he looked around, not at the plaster dust on the Ansel Adams prints, not at the Matisse lithos nor the Rembrandt copy. Even the garish Eisen *spatiale*, one of Jeannie's few lapses, did not attract him. Barry was looking hard at the cracked and shattered moldings.

"A drink?" Cocci asked.

"Is this room safe?"

"The foundation's cracked, the walls need bracing and the plumbing's shot. But the roof won't come down tonight."

"No, I mean . . . 'devices'?"

"You mean bugs? I should hope it's safe. My corporate security staff sweeps every month. They've never found anything."

"Can we walk in the garden? I'll take a drink later, if you like."

Cocci gave him a long look. "I'll get a sweater."

The garden was a brick-walled postage stamp hanging on the edge of the hill. The two men could stroll around it in forty-five seconds. They were into their second circuit before Barry spoke again.

"Your house isn't safe, not if your men haven't found our monitors."

"*You* have—?"

"Of course. My, ah, superiors trust you too much to trust you completely."

"I see." Cocci was at once furious and sick to think of the contamination of his home. "And what have you come to ask this time?"

Barry paused. "This meeting will not have taken place."

"Of course."

"No. I mean, even to my department. To your Defense contacts, in particular."

"Defense? . . . All right. Say what you're not going to say."

Barry sat on a wrought-iron bench, balanced his attaché on his knees and snapped it open. He took out a sealed folder and handed it to Cocci.

"Read that," Barry said.

"Out here? Look, it's getting cold and the light is going. Couldn't we—"

"You read the first paragraph of that report, sir, and I promise you won't mind the light."

Barry spoke with an unusual intensity; Steven Cocci glanced down at the folder. "Top Secret!" "To Be Opened by Addressee Only!" The addressee was Secretary of State Franklin. Cocci broke the seals.

Inside were two sheets of bond with fresh typing on them. They had no title or heading.

In nine paragraphs the paper outlined the facts, much as Cocci's people had first assembled them, on the micro black hole. This document was far more detailed than any residue of that abortive talkie Ariel Ceram had let herself be humiliated with.

However, the report was still old data. The numbers crunching the hole's orbit were even more approximate than the first guesses Ariel had made. They were positively crude in light of recent corrections to her computer program, based on her charting of the Honda Fusion accident and other strange incidents along latitude thirty-seven degrees thirty minutes. To these incidents the State Department report made only the most passing reference.

It also held no approximation of the danger Jason Bathespeake predicted. The fact that Hawking-1 was sucking up the Earth like a vacuum cleaner going through a pile of sawdust—and would finish the job in seven years—wasn't even mentioned.

Nor was there any mention of capture plans—let alone Jason's latest and almost-developed idea for shifting one of the moons of Mars.

Cocci remembered the bug they had discovered at the end of that first exploratory meeting with Ariel. He looked up from the paper.

"How did you acquire this information?"

"I—uh—intercepted it."

Cocci made a move as if to throw the papers away in the bushes.

Barry reached quickly. "That report has to be on the Secretary's desk by eight o'clock tomorrow morning."

"Can you duplicate those seals?" Cocci asked.

"I put them there."

"What's the source of the original data?"

"It's a collation from several independent sources."

"I'll bet it is. And why did you show this to me?"

The man named Barry stood up and looked off over the brick wall, into the fog coming through the Gate.

"We have reason to believe that people in your company may know more about this than the Defense Department."

Cocci folded his arms to conceal a shiver. Was this his chance to get access, right to the top, with the black hole story? But alarm bells were going off in Cocci's head. He played cool. "Reason to believe . . . ?"

"It's implied in our sources."

"I see. Still, I make industrial automata. Why

should I be interested in an astronomical phenomenon?"

"We ask ourselves the same question. Among others. We believe you have further information that would give this 'micro black hole' a number of interesting potentials."

"Such as?" He wrapped his arms closer. Sang-froid, he whispered to himself, be cool.

Barry shrugged. "If one could determine its exact speed and location, one might be able to shift its orbit to a more useful latitude."

"Define 'useful.' "

"A degree or two to the south might target the capital of New Persia."

"It might eventually, but with what effect?"

"Well, certainly, a complete black hole, dropped from orbit into a major city . . ."

"I doubt—" Cocci bit hard on his tongue. He was about to say the hole had flown directly through the wrist of his chief engineer and the man was still alive. That information was evidently a card Barry's people did not hold.

And in a couple of years? What would the black hole's effects be then? However, that line of conversation might make a case for, in Barry's terms, some "useful" action. Steve Cocci hesitated to disclose the object's destructive potential—and the doomsday it implied—to people who wanted a weapon.

"Well," he continued lamely, "the black hole would also fall on many other, innocent places."

"Twenty degress to the north," Barry went on smoothly, "and we could target Moscow."

"Yes, and Copenhagen and Glasgow." Cocci made his decision: he handed back the folder. "This meeting did not take place."

"But . . ." The young man seemed disappointed, but not disappointed enough.

"You have a plane waiting." Cocci said cordially. "I will think about your 'potentials.' "

The man whose first or last name was Barry turned with a bow and walked from the garden. Both he and Cocci harbored secret smiles.

Cocci was still awake at two the next morning. He threw back the covers, put on his robe and went barefoot across the hall into his den.

The ranch's east-facing windows looked across the Napa Valley to the street lights of St. Helena, dim and cool in the September night. He reached for the desk lamp, then paused. In the semi-darkness he sat down in the cold leather chair and pulled a lined tablet toward him. The shaft of his old-fashioned fountain pen came into his hand. Then Cocci turned on the light with the shade bent low to the blotter.

He began doodling on the tablet. It was an old habit of his to work out a problem with pen or pencil. Doodling had helped him solve the leg motions of the Courier, a cheap and expendable automaton to compete with the city's corps of suicidal bicycle messengers. Cocci had been working for Handybot at the time. Two years later he bought out the company to expand Pinocchio, Inc.

Tonight's doodling turned to the long, elliptical loops of an orbit around and through a quickly sketched Earth.

If Defense was interested in the black hole, it was very bad. Of course, such interest might ultimately spell a commitment toward the success of any recovery effort. Of course, there would be rich, cost-plus contracts for everyone involved. Of course, there would be plenty of work for automata.

There could be a problem, though. The U.S. Army Arsenal at Bay St. Louis produced robotroopers that were almost the equal of Pinocchios. Designed for combat, they were sealed and self-powered, just like the space-borne Fixits. It wouldn't take much to modify them for the mining and structural work that would be required on Phobos.

His doodling on the pad became the prehensile arm of a Fixit, swivel-jointed and fitted for grasping.

If Cocci wasn't careful, Defense would take on the project itself. First for a weapon, then to save the world, once the generals had all the facts. But Defense would put it under security, probably with a secret classification system all its own. Pinocchio, Inc. might go under military authority—just for having discovered the hole—and still not get a contract that would show a profit.

He doodled a beartrap clamping down on the Fixit arm.

How do you fight that? First, *should* he fight it? With the world at stake, why not play up to Defense and its vast resources? Because . . . because, with the project under deep security, success or failure would rest on the judgment of a very few. And soldiers at that, not necessarily engineers. Humanity might strike out against the black hole and no one know until too late.

And why *shouldn't* everyone, including Pinocchio, Inc., have a chance at bat with this thing?

He doodled a crablike Miner in a Giant's cap with an oversize baseball bat.

So—how do you fight the security apparatus?

With publicity. Ariel Ceram had started on that course: make the black hole a subject of popular curiosity. Make it a common, everyday news item. A regular roving tourist attraction, like Kilauea or Old Faithful—with wings.

Even if it started a worldwide panic?

Hell, the black hole would become that anyway, when other bright boys with calculators began figuring the nibbles it was taking out of the Earth. This was stuff for the hysterical newsheets at the checkout stands: "Earth Invaded by Black Hole, Will Your Town Be Next? See Page 3!"

Cocci doodled a plunging comet, falling on a rabbit-faced, rabbit-eared woman pushing a shopping cart.

He ripped off a sheet and started a list. People to contact, things to do.

Did he know anyone on the editorial board of *American Scientist*?

Yes, but only noddingly, from industrial conventions. Well, it was a starting place. Ariel Ceram wanted to get into the history books, let her begin there. She should coauthor with someone from Pinocchio, of course, to link the company's name firmly with the black hole. Who? Why not Bathespeake—he was a natural as a word processor, if not a writer.

Cocci sketched a bony head with blank Little Orphan Annie eyes behind black goggles. A strip of paper was coming out of its mouth.

What other angles were there? The Astronomical Sciences Section of the American Academy, of course. The ASSAA would take professional interest in a captive black hole. And Cocci's address book was full of members, after the work Pinocchio had done for the Farside Observatory.

Cocci sketched the linked hexagons of the Observatory's antenna array.

And the National Authority for Space Power Facilities could be lured into the project. Hawking-1 was an object of incredible potential. Whether as a navigation hazard, a competitive energy source or a permanent disruption to their worldwide power monopoly, it was a danger to NASPFAC. Dangers to NASPFAC were quickly attended to, Cocci had found.

His doodling showed a full-rigged solar station with its microwave beam putting the zap on a crouching figure.

And whom did he know in Congress? Politicians

were usually an effective antidote to the Pentagon. Despite the blurred lines of authority, they all knew which side of the budget their butter was on.

He started to sketch a pig but stopped with the first rounded strokes.

Cocci pushed back the pad and snapped off the light. Now that he had a course of action, he could sleep out the night.

"All you really have, Dr. Cocci, is two mysterious accidents and a great deal of theory."

Gregory Domkin's voice rumbled across the walnut desk and echoed among the plaster columns of his mock-Colonial Washington office.

The chief of the ASSAA Exploration Section was of indeterminate nationality. Some kind of Slav was hinted in the cheekbones, the straight blond hair, the burly shoulders. The man's accent was neutral, although a little flat in the vowels.

"If you could show me some *real* evidence . . ." Domkin paused, expectantly.

"We do have the seismic recordings."

"Ah yes. The seismic . . . recordings." The man's fingertips came together in front of his mouth. "As a businessman, you deal with facts that are always consistent and checkable—"

"Not always."

"Yes, but you may not appreciate how speculative— open to interpretation—a compilation of laboratory data such as seismic accelerations can be. We do not comprehend by any means all of the forces at work during a seismic event. What your Dr. Ceram's computers have shown is not necessarily a real situation."

"A cyber who works for me reviewed the professor's program," Cocci said. "He is satisfied that it is accurate."

Domkin's nose wrinkled.

"He may be satisfied that *the system* is functioning, but is he trained in the geological sciences? Does he know what the system is trying to interpret? I think not."

"The computers do show a recurring pattern of disturbances. And the pattern is consistent with—"

"It is consistent with an orbit that was computed from the seismic pattern, yes. If you'll pardon a wretched pun, Dr. Cocci, your argument is circular."

"You must be aware of the growing number of independent sightings along the same latitude. They confirm impact and breakout, according to the theoretical orbit."

Domkin looked weary. "UFOs . . ." He actually said Ooo-eff-ohs. "Do you have any idea how many strange reports my section is inundated with every month? It doesn't surprise me that this year some of them seem to congregate along a certain latitude. No more than, in other years, they all seemed to fit into the Bermuda Triangle."

"Then what evidence would satisfy your committee?"

"Some independent means of detecting the presumed black hole. One not linked so directly to your company's, um, directed efforts."

"There are still the two incidents, both independently verifiable. In the jumpjet, where it seriously injured two of my people. And, of course in the fusion lab."

"One would hardly accept stray radiation at a ruined fusion lab as evidence of anything but an experiment gone terribly wrong." Domkin grinned. "And of course what happened to your employees could easily have been a technical malfunction aboard the plane. Do you have no other records?"

"What about the hole under the reactor?"

"Flying debris from a subnuclear explosion."

"And the holes in the plane?"

"Flying debris." Domkin shrugged.

"I see."

"We accept your report with interest, Dr. Cocci. There are many unexplained events in the physical world around us. These occurrences may remain among them."

"And the threat to the world is . . .?"

"Beyond credibility. Hmmph. At this time."

"Are you blackmailing me, Mr. Cocci?"

Peter Kriegs' thin face held the same ironic smile with which he'd opened the interview. But the flat gray eyes were steady and hard.

"National Space Power offers an important, a vital energy service to this country," Kriegs continued. "It's damned irresponsible of you to suggest that we do not make the fullest use of available space resources."

"I'm not suggesting you don't," Cocci said. "Simply that there's an opportunity here for an almost unlimited power supply."

"Yes, I've read your report." Kriegs tapped it on the desk between them. "Once we've cornered this black hole of yours, we're supposed to feed material into it—"

"*Any* material. Rock dust, atomic wastes, garbage, raw sewage—"

"And it returns a flare of heat that we can tap for power." Kriegs sat back in his shellform, gimballed chair and looked up. Cocci had noticed when he first came into the office that the ceiling was covered with mirrored facets, like thousands of tiny heliostats.

"The power source is the black hole's gravity well," Cocci said patiently. "Any material that falls into it accelerates toward light speed. The hole expends no energy itself, and so it never is used up or worn out. In fact, the more material it absorbs, the more powerful it becomes."

"I *said* I'd read your report." Kriegs gave him another glittery, hard smile. "The problem seems to

be capturing the black hole in the first place. First
we go to Mars. Then we bust loose one of its *moons*
with a fusion engine. Then we bring it back to Earth.
Then we line it up with your black hole's orbit and—
and *plink*, the black hole falls into the moon. Correct?"

"Essentially, yes."

"And all of this costs us maybe half a trillion, give
or take ten or a hundred billion?"

"I think it could be done for less."

"Of course, *take* that hundred billion. And with
that we would have how much power? A couple of
hundred megawatts at most?"

"But the power would be increasing every year,
available forever."

"And forever is about how long it would take to
amortize that kind of original investment. Come on,
Cocci! You're a businessman. You've got a compucalc
on your wrist, same as I do. Having a free source of
energy isn't everything, not if—and I'm making a
pun here—it costs the Moon to get it."

"People might have said that when you put up
your first solar station."

"Yes, but the technology was already in place. We
had a military presence in space. The solar power
potential was almost an afterthought.

"No, perhaps your scheme would work in a hundred years—when and if we can find a valid reason
to go to Mars. Until then . . ."

Peter Kriegs made a gesture over the report, one
of pouring sand from his open palm.

Cocci reached forward and caught the man's wrist.
"What about the danger? If the object isn't stopped,
it will continue tearing up the Earth. Where will *you*
be then?"

Kriegs slipped his arm free and shrugged.

"Our technical people have studied this document
in detail. They simply do not agree with your risk

assessment. They say any danger to the planet is on the order of thirty billion years in the future. . . . It's really not worth our time."

Congressman Winkle was backed into a doorway between two soaring marble columns. From his glances to right and left, he obviously wanted to escape across the Rotunda.

"Cocci, I don't care how good it's going to be for the business in my district. There is no way this side of Heaven we can get an appropriation for some junket to Mars."

"A feasibility study. Is that too much to ask?"

"Hell yes! A study on a trillion-dollar project is going to run tens of billions. You know that."

"Less, certainly."

"And less is just what you'll get. Haven't you been paying attention? We're in a dry cycle up here on the Hill. We just turned down a twenty-billion-dollar proposal to reseed the Allegheny Plateau. That land's been dead of pollution for a dozen years. All they wanted was starter domes to protect ten acres in every thousand. And could we give them that? Not even a close vote!

"And now you want—you'll pardon the expression—*seed money* for gallivantin' to the stars, chasing a thing you can't even touch with your bare hand.

"Why don't you go home, Cocci, and invent a robot that will scrub hydrocarbons off of pine needles."

"In seven years, Congressman, it won't matter about the trees on the Allegheny Plateau. It and the rest of the Earth will be just a jumble of rocks orbiting the sun."

"Yes, and in seven years it won't be an election year. So we can talk about it then. Okay? Now if you'll excuse me . . ."

So Steven Cocci did go home. And under his

guidance Pinocchio, Inc. tended other gardens, although not the conifer forests that the congressman had suggested. Cocci had planted the seeds of suspicion—possibly competition—in Washington.

Now, how could he help them begin sprouting?

Chapter 10

Eldon Richardson: BIG TIME

Eldon Richardson was fascinated by the reception-ist that met him in the lobby and led him up to Mr. Steven Cocci's office. The leg motion in particular was driving him crazy.

The machine walked on sliders and joints like two legs chopped off a spider. They reached impossibly far ahead of the thin, sensor-studded body but never actually passed under it. It was a clicking, hissing parody of a hand finger-walking across a table. What held the trunk in balance, kept it from falling over backwards, Eldon couldn't guess.

"Gyroscopes," Cocci told him as the Courier pir-ouetted in the office and strode out the door. "We wind it up every morning to about fifty thousand revs, but by three o'clock it's wobbling and crashing into doorways. That model never got out of proto-type. Now we let it run around because it's fun to watch. Can I get you a drink?"

"You have a robot bartender, perhaps, that sneezes tonic out its nose?" This was more fun than Whee-B-Toys.

"Tonic, gin and tonic, whiskey and soda, or champagne."

"It's a little early for me. Coffee?"

121

Cocci nodded and pressed a button. "You've been on the thin edge of it, haven't you? Ever since that tape from Japan?"

Eldon sighed. He wondered if this interview was going to end before it began. When Cocci had called two days ago, he'd implied some kind of corporate PR offer. Not really exciting stuff, in Eldon's frame of reference, but still a job. This conversational gambit, now, didn't look hopeful.

Well, take it straight.

"I'm officially on leave from the station."

"And unofficially?"

"I'm a looney-toon who'll be escorted to the Kansas border with due ceremony—that is, chicken feathers, tar, and a torchlight parade—if I ever pull a whizzbang like that again. End of quote."

"How do you feel about that?"

Eldon tasted bile. "How would you? Angry! Frustrated!"

"Foolish?"

"I saw those holes. In person. At least the one in Kansas. And everyone else by now has seen holopix of the other, in Japan. Something mighty big is punching mighty deep potholes."

"From the sky, you said."

"Yeah, sure, well, up from under the ground is *crazy*."

"Improbable, yes. Crazy, perhaps. But also true, I so swear."

"And who are *you*, sir? A rich man, head of a company that tinkers in robots, sure. Steel-collar boss of the western world, if you like. But an instant expert on the Defense Department's shenanigans or NASPFAC's fox passes? I doubt it."

Cocci made a brushing motion across his desk. "We have our sources. This story has landed you in hot water up to your eyebrows, but there's a key to it. And I happen to hold it. You got the facts about half right. Now I'm going to give you the other half."

"And in return—?"

"You're going to tell it. Persuasively. Powerfully. To every net and cast service that'll pick up a non-syndicated tape. You'll have Pinocchio's full resources— data, simulations, expert testimony, technical support. Just get the story across."

Eldon thought about it for two seconds. "My fee is five thousand a day," he said, using the first number that came into his head.

Cocci just laughed. "I thought, in view of your current position, I could name my own figure. But, yes, five thousand is acceptable. You'll earn it. Come with me."

The dapper little man led Richardson to an adjoining conference room with full vid and holo effects. It was already darkened.

"The first tape you'll see is raw data. It's a computer interpretation of seismic read-ins from around the Pacific."

He proceeded to show, rather proudly, a really bad computer simulation. It was crudely drawn and, about halfway through, broke up in a kind of static. Cocci was absurdly intent on some mark that only showed up at the beginning and the end of the simulation. He went on and on about how it was the key to the whole mystery.

Eldon just nodded and looked as if he understood.

A black hole. Yes, of course.

The second clip was of a woman in a wheelchair. Pretty lady, perhaps once. But now she was obviously sick. For some reason her hair was in a crewcut, like a punker from the eighties. Or a Dachau survivor.

She was telling a story—in the subdued, rehearsed cadences of a police witness—about a jumpjet accident. Someone had been hurt by a flying object and she'd had to tourniquet him, in two places. She had later visited the plane in quarantine and obtained holo evidence that something from outside the fuselage entered and exited the passenger space where the man had been sitting.

The holo unit lit up with straights and pans of first one hole then another in a commercial jet's metal skin. They looked like bullet holes.

The third clip was based on Richardson's own piece from Japan, but with much better and closer examination of the Haramachi hole. Then there was the familiar sequence of the techno-san, grinning behind the face plate of his radiation suit, releasing his brightly ribboned probe in slow motion and it sliding smoothly down through bedrock. The clip's ending, where Richardson talked about a force coming down from the sky, was omitted.

The fourth clip was another computer sim. This one was very professional, done on the holo. It claimed to show a black hole in action. The audio's voice-over said it was magnified about a billion or a jillion times. A gray pearl was embedded in a vortex of fire; the voice called this the event horizon. As the focus pulled back, the pearl disappeared and the fire quickly resolved into a disk and feather-fountains of blue-white gas. The voice now said this was the actual size. The disk was about eighteen inches across.

Uh-huh. Yawn.

The audio effects were intended to be one continuous wave crash. Someone had taken the surf track from *Midsummer Moon*, last year's Caitlin Amor sexstravaganza, and rolled it into one long crescendo. But Eldon's trained ear could detect the splices. The thing needed a lot of work.

The final clip was another holo sim. It showed the Earth against a starry background, being gouged repeatedly by a line of white fire. The line looped in and out, around the top of the planet, through the U.S., China, the Mediterranean. Another voice-over explained that this was a perfect elliptical orbit, with the perigee embedded in the Earth near the core. It looked like someone was walloping the bejeezus out of a beach ball with a length of silver chain. The sound effects were the whump-whump of a small car running on a flat tire. After a span of time the audio called six and a half years, the ball started to sag and collapse, then fragmented. Orange globs burst forth and solidified into tumbling asteroids.

These were just dumb, pre-*Star Wars* visuals. Antique.

The lights came up and Cocci beamed happily at him.

"Quite a story, isn't it?"

"Oh . . . yeah. Just—what did I see?"

Cocci frowned mightily. It made him look like a disgruntled apple doll.

"That's our evidence. We've got proof that the Earth is being subjected to repeated bombardment by a tiny black hole."

"Proof . . ." Richardson's shoulders slumped. Here he'd thought he had a job almost lined up, and he was dealing with a crackpot industrialist with a scientific bee in his pants. This project was just an old man's fantasy trip, which would collapse as soon as they started on backgrounding. No wonder the guy would accept his fee of five thousand. Eldon should have asked ten or fifteen and would probably have gotten it—for a while.

Unless the man was right, of course, and the world *was* going blooey . . .

"All I've seen," he said carefully, "are a series of computer simulations, some of them fairly corny. And one woman, who may or may not be able to stand up from that wheelchair, talking about a freak accident on an airplane. That's not what I call proof."

"You said yourself, you saw those holes."

"Of course. But they could mean a lot of things.

They don't prove anything about this whumping black hole you claim you've found."

"We do have a technical report. I thought, however, you'd find it rather dry."

"More words. More computer simulations. Those aren't going to prove anything, are they?"

"I wasn't aware that a journalist's standards of evidence were so high," Cocci said stiffly. "Especially not after your report from Japan."

Ah, that was a low blow.

"Look," Richardson started over, "for whatever reasons, you seem to want a case made for the world coming to an end in six or seven years. Maybe you have a stock deal planned, I don't know." He took a breath. "But before anyone will accept your story, first, you've got to be credible and, second, you've got to be plausible. That bunch of stuff wouldn't convince a ten-year-old to buy bubblestix."

"I take it you're refusing this assignment?"

Eldon paused. "I don't know. Let me read the report. Maybe it will suggest something."

Cocci seemed to unchill a bit. "Good. I'll have a copy sent around to your hotel."

The little man started to turn away. Richardson, against his own better judgment, still wanted to press the point.

"It would really help me to understand if I knew exactly what you're trying to do. What's the punch line?"

Cocci grinned up at him. There were wrinkles in the creases around his mouth and beside his eyes. The man was older than he looked. Or, for just a moment, looked older than he was.

"The world actually is going to end in seven years. And the people who can do anything about it remain as unconvinced as you. So I'm hiring you to play Chicken Little. Maybe they'll believe a professional media caster."

*   *   *

The report was as dull as Cocci had promised, full of equations and calculations. Richardson got to the end of it only by skimming the last half, and even then he finished after midnight.

It still didn't convince him. But if Cocci was playing some deep game, he was putting a lot of time and effort into it. And the numbers, the jumble of physics in the report *smelled* real. And the simulations he'd seen in Cocci's office had, on reflection, the eerie feel of some earnest amateur who believed in his work.

Over the next week he met with Grace Porter, the woman in the wheelchair, with Jason Bathespeake, a cyber with goggled eyes and whispery mechanical voice, and with Ariel Ceram, who supposedly discovered the—um—black hole. They all seemed to believe the story with a candor and an innocence that Richardson found almost convincing.

Finally he decided that, whether the story were true or not, provable or not, he could still earn his fees. He would package it, dribble it out, make it plausible, raise a fuss that wouldn't quiet down for weeks, maybe for months.

At the end of a week he unfolded a plan of campaign to the group in Cocci's office.

"All the pieces have to look like they came together independently," Eldon insisted. "Ariel publishes her new monograph. In the *American Scientist*, if you can arrange it. She doesn't tie it to the jumpjet or anything, just fudges the numbers and calls it a black hole. This time she reveals the speed of the thing and talks about its being in orbit, endlessly returning.

"The second attack is your lawsuit. We push as hard as we can on the fact that AmAir concealed the damage to the jumpjet."

"Whom exactly are we suing?" Grace asked.

"It doesn't matter. The Federal Air Safety Advisory Board, for letting the plane fly into a black hole. Or AmAir, for failing to advise you about the radiation hazard. Just so long as you get a second slice on the story. This picks up about two-point-eight days after Ariel publishes."

"Do we sue in Pinocchio's name?" Cocci asked.

"No. Grace and Kornilov can sue privately, even separately if you like. It's just a nuisance suit to get the word out. You abandon as soon as the networks and beam channels pick it up. Then the third—"

"What about bonds-in-earnest and court costs?"

"Price of doing business," Elson said quickly.

"What about countersuits for litigious harassment?" Cocci persisted.

"Look, the suit is just a media hook. You don't talk to anyone except reporters. I'll find out who's local and should be bird-dogged on the story. Third, we get Jason involved. The voice and those goggles make him scary as hell. He's our—"

"Thank you, I'm sure," Bathespeake said. He sounded amused, but with that voicebox who could tell?

"De nada," Eldon said. "You're the oracle, the voice of the god Science, an acolyte with x-ray vision who can see the Real Truth. And you push the end of the world in one act. You narrate the computer sims. You hit the talk shows and give them the whole line. Right up to blooey. Think you can handle it?"

"I already rehearse it every night."

"Right." Eldon still wasn't sure of the mechanical man. Deep things going on there. "Finally, we all get together—geoscientist, victims, oracle—at a site we'll announce *in advance*. And there we all witness once again the horror of the roving black hole. On primetime vid. Can you do that, Ariel?"

"What, predict a point of impact? With what we got from Japan, you give me a date and I'll give you a time and a place to within four feet." Ariel casually breathed on her fingernails and pantomimed buffing them on her lapel.

"The date will be four-point-seven days after we launch this thing," Richardson said.

"What's the point of the site visit?" Cocci asked.

"No point at all. It's a classic media event.

"By that time," Eldon went on, "if all the theory I learned in Media Arts 101 still holds, we should be reaching about four hundred million people in the industrialized world, about half that in the non-aligned, but only about forty million in the Third World.

"We should have a credibility reading of twenty-eight percent, average. That sounds low, I know, but it'll be a prime audience. The theory says that on hard-science stories like this one, the cred inverts and lodges with your best-educated segments."

"What could we do to widen the reading?" Cocci asked.

Eldon shrugged. "A docudrama about the black hole, running in five parts on primetime. Or introducing it as a key-concern reference in the story lines of two or more major soaps. But you don't have the time to prepare the one, nor the bucks to buy the other.

"Although the visit to a predicted impact site will help, it would really be convincing if you could capture the black hole and display it in a cage. But if anyone could do that—"

"Right," Cocci agreed. "We wouldn't need to go through this exercise. Is that the whole program?"

"That's what we've got. It's a little ragged. For instance, if you could hint at a resolution, give the viewers a plan of action—"

"If we had one, we certainly would," Cocci said blandly.

Ariel shifted in her chair. "What about—?"

Cocci's voice rode right across the professor. "But

there is no known way to stop or contain a black hole, is there?"

"Then I'm still in the dark," said Richardson, "about what this campaign is going to do. Except cause a worldwide panic in every metro center that gets channel cast."

"That's all I'm paying for." Cocci's smile was hard and bright and final.

Chapter 11

Alex Kornilov: ON SITE

Alexander Kornilov was not a musical man. It wasn't that he was tone deaf and the sounds made no sense to him. He just wasn't interested. Of the current popular music on the channels he might hear one song or another that would catch his ear, but music as a subject and a study was outside his world.

When his hair stopped falling out and he started to regain his color, the doctors said he needed physical therapy and training for the mechanical hand they had attached to the steel bars in his wrist. So they decided he should learn to play the piano.

Kornilov thought of it as punishment.

Three times a week he went to the rec room for a half-hour contest with Madama. She was a plump Austrian with an out-of-date PonyBoy haircut. She wore black polyester bag dresses that chafed her neck and upper arms. She scolded and petted him and made a fuss. But she taught him fingerwork.

Kornilov hated it. But he learned.

He learned that his meat left hand was stronger and could bang the keys harder. His mechanical right hand was quicker and had more stamina. When he played rhythm right against left, the metal hand ran away from the meat. With its pistons and levers

131

Kornilov could run through scales and trills and chord changes for hours without tiring.

Steve Cocci came to visit, and Kornilov grumbled that the hospital routine was wasting his time. He was ready to go back to the labs. Cocci pursed his lips and said something about when he was fully recovered.

Grace Porter came to visit, and Kornilov fell over himself to show off his new talent. He played nocturnes that sounded like dirges. And she bit her full underlip while smiling at him with squinty eyes.

Jason Bathespeake came regularly, and somewhere in that computer-bruised brain of his, he heard music in Kornilov's thumping. He seemed to enjoy it.

Madama, it turned out, didn't care a bit about his music. She studied his technique. At the eighth lesson she opened the carpetbag she carried for a purse and pulled out a pair of calipers with laser teeth. While he pounded through a Scott Joplin rag, Madama sighted along the keyboard and measured the lift of his second knuckles.

With a satisfied chuckle she waved him to silence and said he was doing very well.

The left meat hand was aching; the right mechanical hand clicked and wanted more.

So the duty nurse took him over to the children's wing of the hospital to learn games: Jacks, Cat's Cradle, Skeedaddle, Whump-Pups, the old and the new coordination builders. In his room, they encouraged him to play solitaire instead of reading his technical journals, because handling the cards was exercise. They fed him everything cut up bite-size and gave him only chopsticks to eat with. When he tried them lefthanded, Korny spilled more; he sighed and switched back. He ate his rice two and three grains at a time.

Finally the day came when they said he was well. They told him to come back on his sixtieth birthday to have his stomach battery replated. Then they wheeled him out to the curb and dumped him—into Grace Porter's hands.

Grace took him to dinner, both to celebrate his release and to bring him up to date on the Black Hole Task Force. She seemed quick and shy and fumbled with her silverware.

Over the first glass of wine, in the uneven light of the candle on their table, Kornilov saw Grace as if for the first time.

She had always been one of the most beautiful women he knew. That made him wary, a little defensive . . . well, all right, sometimes abrupt and cold. Korny had a reputation to keep up, one carved in the hearts of at least two generations of Pinocchio's willing female technicians and secretaries. But confronted with this amazing woman, who had beauty, poise, savvy and executive-grade balls to swing, he hesitated. He felt like a schoolboy whose pass—if one were attempted—would be knocked rudely out of bounds. This defensiveness was his own brand of shyness.

Now he saw her with the eyes of someone who shared with her a mystery and a tragedy. One way or another, it was a bond.

Grace's face, he recollected, had once had the precise, metric angles of a fashion model of the late '90s: firm jaw, high cheekbones, long nose, full-bow lips. As precise as the curves of a supersonic racer. Now there was a roughness to the skin, a hard taut-ness that came with trauma. Or with age.

Tiny wrinkles marked the skin around her eyes and mouth; they made her look more . . . thought-ful. More a person with experience in this world and less a sensual innocent from the fashion page.

Her hair, which had once flowed around her shoul-ders, was now cut into a tight, layered cap. It was a new-grown legacy, he supposed, of her radiation sickness, and it heightened the Nineties Look. But while her hair had kept its rose-gold color, silver-white streaked Grace's bangs and the quarter-curl before her ears.

Other damage was there to see. Her body still had the straight shoulders, small breasts and long legs that went with the Look. But her neck and arms were thinner—almost bony. Her wrists and fingers had lost the micron-thin layer of subcutaneous fat that in a woman divides "slender" from "scrawny."

Grace had been talking quietly under the restaurant noise about a plan to capture the black hole, something to do with Mars and its moons, Jason's idea, which Cocci had declared a supersecret for now. . . . She paused at his calculating stare and gave him a brief smile.

"Do I pass?"

"Sorry," he said, ". . . thinking about something." About the day she had taken that dose of radiation, and whose life she had saved in the process.

"You were counting the wrinkles like the rings on a tree." She sighed. "I'm forty, Alex. I've been sick. It shows."

"You're still the neatest lady I know," he said gallantly.

"Words . . ."

"You saved my life. When anyone else would have dithered or fainted, you did the right things. Fast. I owe you . . . And I'm glad it was you."

Kornilov felt a sudden confusion and knew he had to back up words with a gesture. He slowly reached his meat left hand across the tablecloth. She took it with a little squeeze that might have been just friendly—and a dismissal. But then she let her hand lie there, lightly stroking the edge of his palm with her fingertips. Her eyes held his for two seconds, then lowered shyly. To Korny it seemed more intimate than a kiss, and he had enjoyed thousands of those.

After a moment she withdrew and sipped at her wine.

"So," he said, trying to sound gruff and businesslike but not quite making it. "Ripping off a moon sounds like Cocci's brand of tactics. Who pays the bill? The Feds? Not Pinocchio, I'll bet."

"Steve is being very close-mouthed about plans. He does have something going." She shook her head and the bangs shifted in the soft light. "Where, I don't know. But whatever it is, he now wants publicity—a big splash, complete with a media fixer he's found. It's the fellow from Kansas who did that scaredevil report from Haramachi. The blitz is already under way. Your part and mine started up yesterday."

"What did we do—rob a bank?"

"Sued the airline. For grievous bodily harm and concealing evidence of unsafe conditions."

"Why, for chrissakes? They didn't have anything to do with the black hole."

"It's a ploy, to get media attention."

"Can we win?"

"Doesn't matter. We'll drop it in a month."

"Then what?" Korny swivelled his mechanical hand over to the right to pick up his knife, then left to pick up a butter pat. He caught Grace staring at the impossible movement. "I said, then what?"

"Oh!" She jumped in her chair and blushed. "Then it's up to Steve to negotiate whatever he has planned."

"And you haven't an inkling—?"

"Well, his phone forwarding shows he was in Washington for six days two weeks ago."

"The Feds, I knew it."

"Not indicated. Every time someone mentions the government he snarls. Besides, the memory tags on his calls show him spending time with the American Academy and with National Space Power. That's hardly government."

"You *have* been snooping," Korny accused her—but with a smile.

"Just making sure that I—knew where to get in touch with him." She returned the smile.

"Unh-huh. Sounds like he's putting together a coalition. But why the big publicity?"

"Maybe it's a reluctant coalition?"

"Reluctant for why?" he asked.

"Jason says there's terrible danger if we use Phobos. Something about the margin for error. He says that if we slip up, the Earth gets snuffed in a few weeks instead of years."

"Weeks or years. That's still not a reason to back out." Korny took more wine. He wondered if it would affect his control of the new hand.

"But Jason also says there are asteroids larger than Phobos that we can use, with a better safety margin."

"Yes, and could we get to them in time? What if the Mechanical Man is wrong?"

"Jason never has been. If he is, then we all meet the inevitable—in a matter of weeks or years. But we've got no one better than Jason for accuracy."

The waiter brought their plates. Korny picked up his fork and did a showoff snap roll to test the balance. They ate in silence for some minutes. Liquor didn't seem to affect coordination on the hand's circuits, Kornilov noticed. For some reason that bothered him. He wanted to understand the wiring Jason had ordered put in his head.

"Does it hurt?" She gestured at his hand.

"No . . . Funny, it never really has. Some aches now and then that the doctors call psychosomatic, that's all."

Grace shivered.

"Does it offend you?" he asked gently.

"Oh no. It's just cold in here, suddenly."

When they had finished with coffee and she had insisted on paying the check, over his mild protests, he offered to take her home.

"All right, but it won't do you any good," Grace said.

"No?" He let his mouth sag. "Why not?"

"Because you have to pack. So do I. We're going on safari."

"Where to?"

"Some place in Virginia. Only Ariel knows exactly."

"More media blitz?"

She nodded. "And a little number-polishing."

"This is becoming inconvenient."

"Oh, I don't know about that." Grace met his eyes again and she was smiling.

In a matter of microseconds, using perceptions sharpened by a dozen similar encounters, Kornilov summed up the meal and the evening. That one touch of hands and eyes, the other banter, the offer and her wry acceptance, all totaled up to a completed pass and, possibly, a technical penalty. But the game, he decided, was on.

Korny could see no special reason for the entire task force to come on this trip, except for psychology—both the media's and their own.

Until they saw Hawking-1 make its mark on the Earth, the team could not be sure they had more than—as Richardson had told Cocci—just words and computer simulations. Also, the amateur sightings were never exactly chronological, never precisely placed. Everyone wanted one more clocking to sharpen Ariel Ceram's model of the black hole's orbit.

Kornilov knew he would be better off spending his time planning the automata to be adapted for the mission to Phobos. Grace, Jason and Ariel probably felt the same way about their respective jobs. Only the technicians and roustabouts were actually required to take an accurate reading. That lanky flack, Richardson, had strongly disagreed. And got his way.

So the whole group had come, except for Cocci.

"Just call me camera shy," Steve had said quickly, when Korny asked.

They might have traveled to the wheatfields of Richardson's Kansas, the stony deserts of Nevada, rice terraces in China, goat trails in the hills of Greece. But they were in a less dramatic but more charming setting: on a ridge overlooking the James River, a few miles east of Fincastle in western Virginia.

It was so cold on this October morning that Korny had expected snow, but all they had was a glazing of frost to stiffen the grass. It scraped on his boots while he was setting up the directional receiver-dish on its tripod. They had forty minutes until—do you call it "expect"?

Grace was back in one of the Jeeps. She was wrapped in a parka and sipping hot coffee. From her previous encounter with the black hole and the radiation sickness that followed, Korny knew she was vastly uneasy about this trip. As the time drew closer, she had quietly faded into the background. But still she had come along.

"Station Two, are you ready to test? Over." Ariel's voice crackled from the talkie.

"Ready. Over."

He made a final adjustment of the dish's gain with the tip of his little finger. He didn't want to jar it.

"Test one, Jason. Over."

Out in the center of the field, Jason Bathespeake fired off a burst from the electrostatic generator. Korny's directional dish swiveled and locked. Around the ridge, half a dozen more were also taking notice of the signal.

"Bingo! Got it. Over," Ariel crackled. Thirty minutes to go.

Korny had some time ago decided that Jason wasn't *actually* taking a risk by standing in the middle of a field where, in half an hour, the most concentrated form of matter in the universe was due to burst through. After all, they had no reason to doubt the timing of the hole's orbit. Still, when he went to check on the other stations, Kornilov preferred to walk around the field's perimeter. His metal hand was starting to ache at the wrist joint. And not from the cold air.

A dozen media vans were parked on the south side of the ridge. Videyes, floaters and shotgun lenses bobbled in the crowd that surrounded Richardson at his press stand. Two men came up and began asking Korny about the AmAir lawsuit. He clacked his right hand at them and said he was busy. Twenty minutes to go.

He stopped by their own vehicles and found Grace with her nose in a magazine. It was *GIGO,* a popular pseudo-science journal Korny knew she scorned. There on the page was Jason's solemn face, the goggles black and menacing. Another planted story.

"Everything okay?" he asked.

"I'm fine. I'm really fine." She never took her eyes off the magazine. Her elbows were in tight to her sides. Her legs were crossed with her feet tucked under the seat.

"It shouldn't be too long now."

"Yeah. Right. Thanks, Alex. Don't miss it."

Grace turned a page. Ten minutes to go.

Ariel Ceram was bustling around in the equipment truck, checking the disks in the recorders, making twiddle adjustments on the seismic readers, spot checking the view from the cameras set up around the ridge.

"Everything okay?" he asked here.

"Great!" She rubbed her bare hands together. "The equipment's working perfectly. The computer model has the place pinpointed to six nines. We're going to *nail* the sucker!"

"Good. I think I'll watch from Station Eight."

"Wish us luck, Korny."

She smiled so nicely that he leaned forward and gave her a peck on the lips. He just caught a glimpse of her widening eyes as he turned away. Two minutes to go.

Jason was at Station Eight. Korny noticed that he had disconnected the plugs at his throat and behind his ear. That was understandable, considering what feedback from an overload on the cyber's prostheses might do to his nervous tissue.

Kornilov quietly unsnapped the D plug at his own wrist.

Thirty seconds.

Despite all the warnings, he slipped on a pair of polarizing sunglasses and looked out across the field. He wanted to *see* this thing, not just study some recording of its passage.

As if they knew something was coming, the birds grew quiet and the wind died down. Korny could suddenly hear someone counting backwards and realized it was Ariel, her voice muffled in the truck's interior.

". . . Two! One! Zero! Huh?"

There was a detonation from somewhere behind Korny. It sounded, on reflection, like the crack of a shell bursting, *followed* by the whistling rip of air that an incoming round makes. From ahead—no flash, no twist of the dish-ear to triangulate on Hawking-1's path.

He turned just in time to see half of an old, spreading oak crash on the last van in line; the other half fell off down-slope. A column of smoke and vapor rose toward the morning sky behind the trucks. Across the field, the vid operators followed it up like a pack of bird dogs on a flushed grouse.

Grace Porter slammed open the door on her Jeep and ran shrieking across the field toward Korny. He caught her and held her close.

"It didn't touch me! Tell me it didn't touch me, Alex!"

"Easy, easy," he soothed. "You were sixty, no eighty, feet away, with six tons of steel trucks between you and it. No radiation hazard at all."

Grace untucked her head from under his chin and looked up at him.

"You're sure about it?"

He nodded.

Bathespeake plugged in his vocoder. "No danger at all, Grace."

Ariel stalked over from her equipment truck with dark murder written on her face.

"Why did this happen? Alex? Jason? The model is good. It checks out. Then we get an observation two or three hundred feet off. Why?"

"The model must be incomplete," Jason said.

"How?"

"Something is altering the orbit. Very slightly." Jason's voder sounded flat in the chill air.

Kornilov considered Ariel's mathematical model. It was a simple program that added and subtracted degrees, minutes, seconds, and microseconds of longitude along latitude thirty-seven degrees, thirty minutes. So much time in the planet, so much time outside, all while the Earth turned at a steady thousand miles an hour. Nothing could vary the orbit except . . . gravity flux? The model accounted for perturbations of the Sun and the Moon, but what about the varying densities of the Earth itself? The basalt masses of the continental plates might have some minor effect.

"Are they in your model?" he asked Ariel.

She stared at him for two seconds, then her eyes

crossed. "That's a geologist's question. I've been playing astronomer too long."

"So!" Bathespeake said. "We just add wobbles to the orbit as it reacts to variations in the Earth's gravity field. It shouldn't be hard to figure out, once we chart the masses and convection currents along thirty-seven thirty."

"You can handle it, can't you?" Korny asked Ariel.

Ceram was looking from him to Jason and back. "Can I *handle* it? Your brain's gone soft, Kornilov. You handle the lady and I'll go punch my computer. Again." She stamped off toward the truck.

"Maybe you'd better help her?" Korny said to Bathespeake.

"There's a choice?"

Later, when they measured the exit crater by the oak tree, they found a hole seventy-four centimeters across. Hawking-1 was definitely growing.

Richardson made sure the video teams got good closeups.

That night at dinner in Fincastle's "de luxe" and only hotel and restaurant, it took three glasses of wine to cheer Ariel up. And four glasses to calm Grace down. Korny counted them.

When they went up to their rooms, Grace was hanging on his arm. So it seemed natural when she invited him in. Natural when he folded her into his arms. And natural when she asked softly, "Have you been taking your Ban d'AIDS?"

Except it made him draw back a little.

"Of course, every morning. And—um—have you?"

Grace dipped her head onto his shoulder. "Why should I? You're the guy with a reputation, not me."

"What's this? A reputation?" Korny pretended to be scandalized. At least, he tried to pretend.

"Uh-huh." Now there was laughter in her smile. "And I want to try it out thoroughly."

"Try it out? Or wear it out?"

For answer, Grace put a hand around his backside and grabbed a handful.

"Whichever comes first," she said.

"Don't you mean 'whoever'?" he asked, low in his throat.

"Mmm-hmmm," she purred in hers.

Conversation languished for the rest of the night.

The voices rose up to the pineboard rafters:

"World's gonna end in *fire!*"

"Fire, brother!"

"*Black* fire from the visitor!"

"*Dark* fire of the Antichrist!"

"Amen, brother!"

"Tell it!"

"Millennium come and gone, but the Lord remembers!"

"Lord God a *Hosts!*"

"Gonna come down and suck the substance—"

"Way down!"

"Substance of the world and the flesh!"

"And the world gonna end, brother!"

"In *fire!*"

In a scented hall of white stone, dry voices in feather whispers discuss the same apocalypse:

"What is the meaning, Ananda, of the report from the Americans?"

"The world was formed on the Wheel and on the Wheel it will also die."

"And is this a matter of terror and despair?"

"Nothing that comes of the Wheel of Life is a matter of joy or despair, terror or hope. Only fulfillment follows the Wheel."

"Very good, Ananda."

*   *   *

In a glass and tile kitchen on Long Island, over the evening's first margaritas:

"Does this mean we *should* accept that second debenture, Geoffrey? Or that we shouldn't?"

"I doubt very much, dear, that many debentures will be offered, once the implications of this catastrophe sink in."

"What implications, Geoffrey?"

"Well, *who* is going to be involved? There will be no Wrigley Wrench Company to make good on them, right? And no Dun & Poor's to rate them, right? And no *us* to collect, right? So it stands to reason that there will be no offering."

"But suppose this turns out to be nonsense? Like all that population-explosion, greenhouse-effect, carcinogen claptrap the Democrats have been spouting for forty years. What do we do *then*, Geoffrey?"

"Then we *take* the debenture, dear, of course."

"You got a promise somewhere that you *ain't* gonna die?" the Cincinnati cabbie demanded of his worried fare.

"Because, if it's written down I'd sure like to see it. I never got one of them. So I guess *I'm* going.

"And it would be nothing but a comfort to know that everybody else is going with me. Fewer loose ends that way, you see?

"But who believes everything you see on the vid, hey?

"Yeah, have a nice day, sir."

Chapter 12

Steven Cocci: THE SETUP

"Dr. Cocci, we must talk."

Domkin's voice, even at three thousand miles' distance, sounded both hurried and hushed, like an undertaker with a distracting itch.

"Go ahead, Gregory, we *are* talking."

"Have you seen the news vids?"

"I generally keep abreast." Cocci was enjoying this. "Any item in particular?"

"You *know* what I mean. It's all over the channels about your black hole. We must have taken over thirteen hundred calls in the last twenty-four hours. Everyone wants to know what the Academy is doing about it."

"Yes? And what do you tell them?"

"Please, Dr. Cocci—Steven. We must discuss your—that very—interesting—and timely report you showed us." Sugar and slime dripped in the administrator's voice. Cocci knew the formula.

"I think we *should* discuss it, Gregory. I can even help you catch the hole. But I want something in return . . ."

"Yes?" The tremolo in Domkin's voice amused Cocci.

"Ahh—let's have lunch."

"Shall I come to San Francisco? Tomorrow?"

"Why don't you."

"Cocci, yóu maniac!"

The phone speaker blared with Kriegs's indignation.

"I beg your pardon, sir."

"Do you know you've got half the world believing the sky is falling?"

"Wait a minute, Peter. *I* have half the world? There is a ongoing natural catastrophe that the channels seem to have become aware of. They are now diligently reporting a truth of which I tried, at one time, to make you aware. Privately, I might add. I seem to remember you characterized it as, quote, not worth our time, end quote."

"Yes, well . . ."

"Shall I assume that you, or someone of vision and imagination in your establishment, now considers it worth some time?"

"Our R&D section—" Kriegs's voice suddenly became casual. "—thinks it might be interesting to assess the situational risks."

"And to do something about them? Your people surely must have told you that the time to act on the black hole is now, when it's small and relatively weak."

"We'll act if that seems . . . prudent."

"Shall I expect you tomorrow? Around lunchtime?"

"I'll catch an evening flight."

Cocci's secretary put its head around the door.

"Congressman Winkle on line one, Steve."

"Tell him to come tomorrow, before noon. And arrange lunch for four in the private suite at Kwan's."

"Kwan's has not reopened since the earthquake, Steve."

"All right, the Mandarin Empress, then."

"Very good, Steve."

"And Tribox—"

"Yes, Steve?"

"Don't call me 'Steve.' "

"Very good, Steve."

"Uh—Tribox?"

"Yes, Steve?"

"Take yourself down to Cognitive Programming on the third floor and tell Dr. Raiker that your erase protocols are for the birds."

"Thank you, Steve."

"Dismiss."

The three men ignored chopsticks and used their hands on the platter of baby quail flamed in rice brandy. Cocci watched with amusement as Winkle gnawed a tiny carcass and rolled his eyes like a starved wolf. Perhaps they did not know that six more courses were to come, including three of Beijing duck. If so, Cocci wasn't going to enlighten them—their table manners were too much fun to watch.

The restaurant had survived the earthquake, although its walls showed plaster patches on their red-and-gold silk brocade, the lacquered screens hid chips with daubs of dull-black paint, and a broken chair was bound with glue and twine. The effect was still dynastic—with a glint of decay.

"What is this stuff?" Kriegs asked, raising his glass of the same brandy used on the quail. "Tastes like gasoline."

"Yeah, but it has a higher octane rating," Winkle smirked.

Cocci explained that it was *mao tai,* a popular Chinese liquor made from rice wine, but he didn't mention it was 130 proof. They would find out soon enough.

Domkin was sipping the white-wine chaser. He'd tried the *mao tai* just once, scritched up his nose, and reached for the Chardonnay.

Cocci, also drinking wine, decided he would have to watch Domkin carefully. The man would be sober.

They were into the limp-fried asparagus spears when Kriegs belched politely and swung his head toward Cocci.

"It's not really gonna be your show, you know. We've all seen your report. We all know about the plan to move Phobos. We could go and get the black hole any old time."

Kriegs snapped his fingers to show how easily it was done, except the quail grease made his fingers slip. He stared at his hand for a second to figure it out.

"Yes, except you don't have the numbers," Cocci said.

"We can get them. We have cybers working for us, too."

That was probably true. Once a solution to the capture was known or guessable, the mathematical details were just skull sweat.

"I don't see why we don't turn the whole matter over to the Pentagon," Winkle said. "They're already in charge up there in space. They have the Corps of Engineers, handy boys who'll tackle anything. Let them take care of the problem."

Cocci was about to frame an answer when he caught Kriegs looking death daggers at the Congressman.

"What do you mean, 'in charge'? Head for head and ton for ton National Space Power has more men and material above the atmosphere than the Air Arm does. We've also got the cash flow. What was *their* request to your appropriations committee the last time they wanted to put a laser platform in polar orbit . . . ?"

"I don't think we want to start a turf battle, Peter," Domkin said quietly.

"The hell we don't. Are you going to listen to this

Pentagon drivel? The Academy has the biggest permanent base in space—the Farside antenna complex at Tchi . . . um . . . Tsiolkovskii. And your funding is only partly public."

"We are hardly equipped to travel to Mars, however."

"Nobody is," Kriegs said. "Especially not the Pentagon. When was the last time the Army undertook a war and did any serious fighting itself? The Gentlemen Volunteers do the real work nowadays. The regulars just staff the bases and parade with the flag. Air Arm's no different. Put their guns in orbit and *sit* on them. Beta Station's got so many null-gee tennis and fliegenball teams it's a—a—health resort."

"All right," Winkle said agreeably. "The Pentagon is out. But how, then, are we going to send a complete work party, in effect a colony, to Mars and its moons? It will clearly take a whole new class of rocket, still to be designed and tested. *That* will take ten years, if my committee experience tells me anything."

"Hear, hear," Domkin said in the sudden quiet.

"Don't think of a rocket as a rocket," Cocci said. "Think of it as a propulsion system. There are many easier ways to move a body in space than spewing out reaction mass. Some of them are a lot more primitive and easier to build than a new engine design."

"Name one," Kriegs shot back.

"A magnetic catapult."

"Phooey. We gave up on one ten years ago. Earth's atmosphere's too dense."

"I didn't say build it on Earth. My thought was the Moon. The Tsiolkovskii crater would make an excellent launch site."

"I think the Observatory would have some objections," Domkin said.

"They work for you, don't they?"

"In the loosest sense of the term, really. Anyone

who gets above atmosphere tends to forget where the money comes from. Isn't that right, Peter?"

"Damn straight," Kriegs affirmed. He took another mouthful of *mao tai*.

"Speaking of money," Winkle began. "Where will it come from for *this* venture? I seem to remember your report had a terabuck price tag, Cocci."

"I think we could do it in the high gigabuck range. And if we all kicked in some earnest money, then taking up a public subscription wouldn't be out of line."

"How 'earnest' were you thinking?" Domkin asked.

"A gigabuck each?" Cocci suggested. The thought of that much money was making the sweat run in his armpits. Still, their commitment had to be convincing.

"A billion dollars!" Domkin squealed. "That's a quarter of our private donations!"

"Funny, that's half of *our* petty cash," Kriegs sneered.

"It could be found," Winkle murmured.

"Spend it today or lose it tomorrow," Cocci said.

"Now, wait a minute!" Domkin tried to kill the momentum of the conversation, but Cocci rolled right over him.

"Shall we meet back here in, say, two weeks with our pledges? In the meantime I'll have our legal staff draft an agreement we can begin discussing."

"Don't like that idea," from Kriegs.

"Then why not all have our staffs put something together and we can compare. Use the best from each?"

"Should I introduce a bill in Congress?" Winkle suggested.

"Could it pass?" Cocci asked.

"With the way people are stirred up? I could propose ritual sacrifice of each member's firstborn male heir and get a majority. It will pass."

"Then do it—whatever the budget will bear."

"Now wait a minute!" Domkin said again. And suddenly they *were* all listening to him. "The Academy just doesn't have that kind of money," he whined.

"We could probably arrange payment in kind," Cocci said gently, thinking of his own position and the number of Pinocchios he wanted to supply to the expedition.

"In kind?" Domkin quavered.

"I said yesterday that I wanted something. You hold the lease on Tsiolkovskii. . . . I want Farside's unlimited, no, cheerful cooperation in this venture."

Color started to return to the administrator's face. "We could possibly arrange it."

"I was sure you could."

By the time the almond gelatin was brought in, Domkin was actually laughing. Kriegs, on the other hand, had glazed eyes and a fixed grin—which stayed on his face as he slid silently out of his chair.

The others didn't even notice.

Cocci decided the party was a success.

"If you had to lay your hands on a billion dollars, Grace, where would you look first?"

It was after midnight. Grace and Cocci had been three days in Washington, negotiating the framework of what he called the Consortium.

Now Grace had accepted Cocci's offer of a nightcap. She sat in one of the hotel suite's easy chairs. Her shoes were off, and she kept a medium swirl of brandy going in the bottom of the snifter.

"Without ending up in jail?" she asked. "Sell stock, I guess. A lot of stock to pump up the company's capitalization. Then sell off assets selectively. That gets money coming in two ways."

Cocci yawned, tipping his head over the back of the chair. "And you don't think you'd go to jail for that?"

"Not if it's done properly," Grace said to her drink.

"Ay-yuh."

"Do we need that much money?"

"That's the ante in this game."

"And it all comes down to what—crew assignments?" Her lips were curling in a sneer.

Cocci shrugged and drank about half his brandy. "At least that's the shape of the fight," he said.

"With the fate of the goddamn Earth in the balance, I think it's immoral. It's like—like some 19th-century polar expedition, deciding personnel for a highly complex mission just on the basis of prestige. Or monetary investment."

"It's more than that. Those on scene with the capture team will have a legal claim—at least in some minds—to the black hole. So the sponsors will measure investment and participation in terms of places in the crew."

"What does it mean for us?" Grace asked wearily. "When the 'fight' is over."

"I think we can insist on one berth just because it's our party and we have the corner on hard data—so far. We'll pay for a second place to cement our right to supply automata to the expedition. When you sort out who's paying for what—"

"If ever!"

"—then I think we'll be money ahead."

"You have any names in mind?"

"Not yours."

"Thank you from the bottom of my heart."

Cocci nodded. "I was thinking of Ariel Ceram. She'd be a good nominee for exo-geologist. A slot neither ASSAA nor NASPFAC would be particularly ready to fill."

"And the other?"

"Korny, of course."

Grace stopped swirling her brandy, took a sip.

"He's the obvious choice," Cocci said into the silence. "He's been a project manager in structurals and has space experience. He'd be a good Iron Boss under emergency conditions."

"I know. What about Jason?"

"Not much call for a cyber-psychologist in our part of the package. The others will send their own brainware."

"Then we send Korny." Grace started swirling her drink again and didn't say anything for a long time.

Cocci had one more contact to make. It wasn't even a satellite call, from San Francisco to the Stanford Linear Accelerator.

"Julius? I have a theoretical problem for you."

Herr Professor Doktor Julius Marienkafer was director of the linac's antiquated colliding beam storage ring.

"You know I hate theoretical problems. What do you want?"

"I want to know how much antimatter you can keep suspended in a magnetic bottle."

"Antimatter? What flavor?"

"Doesn't matter. Positrons, negatons, antineutrons, whatever you can isolate. Only hitch is, the bottle has to be portable."

"That's the only hitch? That's what you think. All right, *how* portable? Put it in your pocket? Or put it on a flatbed crawler?"

"Put it in the Shuttle and boost it into low orbit."

"You're talking a couple of tons then."

"Of antimatter?"

"No, you fool, of equipment to insulate and support the bottle. Of antimatter, you'll get maybe a couple of grams, in theory."

"Is that all?"

There was a cold silence on the line. "We usually get to work with *micro*grams, Steven."

"Well, I need *a lot* of antimatter."

"What for, if you don't mind my nosiness?"

"A bomb."

"No kidding. A couple of grams of antimatter would make a *boom* you don't want to be within a hundred miles of, believe me."

"It's not for me. Anyway, would you work up the specs for the bottle and see about producing the stuff."

"Steven! We're talking theoretical, right?"

"Wrong. I really do need this bomb."

"Unh. Let me discuss with my staff—"

"Discreetly."

"Of course, sure, discreetly, and then we'll work up some numbers. By the way, what do you want this *bomb* for?"

"Think of it as a dose of ipecac."

"Ipecac . . . ? All right, I *won't* ask."

After a month—fast work for so many competing bureaucracies—the bid package came in the mail. It asked for Pinocchio's proposal to design, with a contingency to fabricate, various automata to support an exploration of the moons of Mars. The purpose outlined in the agreement's introductory letter was the capture and use of a celestial object, potentially identified as a micro black hole and offically designated Hawking-1, determined to be in close orbit around the Earth's center of mass. The initiating authority came from the National Authority for Space Power Facilities, a quasi-government agency.

This was all a matter of form, of course. The agreement had been locked up for weeks.

It was late in the evening, after the office staff had gone home, when Cocci reviewed this document and began outlining a pro forma response. There was a tight smile on his face, a sense of fullness in his heart, as he began drafting his proposal on a lined tablet.

A knock at the inner door of his office interrupted his thoughts.

"Come in?"

A sallow-skinned man wearing a gray suit of the latest nine-button style let himself in and closed the door.

It took Cocci a minute to place the face.

"Henry? What the devil are you doing here?" Cocci sat up straighter in his chair. "How did you get into the building? We're under full security after six p.m."

"It's been a long time, Steve," the man said, smiling. "But it was very important that I see you."

"I didn't think we had any further business, after Riyadh," Cocci said drily.

The man came across the room, set an old-fashioned expandable leather briefcase on the desk, opened it.

"A loose end, Steve. Just a thread—a teensy frayed thread." From the case, he drew a device—obviously a weapon. "You've been dabbling, Steve. It's a bad policy. You're out of your field entirely. You've been trespassing."

"On whom?"

"The people who employ me now . . ."

He pointed the weapon. It had a pistol grip, a flaring mouth like a bullhorn and, at the operator's end, some kind of electronic meter. He aimed it at Cocci's forehead.

"What is—?"

A shrill buzzing sounded in Cocci's skull. A pain started from deep behind his eyes.

Chapter 13

Grace Porter: EVASIVE TACTICS

A young Pinocchio aide with a somber face took Grace into the hospital room. Steve Cocci was dozing on the only bed. One arm was lying on the sheet, palm up. The other curled against his chest. His lower lip hung open. It dribbled.

"How bad is he?" she whispered.

"They can't really test him except electronically. The stroke was too massive. . . . His EEG is pretty flat."

Grace knelt down by the bed and ran a gentle hand back over Cocci's head. There was a dew of sweat on his bald scalp.

"Steve . . . Steve, do you hear me?"

The left eye snapped open and rolled around. It found her face and fixed there.

"It's Grace," she whispered. "You're going to be all right, Steve."

The eye stared at her, wandered briefly to the side, then came back to stare again.

That was all the response Grace had. If she let her imagination work on it, she could read pleading, anger, relief and pain in the focus of that single eye.

She preferred to believe in random movement.

Cocci was all but dead.

"Will he get better?"

"The doctors give no hope at all. If anything, he's deteriorating. The blood supply—"

"They found him at the office?"

"Yesterday morning. From the bruising, they estimate he'd been lying there for some hours."

Grace nodded, turned away. She felt the tears coming.

"There was an envelope for you among his current papers," the aide said. He pulled it from his side pocket.

Grace accepted the impervious, ivory-fibered Notevelope. On the front, in Cocci's block script, were the words: "For Grace Porter in the event of my death." When she touched it, she thought she felt a lumpiness.

Grace turned and ran out of the room half-blinded with tears.

The bank vault three levels below the street was cool and brightly lit with fluorescent strips. As she approached the guard's desk, Grace held out the scrap of paper in Cocci's handwriting, which had the bank's address on it. Taped to the note was a flat steel key.

The guard took the key, nodded at the number on it and gave her a card to sign. He studied her signature, compared it with another in his file—how he had it Grace did not know—and seemed satisfied.

He led her through the round steel doorframe into the vault itself and over to the side where the biggest boxes were arranged. The guard's key and hers opened the engraved panel and he pulled out a black box with a hinged lid. The guard carried it for her out to one of the privacy booths.

When he had gone, Grace took a deep breath and opened the box.

They looked like theater tickets. Hundreds of them

were bundled together with rubber bands, then the bundles were stacked in layers to the depth of the box. When she pulled one bundle out, she saw the tickets were computer-printed certificates of common stock in Pinocchio, Inc. On the back of each ticket was the phosphor-etched NYSE authorization code. Each was good for a round lot, one hundred shares.

A piece of paper was folded on top of the stacked tickets. In the same block script, it said, "51.275 percent of the firm. Stay out of jail.—Steve."

The first attack came four days after Cocci's funeral.

Grace was crossing Market Street on the green during the lunch hour when a gray sedan jumped the light and came at her, engine screaming, blue smoke wreathing out of its wheel wells. She took three long steps and landed on a Muni safety island—and the car swerved to follow her. At the last second, with the front edge of the hood not eighteen inches from her hip, Grace jumped back. The car went right up over the island, clearing out a row of safety reflectors and a bus sign. She stumbled backwards across the traffic lane and fetched up in the gutter, against the curb she had stepped off five seconds earlier. The other pedestrians gathered around her, concerned, as if she had actually been struck by the car. Grace's first coherent thought was that, by golly, somebody really does tell the crowd to "step back and give the lady some air." Then her back muscles started to hurt. Her second thought was that the car hadn't been stopped in traffic for the light at all. It had been parked along the street.

It had been waiting for her.

The next attack came two days later, as Grace walked from the Muni station to her building in the early morning. She paused and turned in front of a shop window to check her hair in the reflection.

Before she could complete the turn, the window exploded in her face, spewing a thousand tiny chunks of tempered glass out into the street. The pieces were still bouncing when Grace went flat on her belly on the sidewalk. She scuttled, rump high, on elbows and knees around into the alley, stood up and took off. There was blood on her sleeves and stockings. Her cheek stung from a cut and it felt like there was something in her eye. Grace didn't stop running until she was in the next block. Then she sagged down in a doorway, breathing raggedly. A man in dark-blue velveteen and fashionable spats reached a hand down to help her. Grace gulped, held her eye, and let him lead her out of the doorway.

"What's wrong, m'dear? Something in your eye?"

Grace nodded and leaned against a parking meter. There was a sickening scratchy feeling every time she moved her eyelid.

He pulled out a lace-edged handkerchief, only faintly scented, and gently removed her hand. He deftly wiped below the eyelid then peeled it back with the tip of his finger. The tears poured out. The man's handkerchief moved quickly and, before she could pull back, her eye felt clear. Tender but clear.

"There you are."

"Why—why thank you. How can I—?"

"De nada, pretty lady. Now, do you need help? Defense against some ruffian? Assistance in the direction of the nearest hostel of the medical profession?"

"I—can you find a taxi for me?"

"Of *course*, m'dear. I *conjure* taxis." Suddenly he let out a bellow that shook Grace and spooked a colloquy of pigeons half a block down. A Crimson Cab that Grace had not noticed before was at the curb two seconds later.

The man—she took in the fact that he had no particular age, clean-shaven with sallow skin, iron-gray hair and the bright, jadestone eyes of a Nieman-

Nakamura teddy bear—was at the door, holding it wide for her. The hand he helped her inside with was as firm and unyielding as the hand of a statue. For a moment she thought he might be one of the Pinocchios in human mold. He slid in beside her and flipped his palm at her, an old vaudeville gesture, inviting her to speak.

"Your choice, m'lady. Hospital, home, or place of employment. The ride's on me."

"Perhaps we'd better go to my office." She gave the driver the address, three blocks away.

He had started to protest when her savior—yes, that was the right word—gave a rap on the glass with his knuckles and told the "hack" to drive on or he wouldn't get the two-dollar tip he so richly deserved.

Since twelve dollars was union scale, the driver raised his volume. Then he caught the bland, green stare from the back seat and shut his mouth.

"I suppose you're wondering what happened to me," Grace started.

"None of my business, really. I assume you were mugged." The man watched the foot traffic out his window.

"I think I was shot at."

"Good heavens, with a gun?"

Grace told him about the exploding shop window.

"On that street? Hardly likely. There's nothing less than fifteen stories there. Not a window that opens, no vantage 'til you get to the roofs. And that's a bad angle. Now . . ." He steepled his fingers and pressed them to his lips. "From street level? Not professional. Too exposed for an ambush with bang-bangs. Unless they were in a moving car. Did you notice a car?"

" 'They'? How do you—"

"Because the lone assassin is an antique, m'dear. Everything is teamwork these days. One to steady the gun and the other to fire it. Or to drive. So—no

car or you'd have said so. Do you often take that
street to work? Every morning perhaps?"

"Yes. Most mornings."

"Then it was a set piece." He snapped his fingers,
and Grace had the odd impression that he was used
to wearing gloves, white kidskin gloves. "A bad lie,
but the only way to take the quarry. Speaks for the
professional under stress. There must have been a
car, you just don't remember."

"There are a lot of cars on the street this time of
the morning."

"That's right, too. Better cover." More steepled
fingers.

The cab pulled up at Pinocchio, Inc.'s building.

"I get out here," Grace ventured.

"I shall come with you. You may need my help."

"Um—who are you, that I need your help?"

"My card." He produced it from his sleeve per-
haps, like a stage magician. It read: "Henry Darnley,
Soldier of Fortune, Survivalist, Security Specialist."
There was no address or phone number.

"Perhaps I do," Grace said. "But how do I contact
you?"

"Merely put out your hand. I shall be right behind."

When Grace and her savior reached the thirty-fifth
floor, she excused herself and left Darnley in the
anteroom with the tribox for company.

In her own office, she put out a priority seek-and-
find for Paul Finte, head of Security. Two minutes
later he was admitted by the tribox.

"Morning, Grace. Who's the scented body in your
outer office?" Then he noticed the bloody rags of her
sleeves and the ooze on her cheek. "And what the
hell happened to you?"

"What happened is why he's out there. I just
about got killed again." She told Finte about the
second attack, watching him grow hard and quiet.

He didn't lighten up when she told about being found and helped by Darnley.

"So you brought the man here?" he asked.

"He rather brought himself. I want you to check him out. If he's clean, maybe we can put him on staff."

"Isn't that a little quick?"

"I don't know, Paul. I feel good about him."

"What were you thinking of—watchman? door guard?"

"Hardly. How about strategic analyst?"

Finte made a face. "Didn't know I had that box in my table of organization."

"Bodyguard? I'm beginning to think I need one."

"Wouldn't you feel better with a Mark IX Rover? This model is right off the line and looks pretty good. Passes for human in all but social situations. Faster reflexes than even the VIIs."

Grace considered having a hair-trigger humanoid armed to stop a third-stage riot following her around like a puppy dog. She thought Darnley would be better company. Safer, too.

"I'll think about it. Why don't you have Darnley inspect one? The Rovers seem to be in his line. It'll keep him busy and maybe begin to repay him for helping me."

Finte's agreement was less than wholehearted.

The first positive step Grace took was to abandon, temporarily, her house in the Haight. She rented an apartment on the eastern brow of Telegraph Hill, using some long-expired identification from her short-lived marriage. The broker hardly glanced at it.

For a hideout the apartment was perfect, at least to Grace's eye. It was the lower floor of a duplex cottage with a bay window that looked up and down the cobbled steps and mossy walkways that were a spiritual extension of Filbert Street before it disappeared over the lip of the hill toward the Bay. The back door let onto a landing from which she could climb down a series of wrought-iron stairs to an alley off Sansome Street, on the flatlands eighty feet below.

She had two exits and a view of the street. She had the sun in the morning and the Bay Bridge's lights at night. She even had a tabby that seemed to come with the place and answered to no name she could give her.

It was perfect.

When Darnley—who was now on the payroll although he made a show of working for what he called "found money"—saw the apartment, he was aghast.

"You're not going to live here, surely?"

"Why not?"

"Well, but, there's absolutely no traffic, no street scene at all!"

"I know. I'll see them coming."

"What? How? Where will you put your paid friendlies? Your blockers and takers? You are perfectly alone here. That's the worst danger you could be in."

"I don't know about that." Grace was feeling stubborn. "I do have a back entrance, a fast way out."

Darnley let her lead him to the landing. He peered over the railing and down, shading his eyes with his hand. He quickly straightened and stepped back as if stricken with vertigo.

"But, m'dear, while you are climbing down all those steps, trying to flee from your assassin, his *accomplice* can pick you off with a high-powered rifle from anywhere in those warehouses down there."

"Accomplice?" Grace felt herself wilting.

"Surely. Remember about the lone assassin being antique?"

"Then this is no good at all?"

Darnley hopped over and put an arm around her shoulders. "Oh, no! It's charming, charming. Stay here by all means. But please don't think you've found your Wolfschantz, because, m'dear, it's hardly invulnerable."

"Perhaps I should get a bodyguard."

"An excellent idea! You should install one of those spiffy big killer robots your Mr. Finte demonstrated for me. If they can't outthink and outgun your lone assassin and his backup, then you haven't got a chance, m'dear. None a'tall."

It was after ten at night when a banging on her door caught Grace as she was preparing for bed. The Mark IX was halfway into its crouch, the taser hooks glinting in its palms, when Grace called it off.

"Cool it, Bruce."

"Yes, Miss Grace. Your visitor is a male of indeterminate age, height approximately 190 centimeters, weight approximately ninety-eight kilograms."

"Thank you."

"Be careful, Miss Grace."

The monster had a submoronic vocabulary and mode of address that Grace vowed would be the first line of regular business she attended to after the Phobos mission was over.

She cautiously opened the door on a walkway full of shadowed moonlight—and Kornilov.

"Alex!"

For six weeks Alex Kornilov had been assigned to the Pinocchio test station at Wallal Downs, along Eighty Mile Beach on the edge of Western Australia's Great Sandy Desert. That was as far out of reach as you could get and still be under atmosphere. He had been tinkering with patches and mods to a team of Light Rock Advanced Miners, preparing them for the work on Phobos. The announcements of Steve Cocci's death and replacement had come and gone while Korny was Down Under.

Now he was through the door and had his arms around Grace fast. He gave her a kiss and a hug that almost broke a rib. The move was too much for the Mark IX, which hooted once and moved like a shadow to within a foot of them, hands upraised as if to strike.

"Jesus!" Korny breathed, catching sight of the Rover. Then he barked, "Raspberry mousse!"

It was the correct and current catchword. In a split second the Rover collapsed into its submissive flex.

Kornilov moved toward it, keeping one arm protectively around her. He satisfied himself that the system was resetting itself.

"What do you need a thing like that for?"

"A lot's happened since you've been gone, Alex."

To Grace he looked tanned and fit for the first time since encountering the black hole.

"How did you find me here?" she asked after fixing them a drink and settling in on the loveseat.

"There was a message on the company refnet that you wanted to see me soonest. The net was corrected for this address, with something about your house in the Haight being out of bounds."

"Damn it! This apartment is supposed to be secret."

He paused with the wine halfway to his mouth. An eyebrow raised.

"Of course not to you, Alex." She put a hand on his chest, saw his look of continued puzzlement. "You don't know?"

"Evidently not. What don't I know?"

"About Steve?"

"I'd heard he was dead. That's all. Well, who replaces him? Eddington in Finance? He always had the inside track, didn't he?"

Grace looked into her glass for two seconds. "I do."

She looked up and saw Korny's mouth almost say "You!" in surprise, but he stopped it in time. He waited for her to go on.

"Steve arranged it that way," Grace said. "With a big pile of stock. The Board of Directors had no choice, because I virtually own the company. As Steve did." She felt suddenly bleak, as if she didn't enjoy it.

Kornilov still didn't say anything, although she saw a brief and furious flash on his face.

"What are you thinking?" she asked finally.

"I'm—I am wondering how you managed to earn so much of Steve's confidence and support. Perhaps 'gratitude' is a better word?"

"And . . . ?"

"And—" He let out a long breath. "—I guess you are your own woman. Certainly. And no matter what Cocci's reasons, he's chosen wisely. You have a good background for the political side of the company. And you're cool under fire—as you showed when you saved my life. You'll be a good chairman—chairwoman—for Pinocchio, Inc."

Grace could hear many unresolved conflicts in what Korny was saying. She decided to accept them. "Thank you, Alex."

"We'll make a good team," he went on. "You take care of the political side and the marketing, and I'll take care of the technical part and the machines."

She understood what Korny had just offered. In his own strong, protective, male way, he wanted to divide the job between them. And Grace was determined to refuse. She had to. She would always have to take the road alone, on her own feet.

"I'll—I'll always value your advice and support," Grace said. Suddenly she was feeling very cold and very much in need of holding.

"Will you follow through on Cocci's plan for capturing the black hole?" he asked.

"There's no choice but to go ahead."

"Who else from Pinocchio is involved in the project?"

"Everyone," Grace said. "We've got the R&D labs working overtime to refit most of our line to meet vacuum and radiation conditions. That's for starters. The Academy and National Space Power are spitting out specifications as fast as they can profile the mission."

"I mean personally involved."

"Our new consultant, Professor Ceram, is going to Mars as an exo-geologist. . . . And you." Grace took more wine. "You're our human Iron Boss."

"Thank you." Korny held her eyes for three seconds. "When do I leave?"

"You stage to the Farside inside two months."

"That fast?"

"Everyone's racing the clock on this project. We have some lags due to orbital mechanics that can't be reduced. Luckily, Mars and Earth are in position for a pretty fast trip both ways. Two years ago, two years from now, you couldn't have said the same."

"Do we have a ship?"

"They're modifying one that appears to have been part of a hush-hush NASPFAC project. I don't know where it was going before, but it's adapted for Mars landing now."

"I'd better get a copy of the mission profile," Korny said.

"I'll have a sealed package sent to you at the office. But first there is other business to attend to."

"What?"

"It's been six weeks since I've seen you, darling. And soon it will be even longer. Did you miss me as much?"

"Naw, luv," Kornilov put on a clipped 'Strine accent. "We 'ad ahhrselves all the 'roo we cud catch, we did."

It was some small sound—not the strangled hooting that followed—which awakened Grace that night. The hooting brought Kornilov straight up out of the bed, even though the noise died faster than "raspberry mousse."

"What was that?" he whispered.

"Somebody got to Bruce—and that's impossible," she whispered back.

"Do you have a weapon here?"

"You mean a gun or a baseball bat?"

"Yeah."

"No. I didn't think I needed one with the Mark IX on the job."

"Okay, I'm going out there." Korny started to gather the bedsheet around his waist.

"Be careful."

"No kidding."

"No need to be all that careful, m'dear," said an awfully familiar voice as the room lights switched on.

Darnley was in the doorway, dressed in black pull-over, jeans, and leather gloves. A pump-action scatter gun was cradled in his arm.

"Henry!" Grace said. "What are you—?" Then she understood the gun. "How did you get around Bruce?"

"The spiffy robot? Your Mr. Finte was more than eager to show me all the wonderful features of the new Mark IX, including the brainboard behind its lightly shielded casing of twenty-gauge aluminum." Darnley held up a device that looked like an electric razor. "I fried it with a high energy particle beam. Micro-miniaturized. Isn't science wonderful?"

Grace felt her shoulders slump. She looked at Korny with a question already forming in her throat about backup systems. He shrugged with a warning look in his eyes.

"And who is the strong silent type, hmmm?" Darnley asked.

Kornilov's fists balled, but Darnley made the barest gesture with the riot gun and Korny settled on his heels.

"This is my friend, Mr. Kornilov."

"Kornilov? Ah, yes. Another one who's in on the plot."

"Plot? What do you—"

From the gloom behind Darnley, Grace caught a hint of movement, a moving gray patch, a dull reflection on metal. Keep talking, she told herself.

"What plot do you mean?" Grace asked, an octave lower.

"Too simple, m'dear. The late and unlamented Mr. Cocci was made privy to classified Department of Defense information which the people I work for have been tracking for some time. Said information he had the bad grace and worse judgment to make public. In short, he started a *media* campaign over a very sensitive matter. One that my employers wished to preserve for themselves: you might say that Old Mother Russia takes a proprietary interest in the matter. So it became necessary to order his—um—cerebral accident. Similar orders are cut for all who accompanied him in the plot. It's been a busy month for the local branch of the—well, never mind. Now you and Mr. Kornilov are to experience a lovers' jealous quarrel." Darnley patted the twin barrels of the scatter gun. "With consequential guilt and then desperate remorse for the temporary survivor."

"How can you—? I thought you were my friend. I called you my savior after that morning . . ." Grace said bitterly. The dull red eyes of the Mark IX were five feet behind and well above Darnley's fashionably slouched shoulders.

"A neat arrangement, wasn't it?" he smirked. "After you proved so agile in the crosswalk. We determined to use the second attempt to lure you."

"We? Then you aren't the 'lone assassin'?"

"M'dear! I keep telling you, that's a myth."

"And tonight? Where is your accomplice?"

"Ah-hah! Caught me! But then, I *am* something of a legend. That's my sur—" Darnley's neck went rigid and his head snapped erect as six steel fingers clamped his throat and the taser hooks pumped 30,000 volts into him in sixth-of-a-second bursts. The gun clattered to the floor; the keys and loose change jingled in his pockets.

"Please do not attempt to struggle, sir," the machine grated in Darnley's ear. "You are in protective restraint of a Mark IX no harm will struggle, sir, protective restraint will come to you if you Rover no harm." The voice dissolved in an electronic burble.

"My goodness, Henry," Grace said sweetly to the still pinned and twitching Darnley. "Whatever you did to Bruce seems to have scrambled his voice circuits. I hope his taser system is still functioning. Is it?"

Darnley glared at her, when he could keep his eyes in focus.

Grace did not know how to be subtle about contacting the boss of a failed Soviet assassin. But the human operator of the old-fashioned switchboard in the consulate on Green Street seemed to recognize Grace's name. He quickly plugged her into "delegate of visiting trade mission, Mr. Viktor Morzh."

Grace could guess that the title was not-too-deep cover for the Commissariat of State Security.

The "delegate," who spoke in a jovial, rumbling voice that had no trace of an accent, agreed to a mid-morning meeting. He seemed apologetic that he could schedule nothing sooner.

So Grace, Kornilov, and Paul Finte shoved Darnley—thoroughly shackled and quite pale after his encounter with Bruce—into the back of a sedan and drove up to Green Street.

Darnley had offered two minutes' worth of sullen protest at their assault on a foreign national who held diplomatic immunity. He stifled that when Grace pointed out whose gummy fingerprints were all over the shells in the murder weapon—that was Finte's surprising find—and offered to let him debate the point with her Mark IX again.

The consulate's roof, Grace noticed as they drove up, still had its circle of radio antennas. But they were rusty now, long abandoned after selective jamming had started from the Mount Sutro Tower.

Grace walked into Morzh's corner office with her best long-legged stride. She took a chair, unasked, sat low on her spine and looked up through her bangs at the man. He was big as a bear, actually fat, and had a Josef Stalin moustache, which must just now be coming back in style. Grace held her look for a three-count and then waved in Korny and Paul with the assassin.

Korny managed a deft trip so that Darnley stumbled to his knees in front of the desk.

"This claims to be yours," Grace said. "Do you want it?"

Morzh's face showed recognition for a tenth of a second before his bureaucratic mask clamped down. Pretty sloppy.

"I don't know whom you mean. Who is this person?"

"Spare us the histrionics, Viktor. Henry here is a real canary. He not only sings when you have a gun on him—he sings when he has a gun on you. Runs at the mouth, our Henry does. If he were mine, I'd lose him. But I don't think you and I have the same standards. So I brought him back. Do you want him?"

While she was talking a tough-looking secretary, male variety, appeared in the doorway and Finte faced him off.

Morzh stared hard at Darnley. "What did you tell her?"

Grace let her eyes cross and laughed inside. This pair deserved each other. If they were a sample, she began to think she could get out of this alive.

"Now, what do you think I told her?" Darnley said, with a whine on the edge of his voice. Taser shock did that, Grace knew. "She and the hunk were dead meat anyway. What would you have had me tell her? Bang-bang thud-thud? Is that a proper job?"

Even Morzh looked disgusted. Canary indeed.

"I do not know you, Darnley. I do not know you at all."

"Listen, my good—"

Morzh talked right across him at Grace: "What do you want?"

She held him with her eyes for another three-count. "I want distance. I want you and your pack off my turf. There is no 'plot,' no 'classified information' anymore. The black hole—which your masters in Moscow may choose to believe is an imperialist scheme, a propaganda ploy or a potential weapon—is an astronomical piece of bad luck for humanity.

"I and the others in your 'plot,' or any of them you may have left alive, are trying to correct the situation. Your hope of continued existence on this planet requires that you do not interfere. I will, of course, see to it that the proper State Department officials assist you in your noninterference. Do you understand?"

Morzh looked sulky. "I do not know anything about a plot."

"Exactly," Grace smiled and stood up. Her skirt and suit jacket miraculously fell into place without a hitch or a tug, completing her image of composure. She turned on her heel and sailed out of the office, picking Korny and Finte up in her wake like well-drilled troops.

Kornilov drove them back to the office. By the texture of his silence, Grace knew that something was wrong. Finally she asked him.

"Well, what did that accomplish?" he blurted. "If anything."

"It bought us time," she answered.

From the back seat, Finte swiveled his head to face her for a minute then continued watching the passing street scene. Finte was a watcher.

"How much time?" Korny persisted.

"If we're lucky, a week or two of free action. If not, then enough to get the car parked and ourselves safely upstairs, where we can begin to plan our next move. Paul?"

"Yes, ma'am?" The eyes left the street for another instant. Grace sensed a new respect from her security chief.

"From now we double the security on myself, Korny and Dr. Ceram. Full baby-sitting with Rovers, plus subcutaneous transponders. And bring in extra human staff for your office."

"That could be dangerous," Finte said. "Any recruits we hired might be Soviet plants."

"Of course. Rotate in trusted people from our East Coast and overseas facilities. Replace *them* with recruits."

"Good enough."

"Korny, I want you to get with Richardson and find a way to break the story on the Consortium ten days early."

"Why do you want to do that?"

Grace gave him a long look.

"I'm sorry," he said in a softer tone. "Eldon will want to know, won't he? There are probably a dozen interlocking pieces to pry apart and reglue."

"You're right. And that's what you're good at, Korny." She touched his arm for just a second. "Fitting all the pieces together.

"What I want," she went on, "is the biggest spotlight you can arrange to be put on us. Maybe if half the world sees you, me, and the other Consortium members as its last personal hope to take out the black hole, then Morzh and his people will back off permanently. They might even play ball with us."

"Guys like him and Darnley? They're long on following orders, short on thinking for themselves. If they have us marked, they won't quit—even if it kills them."

"They haven't marked anybody. It's the people up their ladder that we have to convince. The ones who ordered this attack can think as well as react."

"Maybe." Korny took the corner into the garage. At the gate an elderly Rover studied their faces through the windshield and then flashed the access code to lift it. Grace made a note to upgrade the Rover and then rearm the replacement with man-killing weapons.

"If *they* can't think," Grace said aloud, "then that country is truly down the tubes."

"How long have you been saying that?"

"Not long enough."

"Where should you put your money, Dr. Havermeyer?"

The stock broker for Dean Witter Block folded his hands and looked solemnly at the middle-aged couple before him. He tried not to notice the cockroach-scramble of green numbers across his quote screen. It was, temptingly, just out of reach on his periphery. So much *money* to be made this morning, and here he was supposed to yank around this veterinarian's twenty-five thousand.

"If I were in your position, I'd run, not walk, to put it in space issues. Lockheed-Douglas, National Space Power, even Pinocchio. With the news that broke this morning, they're all going to take off like a, pardon the expression, rocket."

He smiled at the doctor—um—veterinarian and his wife.

They didn't smile back.

"You haven't heard the word, son?" the vet said. "This is supposed to be the biggest hoax since the two-headed ram. Just another way to make a killing in the market. That's what Emma and I heard. Who should we believe? We read in the business page that everything was falling like a stone. Now I ask you to tell us where to take our money while this thing blows over, and what do you say?" The man curled his lips. "Space! So we can get burned along with everyone else."

The broker grinned behind his hand. Didn't this piker know the time to make big money was right when the market had big movement, up or down?

"Well, Doctor, that depends on whether you believe everything you read. Perhaps it is a hoax, perhaps not. But what's happening to your stocks today, and what's also happening to the space issues, these are real events. And you can make money on them."

Some, he reminded himself, and a paltry commission. He let his eyes swerve to the quote screen and sensed that the numbers were flipping by faster. The morning was slipping away!

"I just don't know." The doctor bared his teeth for an instant, as if adjusting a partial plate, and the broker saw a gold tooth, up front. "What do you think, Emma?"

"Whatever you think is wisest, Daddy."

The broker felt a flush of sweat on the inside of his thighs. These fools were wasting his time, his money. Women who called their husbands "daddy" were useless. Useless.

"Yep," the doctor said finally. "I think the market is too hot for us right now. Too hard to know what's right. So I think I want to move our nest egg out of stocks and into bonds."

"Bonds are falling now, too," the broker said. Half his brain, the half that wasn't glancing at the green numbers, was calculating the time it would take to shift this veterinarian's portfolio out of the market. Twenty minutes. Maybe half an hour. But he could swap stocks around as fast as he could rattle the keyboard.

"Municipals, then," the doctor said agreeably.

"The municipals most of all."

"Then . . . maybe . . . we better just take our cash and ride out the storm."

The broker almost shrieked aloud. Closing the account, moving the paper around, fetching the cashier and signing the receipts would take at least forty-five minutes, maybe more.

"You're sure?" he asked, trying to seem calm. "You might be losing a golden opportunity. The market hasn't been this active in . . ." Suddenly the green numbers flickered and seemed to double their pace. "In a decade or more."

"Yep. My guts tell me that's what we should do." Damn!

"Very well. We'd better start right away."

The broker turned to his keyboard and willed his fingers to move fast and unerringly. He was going to miss an hour of the best trading in his career. Damn them!

"So someone is actually going to try and *get* the black hole," the Cincinnati cabbie told his fare. "With a moon from Mars yet.

"Believe that when I see it.

"But you can bet someone's going to make a pile chasing it. Won't be me, of course. Myself, I don't mess with stocks.

"I play the ponies down in Lou'a'ville, though. Always put a hundred on the Derby. Even won once. Ponies are safer than the market. Fewer middlemen. And they even get checked once in a while for stims and dope. Not often, but a sight more regular than those brokers get their tree shook.

"You can bet that this flier, now . . . This 'Phobos Project' will leave a bad taste for a long time."

Chapter 14

Alex Kornilov:
OUTWARD BOUND

Kornilov walked the Ramp at Tsiolkovskii.

The leveled and graded pathway began on the floor of the Farside's most prominent crater, on the eastern side at three o'clock. It ran north around the upcast mountains, then west, then south. As the Ramp circled the crater, it rose up the wall, like the tire marks of a truck that has hit a curve too fast and ridden the embankment up, around and up.

The Ramp was blasted out in some stretches, filled in others, tunneled through stone shoulders in a few spots. And it rose smooth as an expressway on-ramp until, at the crater's south side, where the wide roadway was leading due east, it stopped abruptly. The smoothed rock ran over a chopped peak and . . . stopped. With only the hard black sky and the stars beyond.

Kornilov trudged the shallow incline of the Ramp, kicking a stone over the edge here, making note of a sag or hummock there. It was strange to walk in gravity—even at a sixth gee—inside a pressure suit. All of Korny's suit training had been in orbit, without weight. It was heavier than he expected and chafed in strange places.

The Moon's rocks seemed almost familiar. They

were fissured and knobbed, like those of the Mendocino Headlands, but these rocks were harsh grays and blacks. Those along the Pacific, in Korny's memory, were a soft saddle-brown with threads of white quartz.

Like the Moon's, those brown, Mendocino rocks had been bombarded for a billion years, but by Pacific waves instead of debris from the tracks of the comets. These gray rocks had also shifted and settled with the tides, but with the pull of the Moon instead of the Earth. The Mendocino rocks, however, had something Tsiolkovskii's never would: patches of green seaweed, crystals of dried salt, bits of shell—all signs of the sea.

The brown rocks were a souvenir in his mind's eye from the last weekend with Grace. They had held hands like a pair of kids and dared the waves to catch them.

They had stuffed themselves on the food in Mendocino's quasi-French restaurants and then wandered the galleries, making note of favorite paintings or craftworks. Korny now wondered what Grace would say if she could see the Observatory's gallery of computer-enhanced radiographs: x-ray images of variable stars, galactic whorls and the stellar nurseries of the nebulae. He thought she'd like them.

At Mendocino Grace had shed some of her professional demeanor, her frightening hardness, and laughed with him like a girl. For a few hours that weekend Korny had been able to think of her as just a woman, not as an executive and his boss. Except for the Mark IX that shadowed her across the rocks like a guardian angel of death.

In the middle of this reverie, on the Ramp's westward turn, he found the surveyor.

Blood had settled around the pressure-suited body in a dark red powder. Kornilov brushed it with his boot toe and was surprised at how deep a layer it made on the black dust and cut gravel.

He bent and pulled aside the ragged flap of suitknit and insulpad across the body's abdomen. Beneath was a crystallized mess, reminding Kornilov of latex-rubber tubing left to glaze and crack in the sun. Vacuum and cold had neatly freeze-dried the corpse.

The solar visor was down on the helmet, so he could not see the twisted face. The name above the visor was Karl Baden's; Kornilov knew him as a surveyor from the Farside Observatory.

That was going to cause problems.

The Observatory staff was already resentful of the Phobos Project's intrusion. The bustle of constructing a magnetic accelerator around the crater wall was disturbing their cloistered scientific routine. When the accelerator went into operation, interference from its stator magnets would fuzz their radio telescope pretty badly for hours at a time. The fact that the Observatory's parent, the American Academy, had pressured them—with threats of funding cuts, so Kornilov had heard—into hosting the Project had not made relations any warmer.

And now a death, one more thing to tickle already flayed nerve endings.

Kornilov glanced sourly at the Pinocchio that stood nearby, humming quietly to itself on the ground equipment channel. It was a Miner type, and its pick arm was suspiciously dusted with a red powder.

That made the problem Kornilov's. He was Pinocchio, Inc.'s engineer/psychologist attached to the Project. He was the Iron Boss.

He straightened and approached the Miner as he would a nervous horse. Its caged photo-eyes swivelled calmly toward him, but otherwise it didn't move.

Warily returning the machine's stare, Kornilov fumbled in his belt kit and took out a logic probe. He patched it into the socket below the Miner's RF transponder. Still the Pinocchio didn't move.

He began taking readings from the brainbox, recording summaries into his compucalc for later detailed analysis. While the Miner spilled its head, Kornilov was reminded of a schoolgirl's question: "Don't you always teach them the Three Laws of Robotics?"

That neat summary of human-automata relations, formulated by the 20th-century author, Isaac Asimov, unrolled through his mind. First Law, to protect humans from death or injury. Second Law, to obey human orders, except when obedience would conflict with the First Law. And Third Law, to protect itself, except when survival would conflict with the First and Second laws.

It sounded like an ideal code—unless you worked with robots every day. Of course they had "artificial intelligence," but that was in no way to be confused with *awareness*. The automata, even in the advanced-stage brains, could not project the consequences of abstract situations representing "danger to human life" or "danger to self."

The most sophisticated automata functioned merely as "expert systems," comparing coded information and sensory readings with masses of stored working data. From the comparisons, they made probability-weighted decisions and then initiated predictable actions toward a predefined goal.

The Rover series, for example, pattern-matched certain movements, objects, and speeds in their environment with stored images of human violence. When there was a match, they triangulated, homed, and struck with whatever weapons the program selected.

In the case of a Miner, the system compared images of its rock and gravel surroundings with stored diagrams of an excavation. From there, the program issued commands like "chop rock" and "move rock" until a certain amount of crater wall had been cut to dimensions x, y, and z.

In every case the defined goal was provided from an outside source, either a human programmer or a boss system in charge of, say, civil engineering. Generalized laws, like "protect human life," were far too vague to be left to the pattern-matching of the expert system.

To protect against accidents, like this one with Baden, there were overriding safety instructions. A Miner was programmed to freeze when anything the photo-eyes registered as man-sized and man-shaped moved into its working area. That was the First Law. Otherwise it was programmed to dig. That was the Second Law. And it was programmed to respond to strain gauges on its pick and shovel arms and other warning sensors that defined its design limits. That was the Third Law.

Kornilov shook his head. Maybe cosmic radiation had skewed the data in this Miner's safety instruction set. Maybe Baden had bent over till he looked more like a rock than a man to the Miner's photo-eyes. Maybe—unthinkable thought!—some human had murdered Baden and framed the Miner with a sprinkling of red dust.

Whatever the truth of the situation, Kornilov doubted that the Observatory administration would sit still for a technical explanation. They would want to find the Miner guilty of a mindless, heinous crime.

And then?

Probably some kind of trial and then an indemnity to be paid by Pinocchio, Inc. And during the proceedings they would order all work on the Project stopped.

With a jerk he unplugged the probe and then, for safety's sake, shut down the suspect Miner. It was a fifteen-kilometer downhill bounce to his tribuggy and from there he could use line-of-sight laser—never radio in this crater, not by Observatory rules—to contact Bubble Base. That was the local name for the Observatory cluster in the shadow of Tsiolkovskii's central spire. The Base Watch would send out a roller with a stretcher team.

As he started down the Ramp, Kornilov was already shaping his reports to the Project, to the Observatory staff, and to Grace Porter in San Francisco.

Twenty seconds after Kornilov had come through the airlock, the full-time astronomer and quarter-time cop filling a shift on Base Watch had thrown him into a makeshift prison, then dispatched a party to pick up Baden's corpse and "deal with" the renegade Miner.

The abandoned hydroponics dome where Korny was put had foamed aluminum walls with a dimpled skin that sweated. The only access was a hatchway that dogged on one side only—the side he was not on. Beyond the hatch was a bleak corridor in partial pressure.

The only light came from a thick membrane exposed to space. An eighth-inch of sealer sandwiched between the membrane's UV-neutral films was all that protected him from micrometeorites. If anything as big as a pebble chose to drift down into Tsiolkovskii, Kornilov would be dead before they could think to cap and flood this space.

Luckily they hadn't stripped him of his pressure suit. So he had plumbing facilities, after a fashion, with a water converter. He had some emergency food syrups that tasted like toothpaste and possibly were. And he had a hope of getting his helmet on and sealed if he met that wandering pebble.

Kornilov had been here three days.

On the evening of the first day, a piece of paper had been handed through the hatch. It informed him that, as Pinocchio's ranking representative, he was under close arrest. The Observatory director was holding Kornilov personally responsible on a charge of criminal negligence.

Three days was the time it took Grace Porter to make passage to the Moon by way of Vandenberg, Stopover, and Mare Imbrium. When she showed up at the hatch of his cell, Korny's jaw dropped—or floated down in one-sixth gee.

"What? Did they arrest you too?"

"Extradition doesn't reach that far." She grinned. "I thought I'd have to offer myself in your place, but it turned out not to be necessary."

"That's very—why?"

"We just nationalized Tsiolkovskii. This is a U.S. Department of Defense installation as of two minutes ago."

"I'll bet the American Academy howled."

Grace shook her head. "Didn't get a chance to. With Hawking-1 growing like it is, we don't fool around. The Academy actually suggested this move."

Kornilov crawled through the hatch and Grace was in his arms in one bouncing step. She snuggled into him for one second and then drew back, her nose wrinkling.

"Korny darling, I know this is a frontier community with all sorts of quaint privations, but do you think we could get you a bath?"

Now that he was out in fresher air, Kornilov could smell himself, too.

"Down this way," he said, pointing toward the dormitory domes. "What about the charges for Baden's murder?"

"The incident has been ruled an industrial accident, with triple indemnities to Baden's widow. We're paying to send the body back to Earth. The Miner, by the way, has had its brain wiped. Case closed."

"How about Morzh and his merry men?"

"They were still hostile, with a few more tricks—"

He stopped in the corridor and grabbed her arm. "Are you okay?"

"Sure, top notch. Paul Finte will be out of the casts in another two weeks. That was after we ran them through four hit teams and two Rovers. Finally we—the Consortium, that is—went through the President and dumped all the hard data on Hawking-1 on them. The Kremlin still wasn't convinced, until NASPFAC reneged on a ten-year contract and blacked out Leningrad."

Korny decided that problems could melt away if you had the backing of the world's largest supra-atmosphere energy source. "Wasn't that extreme?"

"It wasn't purely retaliation. The Project just upped the schedule on shifting those three beam stations to power the accelerator." She paused with a finger along the collar of his pressure suit. "The one that's going to whip your ass halfway to Mars."

He peeled out of the suit and stepped into a sudsbag. Inside of two minutes it had him clean and dry. All the time Korny was doing arithmethic in his head, and the numbers came up close. Too close! "If they've already started blacking out cities, then the stations must have been ready to move. They don't waste a second of beam time."

"Sure, they're moving already."

"So when are they due?"

"The day after—no! Today, at three o'clock."

"Three on whose time?" Korny felt a sudden tightening in his stomach.

"Universal Mean, according to the last inter-Project bulletin I read on the bounce here."

"That's an hour from now. If they're following the original plan, we should be able to see the stations from the crater."

"An hour?" She put a long-fingered hand on his

bare shoulder. "We've got lots of time. Are these cubbies really private?"

In answer, Korny pulled across the curtain and sealed the velcro with one hand.

"Now, hurry or we'll miss the show."

"Oh. Right. Sure." Kornilov watched Grace come out of her light doze like a cat.

He gave her a fifteen-minute, hands-on demonstration—with several coy nips and pats—of how to put on and wear a pressure suit. Partway through she had to put his hands aside, promising she would learn all about it later. To solo she would need the full ten-hour course, Korny knew, but for an accompanied walk near the domes she had the bare survival basics.

Soon they were out the nearest lock and standing in the shadow of the spire.

"The shuttle pilot said we'd be able to see them in the west," Grace said over the private circuit. "Which way is that?"

Kornilov faced her around away from the sun. He reached into his kit pouch and brought out a pair of helmet binoculars. He scanned the quadrant over the western rim of Tsiolkovskii and handed them to Grace.

When she turned them over uncertainly, he took them back and fitted them into her helmet bracket right side up. Then he took her head in both hands and aimed them.

"Look up there, just past that bright star. You should get a glint from the solar sails."

"Korny?"

"Yes?"

"That's a funny-shaped star."

He stared at it, naked eye, and could just make out . . .

"It's moving," Grace said. "Very slowly. Why don't you take these things and see."

Korny fastened the binocs on his own head and saw Baltic Two. Its power converter and beam projector formed a tiny black hull, like the lean keel and topsides of an ocean clipper. The silicon panels looked like course upon course of sails rigged for a fair wind.

Tiny yellow and blue flares winked like riding lights on the periphery of the rigging. Korny knew these were reaction thrusters slowing the station and berthing her in a new orbit around the Moon.

In the velvet behind her, two more stars were moving.

Somewhere west of Tsiolkovskii was a new antenna complex built to take Baltic Two's and her sister stations' beamed power. Each one could put out almost 5,000 megawatts. The total would be enough to "whip his ass," as Grace put it, along with the rest of the Project team off to Mars.

Korny put an arm around Grace's shoulders and clipped the binocs back on her helmet.

"There. You were right, that star is our platform."

Grace got it in focus and cooed briefly at the sight. "How close to finished are you on the ring?" she asked, suddenly sober.

"The Ramp is all graded. All we need to do is mount the stators, wire them up, shoot a couple of loads for practice, and then . . ." He smoothed some moondust with his boot.

"And then you go. How long?" She turned to face him.

"Six weeks at the pace we're working. Maybe five."

"I'll be here for the grssgmble." A rare burst of static took her last word.

"For the what?"

"The launch," she repeated. "I'll be here."

"I know. I love you. I'll miss you."

Through the faceplate Korny could see Grace open

her mouth to answer. What came through his helmet phones was a gruff male voice.

"Go ahead, lad. Take her inside and kiss her. We'll all miss you."

"Woo! Woo!" another voice came in.

"And remember, Earthie, how private the suit circuit really is."

The rest dissolved in hard-edged male laughter.

There wasn't much to pack.

Korny wandered around his cubby, actually turning on one heel, looking for things to put in his case. The personal allotment was fifteen kilos. His shaving kit and a change of clothes? For the next thirty months he would be under ship's housekeeping, which covered everything from tooth floss to tea bags.

He had no hobbies to take along, no favored books, no music. The ship's wafer library would take care of all the recreational materials they would need. He'd get all of his technical journals from there. And there would be plenty of work to keep them occupied on the trip.

He did have his electronic keyboard, a gift from Madama with her injunction to "practice, practice, practice" if he wanted his hand to remain strong. It was designed for minimum mass: just a stretcher frame and a contact membrane with detachable, mock-ivory key plaques. Ever the tinkerer, Korny had jiggered the electronics until he could make music by connecting the D plug from his wrist into its back. That had amused him for a day or two. Anyway, his hand got enough exercise and "remained strong" with his regular work. He decided to leave the keyboard.

On the bookshelf, he found the Fixit paw that he'd meant to adapt for a suit glove. Korny put it in the case. Maybe on the flight he would find time. Once he got his hands on the pressure suits they would be using, he would work on that.

It didn't seem like much of a life to leave behind. A professional engineer, always traveling on assignment, never had much of a garden or too many pets.

Korny regretted only one thing: Grace Porter.

There was, he sensed, an opportunity in the losing. Grace was no shy girl used to waiting for a man. She was the elegant sort of woman who made her way on her own terms. For one minute or a month, she had chosen him. In another month it would be someone else. Story of Kornilov's life.

He zipped up the case and set it, almost empty, on the foot of the bunk. He slipped out into the cooridor and down to the director's suite, reserved for Grace's use when she was at Farside.

The accelerator, dubbed the "slingshot," had been busy loading and shooting out payloads all week. The first were just light canisters of rock to test the stators and calibrate them for even acceleration. All had gone over the edge of the crater wall to crash somewhere in the lunar rubble to the east of Tsiolkovskii.

The next series had carried dummy electronics into lunar orbits. If the signals from those cans remained clear and readable, it proved that the gauss of the stators' magnetic fields wouldn't burn out shipboard computers and communications gear. Probably.

In just twelve hours, after a long good-bye from Grace, it would be Kornilov's turn.

The ship—first of three that would be sent from Tsiolkovskii—looked like a terrible mistake. Resting at the Ramp's lower end on its starter cradle, it reminded Kornilov of some half-finished submarine about to be launched with a brass band, only to sink with a gurgle in the dockyard basin because the builders had left off its steel skin, diving planes, decks and mast.

A dozen small tanks of fusible mass clustered around the terribly naked stingray engine. Forward of that was the truncated melon-slice of the life-support pod, welded to the engine with just a few alumetal girders. The airlock grew like a tumor on the near side. And covering every surface were bolt ends and studs, like some prickly disease, where the rest of the ship would be built in flight.

The Phobos Project was going to Mars in pieces. Over the next four days the Tsiolkovskii Accelerator would sling this mess—along with its two sister messes and more than a hundred canisters and bundles—out of the Earth-Moon gravity well. Like David aiming pebbles at the War God. They would follow long solar orbits, outward bound along truncated ellipses with Mars at the other end.

Each of these warty little half-ships would hold people. They wouldn't wear shirtsleeves, sit in form-fitted reaction couches with safety harness, and punch buttons on the way up the Ramp. Oh no. It was suit up, lie against a bulkhead with a padding of raw insulation material, and take a strap of webbing across your torso. The strap was anchored to a bolt, welded six inches out of any comfortable alignment, on the steel beside you.

Everything, even cabins, would be erected from prefab in the long orbit to Mars.

The delicate cargo—mostly people—was launched first and gently, at relatively slow speed. The hardier cargoes—ship parts and materials, bundles of structural and sectional pieces, tanks of breathable and fusible, electronics, and all the equipment the Project would need on Mars and later on Phobos—came out of the slingshot faster and faster. The outsides of these packages were studded with maneuvering jets and connector stubs. The object was to rendezvous in transit, assemble the half-ships into three identical craft, wire up the booster/braking rockets, assemble the airfoils—and then ride them down into the thin Martian atmosphere.

As Kornilov walked toward the airlock, he saw a trio of Pinocchio's Artificers bolted to the side of the pod. They hung like beetles mounted in a collector's case, their agile, inquisitive arms now stiff and unmoving. He knew their brainboards had been removed and stored in gelwax inside the pod. These three were the backup team, the last hope in case the Arties in the other cans were damaged or lost.

Three Arties was the minimum. Three could do the work of twenty humans in pressure suits. They didn't get tired, or stop to gaze at the stars, or come in for food, rest, or hygiene. They didn't need the company of their own kind. But they did need an Iron Boss.

That was still Kornilov. He would be key man in the assembly sequence. He would pamper, push, and, if necessary, reprogram the team of Fixits and Artificers doing the heavy hauling and the tight-quarters connections.

Once through the pod's airlock, he found a place against the bulkhead between Priscilla McQuade, the Project's groundside construction manager, and Ariel Ceram, their exo-geologist.

McQuade passed him the web strap, held up four fingers, then did a half-twist with her thumb. That was spaceside handtalk for "four minutes." A half twist with her little finger would have meant "four seconds." Sign language held down the chatter on the suit channels.

Korny acknowledged with a nod, turned to smile at Ariel. She was looking grimly ahead through her faceplate. He could feel her tension in the elbow she had dug into him.

"Is this the best they've got? Bare metal and no

facilities? You'd think this team deserved better." Ariel was talking to herself in a steady grumble, but she'd left her suit on the open channel. "Going off like sausages in a can. At least they could've—"

Korny reached across and punched the quiet button at the base of her helmet. She glared at him for a moment and he just smiled back.

In another minute the ground crew sealed the lock and a minute after that Korny could feel a tug as the ship budged on its cradle.

That was all they felt, except for a steady, comfortable pressure against their backs. No roar of engines, no eyeball-shaking vibration. Just a long heaviness.

In the fragment of view out the tiny porthole beside the lock, Korny could see the arcs of the stators flash by, with a gray blur of rock between them. He imagined he could feel the pod roll into the sideways, centrifugal pressure as the Ramp curved around the crater, but it was an illusion. The curve was much too gentle, the forward acceleration much too strong.

Then, beyond the porthole, there was blackness. The pressure fell to nothing. Korny imagined a soaring sense of lightness as they crested the crater wall and began the long journey. What he was actually feeling was the old zero-gee.

He unstrapped, floated free, and began rolling up the insulation padding. Time to get to work.

After four weeks Kornilov was running on pills and will power. For one incredible ninety-hour stretch he never left his suit or touched a sleeping harness. His exercise schedule went to hell and the two ship's doctors nagged him about it.

The Project's ships had been designed—or rather, redesigned—by a committee in a hurry, and they looked it. While Korny had expected to find mistakes, he had not imagined that quality control could break down so completely. Four separate times he'd had to override the Pinocchios' boss system and reprogram the work orders.

They had jockeyed the three ships into rendezvous with braking jets and then collected all of the bundles and cans. They lost only two of the containers—one of electronics, the other of fusible mass—through docking errors. Kornilov was able to identify spares and thanked his personal gods for the space program's tradition of redundancy.

Their first task was to link the three ship skeletons in a "Y" configuration, a huge space-going bolas, and set it spinning. This maneuver, though it made the assembly process fifty times more difficult, created a fractional pseudo-gravity. Without it their bones would drain of calcium and a horribly crippled crew would land on Mars—if they made it at all.

Kornilov had expected the complications of spin. He had expected to lose some of the canisters. What he had not prepared for was the incredible number of parts shortages or outright omissions. They were so common that Korny began to suspect that, as he griped to Ariel one midwatch, "Some people will even try to make a buck on the end of the world."

She screwed up her mouth and barely nodded.

Ariel was recircuiting a spare thruster-cluster block to serve as an aileron control board, and she had to do it the hard way—with only a logic probe and an oscilloscope to guide her. When she finished that one, she had five more to do.

Kornilov studied Ariel's face while she worked with such intense concentration. He noted the boyishly short hair, the sharp eyes, good mouth and a strong jawline. Once again he discovered that when you shared time with any woman, however plain, joined her in frustrations and successes, came to trust her, she became as beautiful as any model or actress. Sometimes even more attractive.

He gave a mental whistle, reseated his helmet, and went back to his problem *du jour*.

In assembling each of the airfoils, a heat-sink manifold had to be connected in a ten-centimeter pocket created by two structural members. It was a piece of design stupidity that would have been caught and corrected if the Project had taken an extra twelve months to test-build one of the landing craft in Earth orbit.

The pocket was two meters deeper than Kornilov's arm could reach but just right for an Artificer's extensor. Down there, however, the Artificer's photo-eyes were blocked by the structural members and its own arm. It could reach the connection, but couldn't see it.

He rested for a minute, letting his mind wander, one hand reflexively gripping the edge of the pocket.

Beyond the curve of the airfoil were the stars. Korny was suddenly aware of them. All that separated him from them were the four inches of air in front of his face, a shield of lexan, and then nothing. A gulf of lightyears, thousands of lightyears, filled only with random dust and gas molecules. For an animal that all its life had swum in dense air, as Korny had, and never felt chill vacuum, that emptiness seemed to shrink the distances, pulling him forward. Drawing him. Gently raising him . . .

An instinctive clutch with his hand—his right hand made of metal—brought Korny back from the thousand-mile stare.

That right hand, which was more machine than human, more himself sometimes than the old meat hand—of course!

By jury-rigging a cable patch through his suit glove, Kornilov could run the Artificer directly to hook up the heat sink's nine pipes and eighteen bolts inside their pocket—while using a second Pinocchio's eyes at ninety degrees to see the work.

He shook himself inside his suit and called for a second Artie.

Six weeks after rendezvous, they had finally assembled all the craft—with an unaccountable, and to Kornilov surprising, surplus of 52 angled bracing plates, 214 eighth-inch bolts, 93 unmatching nuts, 1,409 still-unmatched lock washers and 2,000-odd feet of service wire that Kornilov never could find a use for.

"What are you going to do with all that stuff?" Ariel asked, staring at the ragged pile in the Two Ship's cargo bay. "It will definitely make some people nervous, you know."

"You're right," he said. "I suppose we could strap on a small thruster and deep-six it."

She shook her head inside the helmet. "Might want some of it later. Waste not—"

"Yeah, sure. We could ignore procedure and just catalog it as spares . . . except Captain Deming keeps the master inventory on that compucalc of his. He'd be sure to notice."

"Could we explain to him . . . ?"

"*Explain* to Detail Dan? He'd have us tear all three ships apart on an empty-socket hunt. We'd go right past Mars in pieces until he was satisfied everything was assembled to spec."

"Then deep-six it," Ariel agreed.

"Wait a sec, I have a much better idea."

Kornilov called up a Fixit and spent five minutes punching a program in on its chest plate.

"What will that do?"

"It will use the plates and wire to build a cat's cradle inside the bay. Nothing too fancy, but enough to look like it has a purpose. That'll keep Deming happy."

"Suppose he notices the other ships don't have one?"

"We'll tell him it's gee-force strapping for 'special stores' and then kind of drift off in the other direction."

"Not bad, Kornilov, not bad at all."

Eight months later they broke the bolas formation and prepared for the Mars landing. On the way in, when they were inside the orbits of the two moons and battening for atmospheric entry, the ships dropped a string of comm-relay satellites in areosynchronous orbit. These would ensure contact with Earth at all times.

Then the trio of ships entered the shallow Martian atmosphere, with the crews' fingers crossed. And the half-orbit landing skims went perfectly, ending in western Aethiopis near crater Eddie. Bubble Base Two, with accommodations for forty-five persons, was built in the lee of Eddie.

The Martian dust really was red. Almost as dark, Kornilov reflected, as the blood of the surveyor that Miner had killed back at Tsiolkovskii. And in both cases the color was a sign of the presence of iron atoms.

There was so much red that, after a while, the mind dismissed it, turning the background as gray as the Moon's stark mountains. Any other color—the blue of domeskin, the yellow and green of gas bottles—stood out in glaring relief against the neutral rocks, hills, and occasionally dust-clouded sky. Finding a ridge of ochre or black rock was a treat to the eye.

As soon as the base was secure, Kornilov and his mechanical gang went to work converting the landing craft to low-orbit shuttles that would reach Phobos. There he would unpack a team of Miners and begin excavating the fusion chamber that would turn the moonlet into a powered craft.

The three lander/orbiters would never leave Mars' gravity well. When the party came home, they would ride Phobos to an orbit around the Earth. If Jason

Bathespeake had coached his computers right, that
orbit would be timed to catch Hawking-1 at apogee.

If not, it wouldn't matter if they never came home
at all.

In the white, incense-haunted hall, the Master
and his disciple considered the news that had been
radioed both from the Moon and from Mars.

"Why is it, Ananda, that the Americans fight so
hard against the end that is their karma?"

"Perhaps *that* is their karma, to fight . . . ?"

The gray head shook slowly in the soft evening air.
"A useless people. A tiresome people."

Outside, on the edge of the village, a small boy
pushed among the waiting cows to gather dungs for
the morning's fire.

Life would go on in the old rhythms. Until it
stopped.

"You wanted proof?" the Cincinnati cabbie demanded. "You thought the black hole was just a
stock swindle, huh?

"So did a lot of other people.

"We all shoulda been warned when National Space
Power moved those stations. When did those goug-
ers ever give up a market rich as Russia, huh?

"Now they've got a team on Mars, just like they
said. That's going a little too far for a hoax, you ask
me.

"Maybe they'll just pull it off. And if they don't . . .

"Here's your address, sir."

Chapter 15

Ariel Ceram: AREOLOGIST AT WORK

If the Phobos Project never returned to Earth, Ariel Ceram might not have cared. She was the first geologist to explore a new planet, and that was paradise—or at least the Plains of Elysium, which was where crater Eddie was located.

While Kornilov tinkered with the ships and the others embroidered the structures of Bubble Base Two or shoveled on layers of red soil as radiation shielding, Ariel spent her days in the field. She was suited against the low-grade vacuum that Mars called an atmosphere, and she already knew—from the long voyage out—how to nourish and relieve herself without having to return to camp.

Alex Kornilov was the first of the reasons, Ariel knew, that she spent so much time alone in the red hills. During the last months of the voyage out, the searchlight of his attentions had turned on her. The advances had been subtle, sweet-tongued, not hard to deflect. But they had been there.

In less confined quarters, with less at stake, she might have welcomed Kornilov as a lover. She would certainly have treasured him as a friend. The Mad Russian was handsome enough, good company, dependable and solid as seasoned oak. And, once she

thought about it, that strange mechanical hand of
his, and his shyness about it, made Kornilov more
human rather than less.

If Ariel thought she could take him away—and
keep him away—from the beautiful, the elegant Grace
Porter, then she might be tempted to respond. But
with a calculation wholly divorced from love or lust,
Ariel suspected that on this trip her only advantage
was proximity. Once they landed back on Earth and
cracked the hatches, Grace would be right there
with the pull of her powerful personality. And Korny
would drift off like a leaf in a swift stream.

No contest for the little prof from Berkeley, Ariel
what's-her-name, nice kid, good in the sack on a
strange planet, but . . .

Besides, Ariel *liked* Grace.

So, once they were down on Mars and had a bit of
landscape to roam in, she put a big chunk of it
between herself and Kornilov on a regular basis.

The second reason Ariel headed for the hills was
the Water Question. Not where could they get it—
the Project was well served by recycling gear—but
where it had gone.

All around Ariel there was evidence of water: dry
streambeds, rounded stones, compacted clays. But
no water was to be found on the surface, no appreciable vapor in the atmosphere. They knew there
was water ice in the polar caps but not enough to
have shaped the land Ariel now saw. Unless the
water vapor had long ago leaked to space, it was still
here somewhere.

She thought it was underground: perhaps locked
in by caprock and aquifer; probably trapped in a
deep permafrost. Either could be detected by a competent geologist—or rather, areologist—and then used
by later expeditions and colonizing efforts.

Like a wildcatting geologist in the Old West, she
set up her seismic recording stations and then blew

off lines of explosive charges. Small charges, because she had to beg from the mining stores Priscilla McQuade had brought along in case they found hard rock on Phobos. (Ariel breezily told her they wouldn't find anything harder on Phobos than cream cheese: the moonlet wasn't dense enough.)

She fired so many shots that the camp wiseguys started calling her "the Terrorist." She grinned at the name and went right on blasting. But she didn't find anything that looked like an underground channel or a porous aquifer. Any permafrost was too deep for her little charges.

Ariel Ceram also went prospecting for sedimentary rocks, the carbon paper of the ages. But all she found were volcanic basalts and high-grade iron ores. She consoled herself with the thought that she was seeing just a tiny percentage of the planet's surface—like the early Viking landers that could only sit where they'd plopped and sample what they could reach with their extended robot arms.

One day, Ariel vowed, she would mount a free expedition and return to Mars for some *real* study.

If Phobos had been a pear—which it very closely resembled—then the top, where the stem would have come out, ended in the jagged crown of the crater called Stickney. Except Stickney wasn't at the top. Because of the irregularly shaped moonlet's orientation toward its primary, Stickney lay along the equator, forever hanging over the shield of Mars.

This mammoth crater, five kilometers in diameter, was easily the dominant feature of the Phobian moonscape. It covered one whole face, from thirty degrees north to thirty south.

It was the obvious place to excavate for the fusion engine.

McQuade and her team set up the Construction Shack on the crest of Kepler Dorsum, the ridge that curved from Stickney southward. For construction power they erected heliostats, like sunflowers of mirrored mylar, along the lower slopes of Kepler. The brains that tracked the sun with these devices, directing the weakened solar rays onto a compact concentrating wafer, were the standard design of a Pinocchio subsidiary. The black box that collected their power and conditioned it for equipment and communications was the product of another Pinocchio clone company.

From the laydown area on Kepler gangs of Miners walked up toward the crater rim as fast as Kornilov and his two teams of Artificers could assemble and check them out. Ariel was working in the crater when the first of the machines, waving its digging tools around and looking stupider than a fiddler crab, walked down the western wall.

Once more she was blasting, but this time with the Project's full approval. She was seeking soft spots, pockets and crevasses under the crater's floor. Ariel had also set up a walking rig equipped with a laser-guided drill and was taking core samples. These she laid in long trays outside the Shack with tags that corresponded to grid points on the chart of the crater.

What she found made McQuade and Kornilov happy. The surface of Phobos under Stickney was a kind of fluffed rock, like volcanic pumice, with about the specific gravity of styrofoam. Ariel's blasting showed the stuff extended down more than 3,000 meters. The Miners would eat it like puffed rice.

Kornilov grinned like a heathen idol and soon was on the radio telling the Project's Mars-side director, Captain Dan Deming, to bump a month or three off the schedule.

Still, Ariel wasn't so sure. The material she'd cored out felt too heavy for Phobos' overall calculated density—which was forty percent that of Earth and half that of Mars. There were some big crevasses somewhere under them.

The trouble started on the first shift of actual excavation.

Kornilov had spent two days punching dig coordinates into the individual Miners and then spacing them across the floor of Stickney according to his master grid. Then he turned their articulated claws and scoops loose on the soft pumice of Phobos.

Ariel was taking a last core with her drill rig, wedged into the bottom of a shallow valley, when a Miner slid down the slope. It was pinwheeling its arms like a drunk on ice skates. It was coming right at her.

Her only warning was the flash of sun off its curved pick. Ariel reacted with a half step and backward stumble that saved her life. The Miner went past her at about twenty miles an hour, gaffed her with a swipe of its toothed scoop and plowed down her drilling rig. The scoop knocked her sideways into a natural ditch.

Ariel lay there, trying to catch her breath. Her side felt cold and wet. It was a precious twenty seconds before she realized that her side was more than wet, that her breath was gone from more than a punch in the stomach.

The pain in her ribs—probably a couple were cracked—kept her from bending around to see. Her gloved hand moved up and down her side, feeling for the leak. How big was it? How fast was the air going out? How much was left?

She was spreading her fingers and numbly holding on, just hoping to cover the outflow, when a pair of boots landed in the ditch by her faceplate. Whoever it was knelt down and slapped her hand aside. What the—?

"Ariel! Let go!" It was Kornilov. He reset her

radio with a stab of one finger while his other hand was doing something to her suit fabric.

In a panic she tried to fight back.

"Stop it!" he barked. "You have to knead the sealant layer to get it to set."

"I can't see. How big is the hole? How deep?"

He finished manipulating the suit fabric and pulled a stick-patch out of his kit.

"Not big—an inch or two," he said. That was a lie, as she found when she got to the airlock in the Construction Shack. The tear in her pressure suit was at least six inches long. It went right down to the nylon undersuit she wore next to her skin. She had two broken ribs and a vacuum burn that would trouble her for weeks.

On reflection, it was a good thing he had lied. If she had known all that while laid out in the middle of the crater floor, she might have died there.

"What happened?" she asked.

"Damndest thing. The Miner took one swing with its pick and went sailing over the ground." His voice went down to a murmur: thinking mode. "It must be the low gravity. I—we—never stopped to think that an excavator uses inertia and friction to anchor itself."

"What's that mean for the Project?" Ariel asked, thinking—just in the abstract, mind you—about sitting up and moving toward shelter. She was glad to have the distraction.

"Trouble."

"What do you mean the Miners don't work? . . . Over!"

Grace Porter's voice, transmitted more than 320 million kilometers from Earth and relayed from Bubble Base Two to the Construction Shack on Phobos, was remarkably clear. Although the twenty-eight-minute lag made direct conversation impossible, it was giving Kornilov breathing space to plan his answers.

They transmitted voice only, not full-vid. Half an hour of staring at faces frozen on the screen—usually with idiot grins—was actually a deterrent to human communication.

Ariel slumped against a wall panel among a crowd from the site team. They were all holding their breath in anticipation. She was holding hers because it hurt to breathe.

"The Miners were never designed to work in zero gee. Phobos pulls so little gravity that they weigh about two pounds apiece. Each chop sends them sliding over the surface . . . Over!"

Ariel wasn't the only casualty. Across the Shack's main room Priscilla McQuade raised a hand roughly patched with pinkish synskin. Another sliding Miner had crushed it, also on their first day in the Hole. The work was like an ice ballet with bulldozers.

Kornilov shook his head at McQuade: he wouldn't waste Porter's time with a catalog of their injuries. Luckily no one was dead yet.

"Anchor them!" Grace said. ". . . Over!"

Twenty-eight minutes for *that?*

"With what? Over!" Korny shot back.

Ariel had a sudden vision of pressure-suited humans working with spades and trowels to dig footholds for each Miner before it could swing its own two-meter pick arm. That way it could take them a century to excavate the fusion chamber. And ninety-three years before then, Hawking-1 would have devoured the Earth.

The room shuffled and whispered while waiting for the signal to bounce.

"With pitons and wire," Grace said eventually. "Team up two Artificers or three Fixits with each Miner to handle the tie-down. Our techs here estimate you can get out 900 cubic meters between anchorings. It will slow your schedule by no more than twenty percent.

"We will transmit unit programs inside of thirty-six hours," Grace continued. "Anchoring specs for Fixits and 'Ficers, patches and mods for Miner procedures, plus Iron Boss programming. . . . Over!"

"Where the hell are we going to get sixty Arties?" McQuade asked.

"We'll strip 'em from Bubble Base," Kornilov said with a hand over the transceiver. "Let them work with their hands for a few months."

To the transceiver he said: "Very good. We will try your solution and report progress in ninety hours. Await your tranning of programs at fifty-to-one speed. Over!"

"Okay. Mama Bear will make fix. Over and out!"

Then the connection went quiet, except for the hiss of the solar wind latent on the carrier beam. Ten seconds later the beam itself was shut down.

After the Phobos Project team had departed for Mars, the Tsoilkovskii Accelerator paused for a prescribed time, an instant of alignment in the Moon's orbit, and then began spitting out more payloads. Thirteen hundred very strange spacecraft were loaded and fired in fifty-two days, all into fast orbits.

They called them blowfish. The only solid parts were a head piece and belly plate of steel faced with ablative ceramics. The main body was a contraption of titanium rings and leaves bracing a glass-fiber skin from the outside. The ships used up six times the world's annual production of titanium and it was rumored that half of the U.S. Air Force had been scrapped to build this fleet.

Back of the head piece, where a fish's gills would be, were scoops with butterfly valves and centrifugal pumps. At the right moment, the valves would open and the pumps start to inflate the skin with whatever atmosphere surrounded the craft. These valves seated outward, designed to contain an enormous internal pressure.

The belly plate supported tiny, stubby wings like the fins of a fish. Clusters of attitude rockets ringed the nose. But there was no main drive engine, either for thrusting or braking.

There were no crews, and no accommodations for a crew to come. The flight path was monitored by a computer brainbox tailored from a suborbital mail rocket's—a standard Pinocchio design.

Jason Bathespeake had personally designed the mission program for each of the 1,300 blowfish. He also had crafted the central pattern, with pertinent deviations, for each of the 1,300 orbits they would follow.

The profile of the voyage was simple: from the Moon, loop out past the orbit of Mars to rendezvous with Jupiter; make one skimming passage through the upper Jovian atmosphere to scoop up the atmosphere as cargo; come back from Jupiter to rendezvous with Mars; make one skimming pass through the upper Martian atmosphere to kill speed; and finish in a stable orbit 5,600 kilometers above the planet's surface. Or just below the orbit of Phobos.

If the pattern was simple, the calculations were monstrously complex. Bathespeake had to consider the current orbital positions of three planets and the Moon; advances in orbit during the course of the operation; the maximum available thrust from the Tsiolkovskii Accelerator; the added mass of the cargo from Jupiter; the pull of the Sun's gravity well coming and going . . . the numbers danced in his head for days. Until they came out right.

And from the immutable requirements of the orbit came the answers for how deeply each blowfish would penetrate Jupiter's hydrogen- and helium-rich atmosphere. Which decided how much internal gas pressure the titanium-leaved sack would have to withstand and how much material each blowfish could bring back. Which decided how many of the craft must be sent to Jupiter in the first place.

The hydrogen/helium mix would fuel the fusion engine Kornilov's Pinocchios would soon begin building in the Hole under Stickney. And the Project's designers knew to the mole how much fusible mass was needed to bust the moonlet loose from Mars' gravity well and bring her to Earth orbit.

It worked out to something over 750 million tons of deuterium.

The string of blowfish would be a year on the outward leg, seven months on the inward. In the loop-and-scoop at Jupiter they would penetrate no more than two kilometers into the upper atomosphere, taking on ambient gas at approximately 350 atmospheres and compressing it several times.

That altitude should put them above the turbulence of storms in the cloud bands. The fins—and later the attitude jets—should be able to correct for any tumbling the fat little fishes wanted to try. The brainboxes had been drilled in simulated recoveries until their confidence index passed eighty-five.

And in any case the Phobos Project engineers had added a margin for error. Although they never told Bathespeake, twenty percent of the blowfish were not expected to survive to a Martian orbit. And the engineers built their fuel margin on *that* expectation.

Just to be on the safe side.

The site team found the first crevasse when the Hole was four kilometers deep—about a third complete and well below the cone of Stickney.

A Miner broke through and couldn't pull back in time. But in the fractional gravity, the wires and pitons held it over the abyss.

Ariel, working nearby with a theodolite, saw the

attendant Artificer try to leap free like a badly frightened monkey. It scrabbled at the edge of the crevasse, then slid out of view.

McQuade decided at the end of shift to slow the work down and let Ariel begin again with her walking rig.

What she found was the true nature of Phobos: a pitted, seamed, fissured mass like badly kneaded bread dough. Evidently the smooth fluff they had found on the floor of Stickney was the cooled plug of molten rock formed by the impact that had made the crater. Phobos itself was a mess.

Ariel thought that would put a dent in Kornilov's sunny smile. There was no way the Miners could work hanging on the sides of slit canyons and pockets. Not that she wished the Project any bad luck, but Ariel wouldn't mind seeing the Mad Russian taken down a peg.

"How many warheads do we have?"

Kornilov grinned at McQuade across the Construction Shack's one cramped conference room.

Ariel thought he'd finally cracked. Why would the Phobos Project be carrying warheads?

Priscilla McQuade didn't laugh. She didn't even look embarrassed.

"Six. All in the ten-megaton range."

Korny looked thoughtful. He was punching the buttons on his wrist calc, but Ariel didn't think it was more than a nervous habit.

"Pretty powerful," he said quietly. "We may have to work out a way to deflect most of the blast up and down the Hole. Don't want to rupture the whole structure."

"What did you bring atomics for?" Ariel finally blurted out. Too late, she hoped the sense of—what? betrayal? awe?—didn't sound too loud in her voice.

"Subsurface caving," McQuade replied in an aside.

"We thought we might need them to cut the fuel chambers."

"But now the problem might be isolating the chambers," Korny said. "Keeping some structure intact so the fusible doesn't leak away . . . Hmmm."

McQuade nodded. Ariel could almost see, behind that high forehead, the blueprints being taken out, unfolded and scrutinized.

"What else have we got in our kit?" Korny asked. "Any Portland cement?"

"We've got some high-temperature, vacuum-setting epoxy that we use on the Moon for binding dust."

"Any good for structural members?" Korny asked.

"Panels, columns, domes. It has about the tensile strength of steel."

Korny was quiet for another two minutes. Finally he said, "Then we can finish this job. . . . I wonder if I can teach the Miners to use a trowel."

Chapter 16

Ivan Turbetskoi: WRONGTHINK

The trip was supposed to be the shortest of Comrade-Commander Ivan Turbetskoi's career. He could doublecheck the essential mission orders in his head: Lift off from the new, temporary, and—admittedly—hastily built rocket center at Ashkhabad. Rendezvous at 88,000 kilometers and match speeds, however briefly. Then brake immediately and return at the start of the next pass, to land at the usual air strip north of Vladivostok.

One wide, elliptical orbit of the planet. Thirteen hours, forty minutes. A snap, as the Americans say.

The *kosmicheskaya vagonetka* lifted with extra tanks of propellant and a reserve set of solid boosters. These were needed both to give additional burn time for the tall orbit and to help with the payload. Built into his ship's hold—actually filling it for the first time Turbetskoi could remember—were four big electromagnets. There were also the steel superstructure that spaced them in a square cloverleaf and the fusion generator that powered them. All of this rig was *heavy*.

And for what? To snuff a candle flame only four meters in diameter. To disrupt an anomaly, a disturbance in the cosmos, that could be measured only in fractions of atomic diameters. It seemed a fool's errand.

But then it wasn't Turbetskoi's place, or his nature, to question the orders of the ministry that sent him into space. Go, they said, and he went.

This time only, they had volunteered the reasons for his mission. It was, they said, to be another triumph of Soviet science.

The Americans, who had discovered and interpreted the anomaly they called Hawking-1, now spoke in desperate horror of the consequences and sent colonies to Mars to steal an entire *lunochka*. Who knew why? To *capture* the so-called "micro black hole"? Or, under a ruse, to set up another orbiting platform? Potentially a new capitalist enterprise zone, hanging there in space above all our heads.

Well, the Soviet superstate would steal the march, they said.

While the Americans pauperized themselves with their foolish Mars project, the Russian people would send just one *vagonetka* and an electromagnet to retrieve the object. When the time was right, they said, it would be paraded—safely caged in magnetic fields—across Red Square and under the Americans' fine, upturned noses.

How was this possible?

Soviet science, they said, denied the true existence of a "black hole" in this space-time. Its mass had removed itself from the continuum, of course. The "object" was merely an interruption of the normal fabric of the cosmos, manifested as a gravity vortex, which itself was defined only by the collapsing matter falling into it.

Just as a whirlpool is defined by the water swirling into it, they said. The rest is only movement.

The "black hole" itself, as the American's declared, had no charge and could not be manipulated. Of course not—because it literally did not exist, except as a physicist's theoretical construct to explain the vortex. But the materials trapped in the vortex *did* have a charge and could indeed be manipulated.

A specialized branch of Soviet physics—hydrosolids—had perfectly described the properties and dynamics of atoms disintegrating under the intense pressures and temperatures at the anomaly's so-called "event horizon." The vortex's embedding matrix of collapsed atoms would respond to magnetic force as a supersolid. The Physics Faculty of Moscow University had then calculated the strength of the fields needed to take and hold the vortex. And suitable electromagnets had been designed and built in the cargo space of the *vagonetka*. The mission was, Turbetskoi decided, a typically Soviet application of hard-headed logic and industry.

It would be a glorious enterprise, they said.

From the Americans' reports on Hawking-1, they had calculated the precise time to fly this one tall orbit. Turbetskoi's *vagonetka* would rendezvous with the anomaly at the exact instant his and its orbital speeds coincided. He would fly beneath it with his pressure doors open. As the anomaly went over the top of its apogee and began descending, it would fall in among the magnet cluster. Their fields would slow it to match Turbetskoi's orbital speed. He would then close the doors and return to Earth.

Just like the goalie Skotina, whose favorite crowd-pleaser was pulling hockey pucks out of the air with his gloved hand. . . . A winning move for the Soviet people, they said.

Now, rising over the blue pearl of Earth on the outward leg of the mission, Turbetskoi felt very good. Everything about the ship was functioning perfectly. The minutes before launch, usually so hurried and uncertain, had gone with the the precision of a military drill. His co-pilot, Alyunin, was a competent younger man Turbetskoi had flown with once before.

He was no good at conversation and telling stories, but he knew his side of the board and that was more important.

"Comrade-Commander," Alyunin now said with correct deference, "is that our objective?" He was pointing generally ahead with his finger.

Turbetskoi looked across the field of stars and could see nothing unusual. He switched the forward telescope into the ship's monitors and focused manually.

"There!" Alyunin exclaimed, pointing at the screen.

It was a dot of light that showed a trace of ragged edge. At this magnification it was less than thirty kilometers ahead of them.

"Excellent, my friend," Turbetskoi told him. "You have sharp eyes."

Alyunin beamed and seemed to stand at attention in his null-gee harness.

Knowing the mission profile, Turbetskoi had of course been expecting the sighting at any moment. But let the other man have his moment of pride.

Turbetskoi ordered sealed helmets and then opened the pressure doors in the hold behind them.

He ignited the fusion generator and ran it quickly up to eighty percent power. The new control panel bolted onto the left side of his board showed everything green. Was it only his imagination, or did he hear a low, vicious humming, like an aroused beehive, coming from the magnets? Surely it was just a vibration in the frame of the ship, but it made him uneasy.

While the stars ahead remained indefinite points of light, the anomaly grew in the screen. It began to show an incandescent disk that, Turbetskoi knew, would never resolve itself into a globe; it would instead remain a flattened plate. Soon, as the ship moved under it, they would see the faint plasma jets where the vortex blew off rejected matter.

It was no color and all colors. They saw it with

their eyes as the purest white, reminding Turbetskoi of a tsarist princess in a satin gown. A pale and fragile thing.

It blared with other colors when he returned to the telescope. In the ultraviolet it was the strongest—a blazing black star, showing a complete globe of radiation. It showed strongly too in the x-ray spectrum and infrared.

Turbetskoi pulled down his visor filters and ordered Alyunin to do the same. He began to suspect that this *anomaly* might not be good for their health. Might they end as another offering to Soviet glory?

Over the top of the orbit, the white disk moved away from them by a few kilometers, then began to close the gap.

Turbetskoi used his thrusters in the last minutes to line up the catch. Through the cameras in the hold he watched the disk drift down toward the dark central space between the dull-gray lips of the four magnets. The outer edges of the vortex bent and began to flow downward into the space. Like the petals of a wax flower melting in a flame.

He would then have radioed the success of their mission, except that the magnets were disrupting the fields around the ship. His exultant report would also have been premature.

The cameras showed it clearly: as the disk descended into that dark space, the exposed surfaces of the magnets began to incandesce. Then their surfaces began to spall and peel like the pages of a book in a fire. The heavy magnets in their steel frame shuddered and collapsed inward.

The camera—all six of the cameras in the hold—went black.

Through his fingertips and boot soles, Turbetskoi felt the shock as the *vagonetka's* bottom—the delicate shield of ablative tiles on which they would have ridden down the atmosphere—ripped away. He didn't have to see it to know that that the *anomaly* had passed through the ship without even pausing.

The goalie had put up his glove to catch the puck and found a bullet instead.

Turbetskoi, with the clean efficiency drilled into him, went over his board methodically. Alyunin was doing the same. Engines—dead. Radios—dead. Thrusters—impaired. Gyros-stopped. Pressure doors—missing. Computers—dead. Radiation level—way above 1,000 rem, a lethal dose for both of them.

Technically, Turbetskoi and Alyunin were now walking dead men from the radiation. But it would never matter.

Long before they began the vomiting and other discomforts of that death, they would endure a long and fiery ride as their orbit took them back to Earth.

Turbetskoi's last coherent thought, before he allowed himself to go mad, was that Soviet physics was . . . well . . . wrong.

Chapter 17

Ariel Ceram: PUFF OF SMOKE

It was late evening, Project time, and Ariel couldn't sleep. She drifted down the corridor to the Shack's comm and rec room. Kornilov was sitting there holding some message hardcopy.

"Letter from home?" she asked, freefalling onto a stool.

"Situation report from Grace on our little friend. Things are getting twitchy."

"Orbit still steady?"

"Yeah. Hard to miss, too. Hawking-1 is pulling a plug of incandescent material thirteen feet across. She says that at night it looks like a shooting star. You can even pick it up at dusk with a powerful scope."

"What about seismic activity?"

"Northern Japan is the worst. The U.N.'s trying to force them to evacuate. Sicily seems to be sinking. And to register to vote in California you now have to waive all rights to disaster insurance.

"Radio interference from Hawking-1 is disrupting the vidisats. So phone service in the Northern Hemisphere is going back to wire and waveguides."

"That doesn't sound too bad." Ariel yawned.

"A Russian *vagonetka* crashed in the Pacific, east of Japan. Latitude thirty-seven thirty."

Suddenly Ariel came awake. "That's on the line . . . what do you mean by 'crashed'?"

"From what Project can piece together out of hints in *Pravda* and one-sided chatter on the Red Army's officer net, they lost contact with the ship while it was still in orbit. It re-entered out of control from about 55,000 miles up. They say the fireball was visible from the Aleutians to Manila."

"That's terrible! Do you think they ran into the black hole?"

"It's *possible* they were in the neighborhood and crossed orbits with it. But I doubt it. For one thing, the Russians prefer polar orbits, since the African trouble. So this mission was out of pattern.

"For another, that ship was way up in no-man's land, beyond even the geosynchronous orbits. You don't put satellites out there: above the Van Allens, the solar wind eats them up. About all that space is good for is passing through—on the way to the Moon, or coming back. The only thing up at 55,000 miles is our friend, at apogee."

"Why would they want to mess with it?"

Kornilov hunched his shoulders and looked at his hands, one meat, one metal. The metal one clicked involuntarily.

"The Russians don't wander into problems—they wade in! From different sources, Defense thinks the *vagonetka* was equipped with some pretty big electromagnets. Lord knows how they planned to use them with Hawking-1. Speculation is, they were trying to take samples of its accretion disk and . . . just got too close."

"They didn't change the hole's orbit!" she asked quickly.

He made a face. "With the mass it's carrying? Not

any more than a freight train would be deflected by running over a baby carriage."

Ariel relaxed. "Good. Wouldn't want them to jeopardize anything we're doing here."

"I feel sorry for the *men*, though."

She suddenly felt very small and foolish. "Yes . . . I'm sorry, Alex."

"S'all right." He folded the papers, stood up and patted her shoulder. Then he was gone, silently gliding down the passageway.

Ariel sat there, hugging her knees in the suddenly cold compartment. She was trying not to imagine being burned alive in a near-vertical re-entry, skin blackening and peeling back, muscle shriveling, tendons contracting involuntarily . . .

Any hope of falling sleep was thoroughly blasted.

She was feeling her own mortality, the pull of time and entropy on her own fragile flesh. For whatever reasons they had all come to the stony ball of Phobos—crisis, discovery, adventure—Ariel suddenly understood they might not be able to thread their way back through the needle. She could well die here. She'd already had one close call with that runaway Miner. . . .

Her body responded with its own logic. She felt a warmth that needed touching, an itch that needed scratching. Her lips were suddenly dry. The same urge that lifts salmon out of their deep ocean home and sends them leaping upstream was lifting her from that metal stool.

Deciding without thinking about it, she stood up and followed Korny down the corridor. She knew which cubicle he kept.

Ariel was part of the grand tour with Project Director Deming, who had shuttled up from Bubble Base Two to admire their work after six months in the Hole.

Helmet lamps danced over the pale, porous rock that showed between the buttresses of Cathedral Hall. Those arches, cast in excavated material bound with epoxy, braced the large central chamber where Artificers were putting the final touches on the fusion engine.

"Are these cracks a problem?" Deming asked, running a shadowed hand along a network of patches in the native stone.

"Just some fill marks," said Priscilla McQuade. "That's about the only solid wall left in this part of Phobos. Now over here . . ." She tried to lead the party to one of the sixteen toroids that would magnetically bind the plasma stream.

The director lingered by the wall.

"Well, it looks pretty shabby," he said with his sarcastic rasp. "Is this blob of stuff going to hold up or not?"

The suit channel carried an audible exhalation, maybe a sigh. It might have been McQuade's sigh.

"The buttresses are bearing the weight now. They'll take a lot of stressing."

"Uh-huh." Deming didn't sound convinced.

"We believe Phobos is now stronger than it ever was."

"Uh . . . huh."

"We've worked out everything. We've had backup from civil engineering studies conducted by eight different cyber programs on Earth. This job is really solid."

Listening with half her attention, Ariel looked around. She suddenly couldn't find Kornilov in the group. He had been right beside her a minute ago, keeping close.

Ariel hoped she wasn't being too obvious with the big, hard-jawed engineer. Pairing was natural on a remote job like this, McQuade had told her. And look at the quiet little programmer Priscilla had taken.

"What about the gas chambers?" Deming was asking. "Are they cracked like this?"

"Don't complain," McQuade growled. "Those cracks put us ahead of schedule. All we had to do was a little local fracturing with shaped charges and pump in a polymer resin to seal the cavity."

"Will *they* hold up?"

There was an embarrassed shuffling. None of the tight-knit Phobos team, who had been through the "ballet of the bulldozers," the work in the crevasses and all the rest, liked to hear their boss put on the griddle like a schoolgirl. Not by a fussy, groundside administrator like Deming.

"Ahh . . . The reservoirs are well forward of the reaction chamber," she said. "If there's any heat expansion, they should still be in stable ground."

"Uh-huh. 'Should be' . . ."

At that moment the argument was interrupted by a call on the open channel from the Construction Shack: "First of our fish coming up on the limb!"

Deming was left in darkness as twenty-odd helmet lamps turned away. The call set off a slippery, low-gravity scramble of foremen and other local dignitaries back up towards the rim of Stickney.

Ariel got there fourth in order and turned her visor toward the sunlit leading limb of Mars, where the fuel boys had always said the Jupiter probes would first enter the planetary system. Because Phobos and Deimos both had synchronous orbits like the Moon's, their primary never left its fixed place, covering a quarter of the Phobian sky just off center over Stickney. The red planet simply turned majestically as the moonlet chased around its orbit.

She held her breath and focused her suit binocs along the Martian equator.

Nothing . . . and still nothing.

She felt a hand close on her right hip with a measured pressure, steadying her. Kornilov was near.

Ariel took a shallow breath and held it again. Then the first spark appeared and faded on the leading limb of the planet. A needle scratch on a red-clay pot. The blowfish had disappeared behind Mars.

That was the whole show, flash and gone. With a few politely disappointed words, the suited figures dispersed toward the Shack. She leaned back against Korny for a minute, then walked away without looking at him. Of course he would follow her.

The probe was chasing Phobos in a lower orbit. It would show again, duller and more redly, at the dark trailing limb in another three hours, forty-nine minutes. The blowfish would then be climbing out of the upper atmosphere, toward the terminator, and heading for its permanent orbit.

And every hour after that, with gaps that told of fish that had not survived the flight, the following ships appeared at first the leading then the trailing limb. Except for one ship that melted or exploded near the end of its skim through the atmosphere. It left a yellow smear on the dark edge of Mars.

In the days that followed, Ariel and all the others kept count of the flashes, the gaps and the explosions. After the twelve hundred and forty-seventh leading flash, with fifty-one intermingled gaps or meltdowns, there came a space of three more gaps. One more than there were ships to fill.

Ariel was outside at the time, working on a sick Artificer with Kornilov. Actually she was just handing him tools. Someone on the suit channel mentioned the inevitable last gap. She then heard another of those audible exhalations. This time it seemed to echo from several mikes—perhaps even her own.

They had their quota of fuel ships. The Phobos Project team would be able to get home.

They were loading one fishful of hydrogen/helium mix for a test firing of Phobos' engine. Ariel was observing the decanting procedure from a toehold along Kepler Dorsum, after maneuvering thrusters had brought the bloated ship alongside the rounded end of the moonlet.

It looked like a goldfish nuzzling a rock.

The fuel boys grappled and snugged the robot ship with lines and winches, then hooked up to the nipple in the fish's nose. The chambers inside Phobos were a high-grade vacuum, so the pressurized gas flowed in quickly.

About two minutes after the pour began, Ariel felt a rumbling through her boot soles.

Probably just expansion, she thought. The gases were finding a new pressure and temperature in the crevices of the fuel reservoir. Perhaps it was a result of the catalysts they had injected to break down the fraction of ammonia and other compounds in the raw Jovian atmosphere.

Possibly it was a simple moonquake—a moonquiver, actually. After all the drilling, cutting and blasting, it would be their first natural seismic event on Phobos.

Ariel dismissed these thoughts when the event failed to stir any chatter on the suit channel. She would remember them later.

The plan was to run the fusion engine up to ten percent, pushing the minimum of reaction mass. It would give them a chance to examine the shape of the plasma envelope and fine-tune the toroidal magnets.

Deming had ordered all personnel evacuated from Phobos and all non-essential supplies ferried down, too. A team of Kornilov's Artificers could start and monitor the engine remotely.

This order brought a fight from McQuade, who didn't want to lose the time. But she finally gave in with much grumbling and packed up everything in the Construction Shack except the radio relays. They even sent the Miners planetside, partly disassembled. The evacuation took fifteen Mars days.

It was a cold morning with a thin, sighing wind at Bubble Base Two when McQuade told the remaining Artificers to open the valves on the deuterium filters and fill the gas charger. Phobos was below the horizon, not due to rise for another eight hours. But it would take that long for the chargers to configure and heat the envelope.

Ariel decided she had time to go out prospecting. She could follow the countdown over the radio net.

Phobos rose in the late afternoon and rushed overhead. Ariel was in a ravine five kilometers south of the base, and reception on her suit radio was slippery. She heard the thirty-second count and paused to listen as McQuade sent the signal that would begin compressing the plasma and ignite the fusion reaction.

She put down her geologist's hammer and straightened, adjusting her binocs. There was the moon, just overhead, with the dark shadow of the Hole pointing down on Mars. Ariel thought she could see a glimmer in the darkness up there.

Phobos sputtered and then exploded.

For a moment it looked pretty, like a Fourth of July firework: a white flash englobed by red and blue stars. The burst left a visible shroud of black smoke and dust that, over the course of several minutes, gradually blurred out along the former moonlet's orbit.

There was silence on the network.

For a dazed moment Ariel had the impression that it was somehow a successful shot . . . as if they had *planned* to blow up Phobos, by the numbers.

Then, as a jumble of voices sounded inside her helmet, she realized that their only vehicle for return to Earth had just shattered into rock dust. The Phobos Project team was stranded.

She began running with long, lifting strides back toward the base, where Korny was. He would know . . . would have a reasonable explanation. What she had seen was some freak of the light, a trick on her eyes. Yes! It was just an illusion, caused by the actually successful firing of the engine.

Kornilov would hold her and tell her that story. And she would believe it.

But deep in her soul Ariel Ceram believed she had received her one-time idle wish: she could now stay and prospect for fossil Martian water to her heart's content.

Humankind's tenure on Mars would have no natural limit. They had their domes and quad-huts, their power heliostats, their tanks of *Spirogyra hydroponica*, their oh-two recyclers, their automata. Other nonessentials could be modified or substituted from existing stores. They could last indefinitely on the Red Planet—until boredom, breakdown, and bad temper wrote their eviction notice.

Perhaps, if they were very careful and lived quietly, they would last as long as six years more. Then they could watch through telescopes as the small, blue dot that was Earth split apart after Hawking-1 had absorbed what it could.

Chapter 18

Eldon Richardson: BINGE

On the day that Eldon Richardson knew they were testing the Phobos engine, Grace Porter called a surprise meeting for four o'clock.

Riding the elevator up to the executive floor of the Pinocchio building, Richardson was calmly expecting a brief announcement of success. Probably there would be champagne, a small party, the usual corporate signs of pride and pleasure. Then it would be his job to spread the word to a waiting world.

Mentally counting on his fingers, he listed the major channels of access: downlinks and beam services, opinion-leader channels, talkies and fifteen-second flashers. They were all as near as his phone.

Although he and Grace had been planning this story for two months, she had never quite agreed to a final budget. And coverage-equals-bucks was the media maven's immutable equation, even when the story was the salvation of planet Earth.

As he stepped into the secretary's bay for the chairwoman's office and submitted to a two-second scan by the Rover standing guard there, Richardson decided to press Porter for a twenty-megabuck authorization. That was two more than the highest figure they had yet discussed, but he figured euphoria and enough champagne just might carry it.

When he got inside the office, he found only a gathering of project insiders from the Pinocchio staff. That was awkward, because Richardson was contract, not corporate. He felt, suddenly, like an outsider.

A polite buzz of unfinished conversation, a patter of expectant laughter, all went still when Porter entered from a private side door in the teak paneling. Her face was set and pale. She faced them with the staring eyes of a starving hawk—so focused that she seemed blind. Richardson couldn't tell if she recognized anyone in the room.

"Some hours ago," she began in a low voice that those in the back strained to hear, "we—um—ran a test-firing of the fusion engine implanted in Phobos. There was an apparent malfunction and the moon has been destroyed. None of our personnel was injured. Bubble Base Two will shortly be sending analog and summaries on the complete sequence."

Grace paused, as if suddenly seeing the people in front of her. She seemed uncertain about saying more.

An engineer in the back called out: "What does 'destroyed' mean? Damage to the chamber? Loss of mass?"

"No," Grace replied, shaking her head slowly like a wounded animal. "No. Fragmented. Totally shattered. Where we had a solid body we now have a dust ring." The strain was carving deep lines in her cheeks, a strange grin. "I'm sorry."

"What about bringing back the team?" someone else asked.

"I've just been in contact with the other Consortium partners. We have no immediate plans for a rescue mission. Now, that's all I have to say." Porter ducked her head, as if to turn aside. "I'm sure we'll have a press conference, or something, later."

With that she walked out the private door.

Richardson stepped forward to follow but too many bodies—frozen with indecision—blocked the way.

He relaxed for a moment and considered what he had just heard. It took him that long to recognize the gap. In someone like Grace Porter the habits of corporate misdirection died hard: even for her insiders she had couched the story in semi-public terms, leaving out the most important part, the obvious implication.

A mutter went through the crowd as they, too, interpreted the news. Eldon heard an AI personality designer standing nearby say, "Game over."

The Earth's one hope for stopping the black hole had just disintegrated in orbit around Mars. Game over.

It was a sorry epitaph for a doomed planet.

By five o'clock the grapevine had spread the story throughout the building, accompanied by a capsule analysis from Mars, based on telemetry from the lost moon.

During the first seconds of ignition, a bulkhead on one of the fuel chambers had given way, flooding the engine with near-liquid hydrogen. Some of the toroids had shorted out, destabilizing the plasma envelope. It blew. And the body of the moon, hollowed to a thin shell like a soft-boiled egg in its cup, had come apart.

That was the story Richardson heard in the hallways. He knew that, no matter how close Grace and the Consortium meant to play it, within a day that story would be all over the city, the country, the world. He would bet, too, that every beam and channel service would get the important part of the message right: Game over.

Outside his own office, Richardson found Gerry Winters, a veteran flash broker from the media team. Winters was leaning against the wall, his mouth opening and closing like a fish thrown out on the dock. His eyes looked down the corridor, fixed on the elevator lights as if on salvation—if indeed he was seeing anything.

Winters was sixty, maybe older, and Richardson feared he was having a stroke.

"Hey, Gerry! Time to go home, man!" Eldon put an arm halfway around his shoulders, cautiously feeling for tremors or rigidity.

The man rolled his eyes at Richardson, his project boss, and just puffed in his face. Sour breath, tasting of fear and laced with fresh whiskey.

"You okay, Gerry?"

"We—we're—going to die—aren't we—El?"

"Sure we are, one day, every one of us. But you want to go home now, and not worry about it. Your wife will be missing you."

He got a glazed nod. Winters straightened, turned about, and shambled off in the wrong direction.

In a doorway nearby, two young writers—known on the team just as Boy Sam and Girl Sam—were openly passing a bong-gong back and forth. Eldon walked over to them.

"Say, Mr. Richardson," Boy Sam said dreamily. "That's bad shit about Phobos, huh?"

"At least, yeah, 'bad shit,' " Eldon agreed.

"What's our line gonna be?" Girl Sam said, squinting against the smoke. "We play it hard or what? Or smooth and kind of slide it out? Do we break it fast or dribble it? Do we—"

"I've got to talk to Porter first," he cut across her word jag. "When she decides, I'll give you the line, right?"

"Sure, right in sight," she assured him. Then her mouth dribbled on amiably, "No fright, not tight. Sail it like a kite. Tonight."

Richardson walked away without being noticed.

He headed for the elevator, deciding that the most intelligent thing he could do was get drunk. A boilermaker or six—that's what he needed. Carbohydrates fortified with vitamin booze. Things would look better when he'd gotten his head clear.

The only trouble with going to bed drunk, Richardson decided the next morning, was it forced you to stop drinking and then you woke up on the near side of sober. *And* sick.

Vague memory snatches floated up with the morning coffee and his stomach. Of hanging onto a brass rail and telling a white-aproned barkeep with purple garters on his sleeves that the world was coming to an end. The man had just kept on polishing glasses and putting up beer and bourbon.

Of explaining to two men and a woman at a table, maybe in a different bar, how the moon had exploded. And getting a five-dollar bill to leave them alone.

Of telling the same story to a rubber tree—*that* was certainly in a different bar—and getting what he thought were sympathetic vibrations.

It had been a wasted night.

Getting dressed was a complicated business. Even taking twice as long over his shave, he went into the office with bristly patches on his jaw. And with fog in his head. At least his shirt was fresh.

Porter's tribox tried to tell him that the chairwoman was taking no calls and the earliest appointment it could record was for the next day.

He told the impudent machine that, if it didn't get him into her office inside an hour, teams of auditors from the Defense Department, the Federal Communications Commission, and the Securities and Exchange Commission would all be asking for simultaneous and conflicting appointments—with Pinocchio's receivership to follow. And what would the tribox do *then?*

This improbable threat slipped the automaton into manual mode and it bucked him onto Grace's line.

"Yes, what do you want, Eldon?" She sounded as if she'd enjoyed as hopeless a drunk as he had.

"Half an hour with you *right now*."

"Can't it wait? We've got serious problems here and—"

"Listen, lady, unless you and I get our heads together and figure out how to ride this tiger, you're going to have a global panic, with a roving riot that will run us both right down to the beach and out to sea."

"*Mister* Richardson—"

"*Mzzzz* Porter, it was Steve Cocci's decision—and yours as well—to use calamity and public fear for financing your Phobos Project, preserving it from total government domination and simultaneously pressuring that same government to back you in the enterprise. Now you *must* keep the show running. Just how the news about the explosion is managed—toughed up, leaked out, or dropped like a bag of stinking garbage—will mean the difference to you between ending this day in control of Pinocchio, Inc. and ending it in a jail cell. Take your pick."

There was dead silence on the phone for twelve seconds. Richardson was counting them.

"Come up," she finally said.

The tribox admitted him to the office with a malevolent mechanical stare. He wondered in passing how much of a grudge a machine could hold.

In conference with Grace were men whom Richardson recognized only from photos and their reputations: Peter Kriegs of National Space Power, Gregory Domkin of the American Academy, Winkle from Congress. They glared at him from around a conference table that, out of the office's corner windows, overlooked the Bay and Yerba Buena Island.

Morning sunlight reflected off the water right into Richardson's eyes and aroused his sleeping headache. Good. It made him mean and brave.

"What is this nonsense about publicity?" Kriegs spoke up with a disdainful sneer. "I thought we had arranged to keep the test firing classified through Defense."

"We did," Porter said quickly.

"Well, then?"

"It doesn't matter how classified you think the project is," Richardson said to the group at large, sweeping their faces. "You can't lose something as big as a moon of Mars and expect people not to find out."

"It takes a powerful telescope, professional quality, to detect Phobos from Earth," Domkin said judiciously. "And certainly the accident yesterday was subnuclear. Hardly visible from this distance. I see no cause for panic."

"Yes, well, you have more than a dozen people in this building alone who were formally let in on the secret," Richardson said. He saw Grace open her mouth and Kriegs turn on her with a glare. "And how many more might know through the grapevine is anyone's guess."

"They can be discredited, " the NASPFAC administrator said heavily.

"What about your own people, others?" Richardson asked. "Surely there must be two or three thousand by now who knew firsthand that a test was scheduled, and they will have correctly interpreted the absence of an announced success. People aren't stupid. They can tell when a project is a failure."

"We have good security."

"Against the end of the world? And when little Phobos doesn't come rolling home in eleven months, as advertised—what will you do then?"

"We're at work on another possibility," Grace said, looking around the table.

Richardson, watching her, waited for the tensions in the others to sort out.

"Deimos, the farther moon," she said after a moment. "It's much smaller, but denser. Weighs about a quarter what Phobos does—did. Its orbit is only eight thousand miles beyond that of Phobos, so our shuttles can get to it. Fortunately, we evacuated all the working equipment before the engine test. And we now have more than enough fusible mass to move Deimos."

"Do you have another fusion engine?" Richardson asked. "Or parts to build one?"

"They could be sent," said Kriegs.

"Do you have *time* to start over again?"

Uncertain glances chased themselves around the table.

"We think we do," Grace finally answered.

"Then we better get the word out."

"Why? We have the situation under control," said Winkle for the first time. "One moon comes back or another—who's to care, or even know?"

And this man was a politician?

"It's a matter of credibility," Eldon explained. "The delay alone will cause questions—questions that would lead to rioting."

"I always said we should never have published a deadline," Domkin said. "Never explain, never complain." He seemed satisfied at being proved right.

"No," Richardson barked. "We tell them what happened at Phobos. Then we explain about the second moon. After that, it's business as usual and we're heroes for having Deimos up our sleeves. I can arrange a press briefing this morning."

He looked around the table expectantly. Their faces still showed reluctance, hesitation.

"It has to be soon," he pressed. "The farther we get from yesterday's test, the fishier it will seem, the more questions—"

"Then perform your function," Domkin told Richardson grandly, waving him toward the door. "Let's be done with this flackery and get on to real problems."

The others nodded and turned away, to begin discussing Deimos.

Richardson, suddenly facing the backs and tops of heads, could only let himself out of the room.

It was an old-fashioned press conference, with flesh-and-blood people crowding into one space and asking questions—across shared air—of Grace Porter and Peter Kriegs. The people there even took some pleasure in elbowing aside the floaters and cobras sent by channelcasters who didn't keep a human representative in San Francisco.

It lasted a long time—almost twenty minutes. Some of the questions became technical, showing the traces of depth-conferencing via pin mikes and earspeakers with science editors at homebase. These reps were primed to ask about Deimos, dig rates, and deuterium content.

It was a media maven's high tea. Everyone was respectful, informed, sagacious. And that made Richardson, standing in the wings and lagging the beamcasters, deeply suspicious.

It didn't do a damn thing to stop the rioting.

The longest-running riot was kicked off in Chicago when the newly formed Church of the Bitter End took their automatic weapons and policy of shared suffering to the streets. Forty days and forty nights of house-to-house "cleansing" all but leveled the Near North Side.

It was *fin-de-millennium* fever all over again. The Earth was going to end in fire and it was God's will so put your hands *up*, stranger!

An outfit in Delaware began advertising personal subscriptions for an O'Neill colony to be built in orbit around Venus. The mailing flyer on it showed lavish settings: stone terraces, crystal fountains, green growing things, healthy tanned people playing in sun-warmed saunas. All of this grandeur hung over a world like a misted pearl.

Richardson actually received one of the flyers—but not directly. It was a sure bet the mailing list was drawn from people whose income was taken in Swiss transfers and stock options—not in anything so grimy as a paycheck.

Even if he could have afforded it, Eldon didn't think he would chance a colony that was organized freelance. The subscription was to be paid in advance. The accommodations were "body only"—which meant buck naked. And transfer was at Tycho. How many of the colonists would actually arrive in this Venusian nirvana? And how many would be stacked like cordwood, white and dehydrated, behind some rock on Nearside? It was a certainty that more subscriptions would be sold than could be honored.

The day after the press conference, the New York Stock Exchange collapsed like a wave on the shore. Richardson didn't play it himself, but he kept an eye on the stocks of those few companies making up the Consortium. They gave him that grimy paycheck. Pinocchio was down by seventy points that first day. Which showed that, regardless of who believed the story about Deimos, the smart money was pulling to the sidelines.

Just where the smart money might go was an interesting question.

The real estate market had crashed when they broke the first stories about the black hole, back when Cocci was still alive. Then you could buy ten acres of prime Oregon potland or a city block in Manhattan for a week's wages—provided you took an option for seven years out. Even in the best days of the Phobos Project only the price changed, not the date on the option.

Escort and guard services had been attractive investments with the increase in casual, animal violence. But they were small businesses, with no aggregate.

Drugs and other distractions had become growth stocks. People wanted to live for the minute and they paid well for the opportune novelties—even paid their life savings.

Suicide cults were doing brisk business but they were hardly capital-intensive. What did you need but a sound stage, some ritual props like a burning skull or a diode-studded dragon's eye, and a gimmicky kicker like timed-release hallucinogens or a silver-plated chainsaw? Disposal facilities, of course—but they could be arranged with the local municipal scavenger.

People with private money were discovering final fantasies to throw it away on. The "Theater of the Ephemeral" became a big absorber of cash. Ice castles at Malibu, with astronomical power costs to keep them frozen. Megasculptures in ice cream, paper, or brie and smoked salmon. Re-enactments of historic battles with real weapons—and indemnities paid to the actors' next of kin. Granite mausoleums erected on the exact line of the black hole's orbit, at a point calculated to be struck in a certain number of days—playing a kind of rigged Russian roulette with the end of the world.

If it was gaudy, expensive, and short-lived, somebody tried it.

Richardson watched all this and more pop out of his channel scanner. It might have depressed him, except for a certain balancing factor: he knew that only a few million people in the post-decadent world had the cash or the leisure time to waste on such frivolities.

Perhaps a billion others across the planet had access to the media—and presumably knew vaguely about the failure of the team on Mars. But for them the impending end of the world was just another inevitable danger in a life of hard edges. If they relaxed their grip on the necessities today, they died tomorrow. Never mind about five years and four months from tomorrow. A near-healthy woman could bear five babies in that time and four of them might die.

The remaining nine billion people living out their hive-horde lives in places like São Paulo, Shanghai, and Soweto would remain oblivious to the danger. The day the Earth collapsed in a cataclysm of molten framents would dawn for them as grimly as any other.

"Do I think everybody's crazy?" the Cincinnati cabbie repeated.

"Sure, but . . . If you think getting buried alive in hot fudge is a better way to go, some kind of consolation, and you want to blow your bankroll doing it . . . well . . . Why not?

"But, then, who am I to judge? I'm still driving this cab, ain't I?"

Brother Mung Xi had the best day of his life. He found one of the cats hiding beneath the lip of his culvert. It was not too wild, not too fast—and not too sick, either. He caught it in his hands and wrung its neck in one motion.

Suddenly Mung Xi's life had a dilemma. Should he share the carcass with his burrow mates, or keep it for himself? To share would win him respect. To keep would extend his strength, perhaps even enable him to catch another animal—though nothing so fine as this cat would come to him again.

It was true, what the Party had always said: a rich man's life is full of burden.

Chapter 19

Jason Bathespeake: BILLIARDS

On the day they tested the Phobos engine, Jason Bathespeake went to Grace's office and stood in the front row of a small crowd of Pinocchio people.

They stood together but he felt apart. Jason wore his mask of loyalty when he came to meetings like this. In private, his face slipped into a sour frown. His work on the blowfish orbits had finished a year ago. Preparing Phobos and pushing her to Mars' escape velocity was simply brute mechanical work. Of course, the team still had to navigate the moonlet back to the right Earth orbit, but Jason had calculated the vectors more than a year ago and filed them away.

For what they were worth.

The Phobos calculations were flawed by the old problem: too small a sweet spot. The orbit that the moonlet had to meet—alignment, speed, timing—to intersect the black hole's path was at the upper limit of human precision. And if their navigation failed to place that three-meter sweet spot on the right track, then Phobos' mass would surely impair the hole's delicate orbit. Then—gulp!

When Grace came into the office and faced the group, it took Jason a few seconds to read the signs.

He had a sober respect for the chairwoman: her head was a stainless steel abacus and sometimes he could hear the beads clicking. Jason would not have believed her personal profile included taking liquor to settle bad news. But now he saw the random movements of her hands and the white set of her face, heard the hesitation in her voice. These telltales gave him sudden insight.

Jason shifted his vision to infrared and saw the heat radiating from her cheeks and temples. She was three drinks down, he judged, and not even slurring her words. Admirable control, under the circumstances.

But she told the story of the failed engine test badly.

When the meeting broke up, Jason left her office with the others. He was walking in a cocoon of private space.

Anyone passing him in the hallway might have read gloom and doom in the forward thrust of his head, the opaque misting of his goggles, the sag of his mouth, his hunched shoulders. Kornilov, seeing the cyber at that moment, would easily have recognized furious concentration. Kornilov, however, was stranded on Mars.

Jason himself was elated.

Of course he understood the implications of Grace's news: that, despite all their work, the black hole would win. Personally, his expected lifespan was now cut by some forty years. Professionally, he would soon be in a position—with the rest of humankind—to observe firsthand the swallowing of an entire planet.

All of that hardly distracted him. In the people moving around him, Jason vaguely sensed the urge toward drunken abandon. He felt none of it.

The Phobos disaster was, for him, a release. Their program had been flawed. Incredible luck had given them a coda—the imperative to return to an earlier stage in their thinking, to make over and do better.

Jason's personal profile, he knew, included a Brahminical patience. The black hole had presented them with a Gordian knot, and he was content to grow gray picking at it, tracing, rethreading, backing up and moving forward. He might even solve it in time.

He went to his computer lair in the basement, closed the door quietly—even thoughtfully—and didn't come out for two days.

When he did emerge, it was to find suddenly smiling faces and renewed hope. And the word echoing in whispered talk was "Deimos."

Bathespeake was moving through Grace's outside office at a dead run when the Rover tried to stop him. Its hand snagged his arm and came within a fraction of closing, but Jason merely barked the stop code "Salmon quiche!" at it and brushed past.

The tall door to the inner office slowed him by a quarter second—turn handle, catch his balance, thrust with arms and hips—then slam it on the Rover, which had almost caught up with him.

Grace looked up from some papers, startled, and then smiled.

"Hello, Jason. Where have you been in all the excitement? I remember seeing you at—"

"Deimos! How was *that* decision made? By whom? It's absolutely the wrong thing to do."

Jason's lungs were pumping, but one of the advantages of cyberhood was that it required no air to speak. He could run a five-minute mile and recite Shakespeare at every step.

Grace slowly put down the papers. "We—that is, the Consortium—met and agreed to proceed with alteration of the second moon."

"Why?"

"Well, we were responsible for doing *something*, Jason," she said reasonably. "The team, all the equipment and the deuterium fuel—or most of it—weren't harmed by the accident. The Project still has to bring back a moon-sized mass. And Deimos is available."

He was scowling deeply at her and didn't care to hide it.

Grace's face stiffened in return. "I really don't know why I'm defending the decision to you. It was the logical thing to do. Politically it was—"

"It's not a matter of politics or persuasion, Grace." He sagged, suddenly tired. "Deimos is the wrong choice. There's not enough mass."

"You're so sure about that?"

"That's not an *opinion*. Phobos was the wrong choice to begin with, and Steve Cocci knew it. He wanted a big project that would profitably use a lot of Pinocchio equipment. He got that. But we never would have taken the black hole with Phobos. As a capture mass, it simply has too little margin for error. And Deimos reduces the margin to almost nothing. The best thing that ever happened to us was that explosion. Can't you *see* that?"

Grace was staring at him. In her face he could watch the emotions flicker—from anger to disbelief, a flash of fear, and back again to anger. She finally stabilized in a half-smile of wonder, as if she were listening to a fragment of inner music.

"Jason, you were—are—my friend. And I know you are not crazy, although you seem to be saying crazy things. You're telling me to stop the work on Mars, is that right?"

"Yes, of course. It's a distraction, a waste of time."

"A distraction from what? Do you have a plan?"

"The same plan as always—before Cocci became stubborn about Phobos."

"Your . . . original . . . plan was to use a large asteroid. And Steve wouldn't accept that. Didn't he say the Asteroid Belt was too far? It's no closer now, and we have even less time to get there."

"Yes. Steve also said a suitable asteroid was too heavy to budge with the forces we had at hand," he agreed. "But in designing the blowfish orbits, I came upon a propulsion system that may work to bring back a large body.

"Now, we could take one of the close-approach asteroids in a near-Earth orbit. But why stop with that small stuff? We can get a much more comfortable margin for error if we grab a really large asteroid. This new system lets us take our pick. We could even bring down Ceres herself."

"Why did you conceal this idea?" Grace squinted at him. "Why not share it with us immediately?"

Jason shrugged. Would it help his cause now to begin a bitter diatribe about politics and profits and other follies? It would not.

"At the time, the work on Phobos seemed to be going well," he said lamely. "You had psychological momentum, something definite to work on. This was just an idea, really, not enough to interrupt the work. I didn't even bother to cross-check the calculations until this setback with Phobos."

Grace looked unconvinced. "That's all? You didn't want to *interrupt* us?"

"Well, the Ceres plan . . . it's dangerous."

"More dangerous than using Deimos?"

"No-oo. Deimos will almost surely fail in capturing the black hole, so that's not really an option. Ceres can easily take it."

"But with a risk . . ."

"All life is a risk."

"That's true enough," Grace agreed.

Robert Elias, Undersecretary of Defense for Strategic Developments, had reluctantly agreed to meet with Grace and Jason. He sat through the computer simulation that Jason had prepared months ago, as a hobby, while Kornilov and Ceram had cut Cathedral

Hall under Stickney. Elias skimmed the columns of readout from Jason's latest calculations. Then he folded his arms and looked out from hooded eyes.

"You seem to be well prepared. Remarkable work for only a few days."

Grace spoke for the first time. "Mr. Bathespeake has been evolving this concept for some time."

"I can see that. It's a pity we did not have an alternate approach in hand before we began the—unfortunate—mission to Phobos."

Grace's eyes slid toward Jason and he merely nodded.

"And now you want us to do—what?" Elias asked.

"The plan requires a supply of thermonuclear devices."

"More than fifty-eight hundred, I see."

"Yes, if they are all at least twenty megatons. If they're less powerful, then more will be needed."

"You have worked out contingencies based on a mix of weapons, of course?"

"Of course. With a safety margin."

"And you realize what this number represents in terms of our national arsenal?"

"Not exactly," Grace said.

"You'd strip the country," Elias barked. "We would be defenseless, totally unable to retaliate. We would have to dock our submarines, ground the remaining bombers, empty the silos."

"In view of the doom we all face in little more than five years," Grace said drily, "that doesn't seem to be an important consideration."

"Nevertheless, that is the single responsibility this office is charged with under the U.S. Constitution. The ultimate fate of the world is not—ahem—on my turf."

"You could continue your patrols," Jason said. "Use dummy warheads. No one would have to know."

"And if there was an incident—?"

Jason tipped his head. "It's been how many years?"

"May I suggest that you are very naïve."

"Then you may just have to begin negotiating a detente."

"Neither is *that* on my turf."

Grace made to stand up. "If you will not help in this venture, perhaps we will find a more receptive attitude in Beijing. Or Moscow."

Jason rose quickly to stand beside her.

Elias looked from one to the other. "We will take the plan under advisement."

"Please don't think long," Jason said. "The next available launch sequence begins in sixty-one days. The one after that will be too late."

For six weeks after the destruction of Phobos, the space around the Earth-Moon system was strangely quiet. And then in the seventh week, the Tsiolkovskii Accelerator on the Moon's outward face began to spit out packages like a St. Catherine's wheel. As they left the crater, some of them spouted fire and whirled off past the Sun. Others were released to coast almost slowly toward the outer darkness.

An alien observer hanging in space above the plane of the solar system might have counted 5,800 of the packages.

An eye projecting their various courses would have found them all proceeding to the dispersed rock garden that humans called the Asteroid Belt. The trajectories were timed to place them all securely inside the Belt at a complex series of critical moments.

Such an alien, with superhuman control of space and time, still would have marveled at the mind that computed those courses. It might have found much to discuss with a half-man, half-machine named Jason Bathespeake.

"Dig in? What does that mean? Over."

The signal from Mars was on the verge of breaking up, a result of Hawking-1's interference.

"It means find yourself a good hard granite cliff and make a tunnel," Grace said with exaggerated enunciation. "Put as much of your life support as you can underground. Over."

The delay, measured in tens of minutes, made Kornilov's questions seem reasoned, judicious. But in his voice Jason could hear the risings of panic.

"We need to know the reasons for this instruction. What do you know that we do not? Over."

"In two hundred and fifty days we will ignite a series of thermonuclear devices that are now on their way to selected points in the Asteroid Belt. These will alter the orbits of more than three hundred large bodies. Certainly smaller ones that we cannot detect from Earth will also be shifted. There is more than a ninety-nine percent probability of a body in excess of one million tons impacting on the Martian equatorial regions. That is, it will come down on your heads. Over."

The delay that followed was a minute longer than the light-speed lag in communications. Jason could imagine the stunned faces in the comm shack at Bubble Base Two.

"What is your purpose in shifting asteroid bodies? Over."

"We hope to perturb Ceres out of its present orbit into a sunward fall that will end in Earth orbit and a rendezvous with Hawking-1. Over."

More minutes.

"Thank you for the warning, NASPFAC Control." The voice was no longer Korny's. Jason thought it might be Captain Deming's. "We copy—and will get our heads down. What plans do you have for a rescue mission. Over!"

"Ahh—no mission can fly at this time because of the scattering this blast series will cause. We will monitor and send a rescue team as soon as the way is clear. Over."

More minutes.

"Do you have a projection on that timing? Over."

Grace paused and licked her lips. Across from her at the communications console, Jason shook his head.

"We can't project until we get further into the series. We understood you had no serious limits on your planetside endurance. Have your conditions changed? Over."

More minutes.

"Only homesickness—now at epidemic proportions. But we understand the reasons for delay and will attempt to endure. Good shooting.

"Private message follows for Bathespeake from Ceram. Quote. Have found evidence of sedimentary layers in outcropping twenty-two klicks northwest of base. Eureka as they say. Will transmit full analysis at fifty-to-one in two days. Unquote.

"Bubble Base Two, out."

"How did you ever compute it all?" Grace asked one day as Jason made his report on the spreading circle of bombs headed toward their appointed places in the Belt. "So many near misses to arrange. All to line up a shower of big rocks across the sunward side of Ceres' orbit. How did you know where to begin?"

There was in her voice a familiar edge. To Jason, it divided friendly admiration and unholy awe: what part of her question addressed his talents as a thinker, what part his *functioning* as a cyber?

Jason sat down in one of the guest chairs facing her desk before he answered.

"Of course, I had the computer to help. The program is like a second memory, keeping track of all the numbers."

"But you still had—how many?—hundreds of

choices for a starting point. I don't understand how you controlled all those variables."

Jason remembered how he had approached the problem, and he smiled. "I worked it backwards."

"Eh?"

"One of the most important lessons in problem-solving, I learned in the third grade. Mrs. Curlow showed me—though that's not what she intended. She had given the class a piece of busywork, a maze, to keep us quiet. We were to solve it with a lightpen.

"While everyone scribbled, ended up wrong and started over, I studied the screen. Then I began at the *goal* and worked backward to the *start*. The traps worked only one way, so I missed most of them.

"So of course I finished ten minutes before the rest of the class. When Mrs. Curlow asked how I had done it, I explained. And she got a strange look and said, very loudly, 'Jason! That's cheating!'

"All the others, hearing only her comment, looked at me as if I was an awful person. But it *wasn't* cheating. There were no rules about how to solve the problem. I had found the way that worked best.

"And it always works: begin with the goal—the result you want—and proceed backwards to where you should be starting."

"So you started with Hawking-1's orbit?" Grace said.

"Yes. H-hour was any convenient time with the black hole at apogee. From there I had a number of 'windows' through which Ceres could be maneuvered. Then I had to work out the configurations of other asteroid orbits that would dislodge Ceres at the right moment. And from there I picked out the right places to nudge *those* orbits."

"And you didn't find any traps?" She smiled at him.

"Oh yes! For example, I still have no idea where most of the main shower will go once Ceres moves out of the Belt. Some of them will undoubtedly follow her down to Earth, but they probably won't find as stable an orbit as she will."

Grace stared at him for a minute. "Are you suggesting that we'd better dig in, too?"

Jason nodded. "We will certainly have some large impacts. Mostly in the ocean, I suspect, with tidal waves and persistent steam clouds. Land impacts will throw up girdling belts of dust. After the immediate death of some hundred millions, I'd look for a long-term climatic change with a drop in global temperatures of some twelve degrees Celsius . . ."

Jason stopped talking when Grace turned away and began punching the phone. She broke a nail on the first two stabs.

For several days Jason thought Grace was trying to stop the detonation sequence.

It was interesting to speculate what she imagined could be done. The nuclear devices were armed and fired on proximity, by on-board circuits tied to radar sensors. Radio signals from Earth were irrelevant. To stop the sequence, each warhead would have to be overtaken and dismantled—a physical impossibility at this late stage.

Of course, for those with drive rockets and maneuvering thrusters, signals could probably be sent to ignite the remaining fuel and change the blast locus. But the result would be chaos. Most of the bombs were already inside the Belt, so scrambling the sequence would still dislodge a shower of asteroids.

To Jason, there was no choice. Millions of humans would die if they brought Ceres down to capture Hawking-1. And billions would surely die if they didn't. That was cold thinking, Jason knew. However, a rational mind would find no alternative but to act.

With the same inward eyes that had created the

detonation program, Jason now "saw" in a few seconds a chain of events occurring several hundred million miles away and actually lasting more than a hundred days. He thought of it as a game of billiards.

Moving at different speeds, arriving at different times, the bombs found their targets: three flashes trailing Pallas well above the ecliptic to drive her sunward; four leading Vesta to slow her and drive her out toward the darkness; individual detonations for Hygeia, Patientia, Bettina, Themis, Diotima, Juno, Thisbe, Eugenia; a rosette on the darkside of Ceres herself. And 5,781 other blasts that would briefly and silently light the tumbling rocks and dark bodies.

To that alien observer, floating above the Solar System, it would seem a brilliant and futile display. None of the targets was shattered, none halted in its forward rush. But careful study in the days that followed would show a pattern, a collective shift here, a drift there.

And then Ceres, queen mother to this jostling crowd, would feel serial pulls from the gravity wells of passing bodies, like hands tugging at her sleeves and urging her toward the light. Already disturbed by the rosette of warheads Jason had placed, she would leave her millennial orbit. She would come sunward.

It was a grim pilgrimage that they made to the top of Mt. Hamilton. While Grace threaded the switchbacks in the single-lane tar road, Jason sat stiff and silent as a statue. If the car lurched in a hairpin turn, he did not feel it. His mind was focused on the coming encounter.

The small optical observatory at Mt. Hamilton had been closed for years. Placed fifteen miles east of San Jose, its telescopes had been unable to deal with the light and air pollution from the fastest-growing urban population in the country. But the directors had agreed to reopen when Hawking-1 began stitching its orbit along a line of latitude twenty miles north of the site.

Grace and Jason had made this trip before. Each time they came to see an enemy they could not touch. But now they knew that, somewhere out beyond the orbit of Mars, Ceres was coming to do the touching for them.

Tonight the black hole was scheduled to rise out of the San Joaquin Valley, east of the observatory. It would pull a plug of rock almost one hundred meters wide—bigger than a football field. The shockwave would be felt from Bakersfield to Redding and break windows in San Jose. The radiation would destroy or alter life within fifty miles of the breakout point.

Jason wondered if the rockfall he had unleashed in the Belt could really be worse than this twice-daily thrashing the planet was now taking.

They parked in the strip along the ridgetop and went to the main building. Under the dome, the crowd was a little larger than usual—mostly professorial types, but a few military uniforms were also present.

A twenty-four-inch Schmidt telescope had been mounted on the pedestal. The clock drive had been replaced with fast-acting hydraulics. In place of an eyepiece it had a splitter that fed into both a fast-decay video camera and a high-resolution image-processing chip. The computer that read the chip could take 15,000 impressions a second.

This was jackrabbit astronomy. Compared to Hawking-1's passage through the Earth's atmosphere, the motions of the stars and planets would seem frozen in time.

Grace and Jason took their places in the theater seats before a wide-screen vid. Jason had a special interface that connected him indirectly to the image-processor. He could not possibly absorb 15,000 impressions each second, so a loop had been written to give him a one-in-forty image sample.

"Two minutes to mark," an amplified voice echoed under the dome.

The Schmidt depressed to its lowest elevation. Even then, it would miss the actual breakout, hidden on the valley floor behind the nearer ridges. The scope would begin tracking as Hawking-1 rose above 2,000 feet and then follow its arch beyond the atmosphere.

"One minute to mark."

"This reminds me of that trip to Virginia," Grace said in a shaky voice.

Jason, who was already hooked up to the interface, turned his blind eyes toward her and smiled. He was watching the far-off streetlights of Modesto resolve into stars as the computer adjusted its image. The town had been evacuated the day before, except for a unit of the National Guard sent in to detain looters.

"Thirty seconds to mark."

Modesto went blurry as the Schmidt shortened its focal length to sharpen on the point in space where Hawking-1 would rise.

"Ten seconds. Nine. Eight. Seven . . ."

Jason held his breath and gave the sort of sidewise glance that seemed to broaden his optical centers.

". . . Two. One. Mark!"

Like a fountain turned on, a rounded head of fire lifted into his sight. Jason could hear the pistons on the Schmidt raising the elevation. The image stayed smoothly centered: a globe of light with its tail thinning and falling back.

A thudding detonation punched Jason in the stomach. It was followed by a crackling ripple of thunder that rattled the dome and jarred the image in Jason's mind. Hawking-1's shockwave had caught up with the pictures they were seeing.

The globe slowly flattened to a disk—almost edge-on

to the telescope now—and the jets of discarded gaseous stuff sprouted from its center. The forward jet ran out and then folded back into the disk. The rearward jet sketched a pencil line down the sky.

Around Jason there was a murmur of admiration from the other watchers. Hawking-1 was a white flower in the night.

As the Schmidt tipped almost vertically to track the black hole above the atmosphere, the disk became a round circle, balanced on the spindle of the rearward jet. Then the circle grew smaller and smaller as it raced toward the top of its arching orbit.

They could watch it for hours, if they wanted. There would be nothing more to see until Hawking-1 tipped over and began descending—but by that time it would have moved below their horizon.

Jason was just about to disconnect himself when the image in his head brightened. From the east, to meet the rising star of Hawking-1, there came a shower of meteors. Glinting trails crossed the path of their black hole.

In a normal shower like the Leonids or Perseids, good viewing would be one a second or two in rapid succession, always radiating outward from a common origin. But it was the wrong time of year, and these came six and a dozen at a time in parallel lines of green fire.

For several minutes the rogue shower continued, then stopped like a faucet being turned off. The white dot of Hawking-1 continued rising.

Jason knew these were the first sign, early arrivals, of the cosmic hailstorm to come. And in their wake was Ceres. As he broke the interface, Jason hoped she would be on time to make the rendezvous.

Chapter 20

Alex Kornilov: THE ODDS

As graceful as Cathedral Hall had been with its soaring arches and cemented panels, so the umbilical pockets that Kornilov's Miners were gouging in Eddie's crater walls were low and ugly. The automata had no elegant plans to guide them, just three imperatives: max depth, max volume, min time.

Deep inside, against a leading face, Korny was fitting a new pick onto one of the machines. Compared to the fluffed rock of Phobos, the rust nuggets and fused silicas of Mars were wearing the equipment at a fearful rate. How much living space the party would ultimately have could be measured in spare parts and carbide tips. When one or the other gave out, that would be the end of the digging.

Ariel came through with a laser theodolite across her shoulder.

"How much rock over us?" Korny asked on the open suit channel.

She paused. "Just going to measure it now. Last survey showed in excess of five hundred feet."

He nodded, although she couldn't see it inside his helmet.

"Are you bolting the roof?" Ariel asked.

"On four-foot centers. Do you think it will hold?"

She leaned over backward to shine her headlight on the flat ceiling, seven feet from the floor. The heavy suit fabric pulled tight across her chest and stomach. Kornilov imagined he could see the swell of her breasts, but it was more like remembering.

"Sure, it will hold." She straightened and smiled at him.

"Is that your professional opinion?"

"Yessir, that roof'll hold up until somebody drops a mountain of rock on the surface overhead. Then it'll come down in pieces that are, oh—" Ariel held her gloved hands three feet apart. "—yea big."

Korny made a face, one that she could see.

"Do you have any suggestions?" he asked.

"Yes. Let's go home. Now."

"We can't."

She took a deep breath that he could hear over the suit mike. Then she looked around brightly.

"What's this room going to be? Our bedroom?"

"No, generator room or hydroponics. We'll sleep with the Second Watch, next pocket over."

"Doesn't sound like much fun." She came over and put her arms around his bulky pressure suit.

"It won't be," he said. "Four square meters apiece, limited hygiene, privacy on a weekly rotation."

"For how long, do you think?"

"Months."

She clung to him with a sudden squeeze. "That's going to be hard."

"Dying's harder," Korny said and squeezed back.

She pulled away and looked at him through the mist inside her faceplate.

"We're going to lose the ships, the fuel, anything left above ground, aren't we?"

"Possibly."

"How will we get home?"

"When it's over, if we win against the black hole,

then the Consortium will send a rescue team. Grace will see to it."

"And if they don't?" she asked.

"Why wouldn't they?"

"Suppose they take a big asteroid strike and the dust cloud kills off all human life. Or it sets civilization back two hundred years. What then?"

"Then we cope. But why are you so worried about the future, all of a sudden?"

Ariel put a gloved hand against the side of his helmet. "I'm worrying for the two of us now. Or, actually, three."

At odd moments Kornilov would find himself distracted—staring at his hands, squinting at the horizon, thinking about the future himself. Of all that he had hoped to find or experience in traveling to Mars with the Phobos Project, a child—and fatherhood—were the last of the unlikely possibilities.

After hearing Ariel's wide-eyed news, Korny had considered, for the space of one swallow, denying the child. But he judged that Ariel was too honest, or perhaps too shy, to carry on multiple relationships. Especially not in the airtight society that the Project had formed. If there was a child, it was his.

A more persistent concern for him was how an educated woman could possibly conceive a child she didn't want. The Project's medical team was fully stocked with contraceptives to suit every taste. She could not have failed to know that. Of course, Kornilov realized too late, he had not thought about using them himself; it had always seemed the woman's choice—and her responsibility.

Therefore, if it was impossible to conceive an unwanted child, then obviously Ariel had wanted it. On a rustball world with low-grade vacuum for an atmosphere, with the last real hope of mankind now orbiting over their heads as a dust ring, under a possible sentence of slow death . . . life would not be denied. And even the shy little exo-geologist had felt its tug.

A dark cloud hovered just beyond the edge of his consciousness. What if the baby were malformed because of cosmic radiation, or the solar wind, or whatever? Both he and Ariel each had certainly picked up a lifetime exposure on the outward voyage and the months of work on Phobos. And this was hardly Kornilov's first assignment above atmosphere.

Well, what of it? The child could be deformed in a thousand ways, for a hundred reasons—blood incompatibility, bad gene matches, accidents, subtle toxins in their artificial environment. Radiation was just one of the risks that Baby X faced.

The child was *life*, a temporary reversal of entropy, reaching for immortality and freedom. It would survive or die on the odds, just as all life on Earth had survived for 600 million years. As it might now survive for another four years, or another 600 million.

At random moments Kornilov found himself distracted by these thoughts. One of those moments occurred while he was reprogramming the sample-and-monitoring system for the hydroponics tanks, now safely installed under GRO-tubes in the pocket cave.

He caught himself and checked the sequence. Of course—that variable measured salinity, not pH. Kornilov tapped in a correction and went on.

Still, it was amazing to think about. Alex Kornilov, a father . . .

Mars was no stranger to meteorites. The proximity of the Rock Garden and the thin atmosphere guaranteed that a high percentage of medium and big rocks came down to the surface. While some of the planet's craters were certainly the remains of shield volcanoes, most were impacts.

The first sizable fragment in human experience,

however, came down just a month after the start of
Jason Bathespeake's detonation series. Eighteen tons
of stone and iron cut a long furrow ten kilometers
south of Bubble Base Two.

They tracked it in, triangulating with the landers'
radars. Deming had decided to put the three ships in
orbit under robot control for safety reasons: moving
targets on different paths had a better chance in the
coming hailstorm than gathered in one spot on the
ground.

A small group of adventurous souls—neither Kornilov
nor Ariel among them—wanted to go sightseeing at
the ditch. But the captain put his boot down. He
ordered everyone into the caves, except on author-
ized topside business. The long night began.

"Yuck! What *is* that?"

Ariel wrinkled her nose at the blue-black slime on
the filter sheet in Korny's hands. It dripped off onto
the rock floor of the hydroponics cave.

"I'm not sure," he said. "It's pretty thick in the
pipes. I think—we'd better get a bio-tech in here."

Five minutes later a shift supervisor from Life
Support was scraping tiny bits into an agar dish. He
didn't look at all pleased as he sucked another sample into a pipette for chemical testing.

He cracked the lid on the tank and, holding his
breath, peeked inside. Korny could see fumes wafting
past his ears.

"I tell you, Kornilov, it takes real skill to kill off
Spirogyra hydroponica. That stuff is recombined,
you know, so it's practically indestructible. What did
you do?"

Something solid flipped over in Korny's stomach.
"Me? What—? Nothing. I just opened the trap to
clean the filters. It's my off-shift assignment."

"Hmph. This batch has been dead about twelve
hours." He glanced at the telltales on the tank. "Tem-

perature looks okay. Valves are open . . . . Who programmed the computer monitors? You did, didn't you?"

"Ye-yes." Kornilov was thinking furiously: did he make a mistake? What could it be?

"Well, then, let's get a data dump and see what the machine knows. I just hope it's a fluke in this tank."

"And if it's not?" Ariel spoke up in a small voice.

"Then I hope some of that *hydroponica* had the good sense to sporulate before it died. Otherwise, we're all going to get pretty hungry."

After they had pumped the last tank of acid-contaminated water and black slime out onto the surface, everyone tried to be nice to Kornilov. But it was clear that smoldering contempt was just beneath their smiles. Except for Ariel.

She sat beside his cot in the sleeping quarters. He lay with the back of his left, meat hand over his eyes. He wanted the world to go away, Ariel included.

"Anyone could have made the mistake," she told him quietly.

"I know."

"It's bad policy to depend on one person for everything. Deming should have ordered routine verification of such an important program."

"I know."

"So it wasn't really *your* fault."

"It was."

"But why?"

"I should have checked and rechecked. It was my job and I blew it. Now the water cycler is down twenty-one percent and it will be four weeks until we can get a new generation of algae up and producing from the spores we could save. It's going to be tough on everybody, staying active on half rations. Everything you said is true. But it's also true that we are in grave danger—which we wouldn't be if I had paid more attention to my job. And if the water goes down any farther, we won't make it. Period. And that's my fault."

"Oh." Ariel reached out and took his hand. "I'll still love you, though."

Kornilov slowly pulled his hand away and rolled over, putting his back to her. After a minute he could hear her get up and walk away.

"Where's Ariel?" Korny asked later the next day. He had not been able to find her anywhere in the caverns.

People answered him with blank looks, some hostile glares, mostly shrugs.

The duty man on the north airlock checked his log. It showed her as signed out to the surface since four that morning.

"On what business?" Korny demanded.

"Says here, 'scientific study.'"

"Did Deming okay it?"

"She showed a pass. Looked like Deming's signature."

"Where did she go?"

Shrug.

"Look, it's raining rocks out there. Was she on foot or did she take a buggy?"

"Checked out a buggy and a trailer of recording gear. Didn't expect to be back for twelve hours, she said. Barely that now."

Kornilov screwed up his face. The right, metal hand was opening and closing slowly. Finally he decided.

"It's not safe. I want to go out after her."

"You have a pass?"

"Well . . ."

"Better check it with Deming."

The captain was as sympathetic as Kornilov had

ever seen him. He refused at first to risk any personnel on an expedition when there was no clear indication of trouble. But when he understood that Kornilov
was volunteering as a one-man search party, Deming
loosened a bit and signed the paper.

Kornilov decided to drive an eastward crescent
from Eddie, tuning across the working channels as
he went. If he didn't find Ariel on the radio he might
pick her up visually.

The daytime sky was etched with white tracks, the
burning of meteorites. Korny began to think that
orbiting the ships might not have been such a good
idea: it robbed them of the atmosphere's protective
blanket, such as it was.

After three hours, with the sun almost setting
behind the crater, he saw a flash of metal in a shallow valley. Binoculars resolved the image of a
smashed-up buggy with a suited figure lying beside
it.

Korny tromped the pedal and felt the motors humming in the frame of his own buggy as it picked up
speed. He slewed down the slope and made a skid-
ding turn near the wrecked vehicle.

The figure stirred and sat up.

"I knew you'd find me," Ariel said.

He jumped down and ran over, meaning to cradle
her shattered body in his arms. But she sprang up in
the point-three-eight gee and ran to him.

It was an enthusiastic embrace, although Kornilov
was feeling for broken ribs.

"You're not hurt?"

"Of course not—oh! I see. You thought I was in
that scrap pile when it happened. No, I was the
other side of the hill placing the last of my portable
doodlebugs. When I looked up, pieces of the buggy
were sailing by overhead. From the size of the hole
under that wreckage, it must have been a rock bigger than a football. Direct hit."

"But you were lying—"

"—down to conserve energy and think out what to do next. You took care of that."

They began walking arm-in-arm toward Kornilov's buggy.

"What were you doing out here?" he asked.

"Prospecting."

"For what? It's a terribly risky time for you to be outside."

"It's the best time." Ariel's voice was sparkling. "This landscape will be getting a terrible thumping soon. Falling rocks are cheaper and more powerful than the pocketful of explosives I had to work with before. The computer will sort out the signal strengths and tell us what's down there."

"But—what are you looking for?"

"Caprock, aquifers, possibly a dome. Any one of them'll resound like a drumhead when this land gets pounded."

Kornilov was sincerely puzzled. "I still don't—"

"Water! What did you think, I'm looking for an iron mine?"

"Water," he repeated. "But it will be underground."

"So? We've got my walking rig stored at the Base. It's good down to ten thousand feet. We'll sink a well for the water we need."

"In the middle of a meteorite storm . . ."

He climbed into the buggy on one side, she on the other.

"Whenever we find it." She waved back at the wreckage of her own vehicle. "That was a lucky shot. The only big rock I see the whole time out here, and it dead-centers on my car."

"Lucky you weren't in it."

"Wasn't I though?"

Two weeks later, with the big rocks falling nearby at the rate of one or two a day, Ariel's equipment chirped a couple of times and drew a waveform she seemed excited about. A week later they had all the hard, rusty-tasting water they could pump into their tanks. The Project was saved.

Life—that strange negative entropy—had beaten the odds one more time.

Chapter 21

Jason Bathespeake: WINCHESTER

It was Christmas, four years and four months after the accidents that led to discovery of Hawking-1. This year there would again be a star in the eastern sky. But unlike Bethlehem's mysterious star of 2,000 years ago, the people of Earth knew its source and its name: Winchester.

Since the billiard game began, Jason Bathespeake had found himself declared a national resource. He was the only human being who intimately understood the jumble of collisions, explosions, interacting gravity fields and crossing orbits that was raining down meteorites and more on the planet. Like the only eyewitness to a ninety-nine car highway pileup, the authorities wanted him available to testify.

It was no good explaining that Jason had calculated only for the final effect—Ceres snug in an Earth orbit with the black hole safe in her belly—or protesting that he didn't *know* where every rock would go. They politely did not believe him: cybers were different; he would remember all the details.

The Pentagon would have slapped him in a jail cell with a Top-Secret sticker pasted on his forehead. Certainly they would have found a cozy, well-furnished cell; it might even have had a view—but one crossed with bars. Only the suspicion that Jason might not cooperate, gathered by two Navy psychiatrists in a twenty-five-minute interview, had kept him free.

Jason guessed that his reputation intimidated them: the Man Who Scrambled the Solar System. They had judged him unlikely to react docilely under coercion. They were right.

His first official act had been to suggest the Pentagon commandeer the Earth's inventory of orbital telescopes to track incoming bodies. They called it the Skywatch Network.

Right away, Skywatch encountered the problem of optical resolution. A tumbling storm of sand grains, gravel, and house-sized rocks had been whipped across the Earth's orbit. The little pieces damaged the equipment. And by the time the big pieces in this litter could be detected and plotted, it was already too late to do anything. Skywatch could only estimate the probable area of impact and turn the matter over to the local authorities.

Three newsworthy rockfalls a day—on populated areas, and not counting ocean strikes or rural impacts—were about average. Cairo was the big loser: nine times in ten consecutive days the city absorbed stony meterorites larger than fifteen tons. Of course, the fact that Cairo stretched north and south for 110 miles along the Nile Valley and Delta made it a likely target.

But Cairo wasn't alone. Asuncion, Boston, Capetown, Damascus, Edinburgh, Florence, Galveston . . . every city caught at least one rock.

The storm soon became so thick that, as flying gravel pushed up the attrition rate among the oribital telescopes and cut into viewing power, Skywatch had to abandon reporting the small stuff. The search shifted instead to masses large enough to do real damage and far enough out to be dealt with.

On that scale, more than fifty possible collisions

and hair-raising near misses had been charted around the planet in the past year. Most had been small, a few hundred meters in diameter. Only Winchester had been tracked on a true collision course, and it was big: 128 miles across.

When the asteroid struck, it would probably do for Earth what the father of Tycho had done for the Moon: fracture a quadrant of the crust, throw up tens of cubic kilometers of debris that would blanket the planet—if it did not rip away half the atmosphere.

Human civilization would not survive this meeting.

To prepare for such an event, Jason had further suggested a hasty amendment to the Dawn Convention of 1992 that would allow for staging U.S. and Soviet missiles above the atmosphere. Bathespeake then ordered the world's arsenals to be mixed; the bomb factories in Russia and the United States would go on triple shifts. The two nations signed temporary pacts, agreeing to withhold hostilities until after the black hole was captured: then they would "re-evaluate" their positions. The armaments this span of cooperation freed up were clustered at the LaGrange points in the Earth-Moon system, and from there the warheads could be sent to deflect or disrupt a body like Winchester.

The missiles were also a reserve force to nudge Ceres into the proper orbit when she arrived two months from now. Jason had calculated the billiard game as closely as he could—and the Cray Omega at Cheyenne Mountain had checked those calculations a dozen times. Still, they had been shooting in the dark, into a jumble of asteroids whose orbits could only be approximated. And Ceres would have come to Earth for nothing if she were ten minutes too soon or two thousand miles out of place.

Some of those precious missiles would now be spent against Winchester.

*   *   *

"Why don't we send them all and split the bastard?" Grace asked in a whisper.

She and Jason were standing behind rows of technicians who sat at scopes and computer screens in the old NORAD command center at Cheyenne Mountain. The center had been converted for tracking asteroids and pushing them aside. "Radar and gunnery," as a gray-haired admiral standing nearby had called it.

Jason exhaled through his nose and then worked his voder.

"Every missile we have—and we need most of them for corrections on Ceres—would not have the power to break up Winchester.

"I could do it with just two warheads," he said thoughtfully, remembering a film clip he had once seen of a non-nuclear approach to destroying hardened targets. "Fire them in tandem: the first to blast a crater, the second to explode inside it. That would shatter any stony asteroid. On a tumbling rock, however, we could never hit the same spot twice.

"And if we did shatter Winchester, all of its mass would still arrive, most of it in pieces big enough to pass through the atmosphere. The Earth would be inflicted with multiple devastating impacts."

He looked away from the spread of maps and viewing screens, toward Grace. She was staring at him with her mouth open. Jason once again silently cursed the cyber effect: he was not and never had been human for her.

So he went ahead, like a teaching automata: "It's better to change the course of Winchester, make it detour around or perhaps even orbit the Earth. If it goes into a stable orbit, so much the better. We can use more real estate—"

A voice from the overhead cut across his explanation: "Coming up on first detonation."

The main screen switched to a long-range view of the incoming Winchester. It was annoying that the orbiting telescope they were using had been fixed in the infrared, showing an image that looked like a distorted negative. All the computer cleanup of its signal could not make the picture convincing.

The asteroid had warmed slowly as it drew nearer to the Sun, but it was still a cold rock, ghostly in the infrared against the no-temperature of vacuum.

Winchester was severely oblate, like a sagging football, dusty and forgotten, long after the Super Bowl. It was rolling, end over end like a football on the bounce, so that Winchester's path seemed to be looping. It was an optical illusion, Jason knew, heightened by their head-on view. Still, Winchester seemed to be bounding toward them like a Great Dane eager to meet its master.

The first warhead struck on the downside. They never saw the missile on the scope, just the explosion. It was an expanding sphere of pure white energy, flattened on one side against the dark base of the asteroid.

This was one of the largest warheads in the U.S.-U.S.S.R. joint arsenal, a special 1,500-megaton device that never would have been used on Earth. It was a little tap, chucking Winchester under the chin.

The asteroid, more than half again as large as the main island of Hawaii, rolled peacefully onward.

Jason and Grace watched silently as fifteen more warheads of equal size, fifteen little taps, hit the same downward side over the span of half an hour.

On the screen there was no appreciable effect.

The cool voice from the overhead after a long silence said, "We're triangulating now. . . ."

Jason imagined somewhere the scan of codes across a computer screen, an incomprehensible gibberish of numbers that defined three or four disparate views of

Winchester's track. Somewhere a machine was knitting them into one picture of reality.

"We have a vector. . . . It's a polar orbit! At least four thousand kilometers at perigee!"

A cheer, somehow thin in the large room, went up from the technicians in their long rows. Grace put an arm around Jason and squeezed. He stood there, stiffly, thinking about how many missiles they had left for the encounter with Ceres.

Within a day the early computer projections were confirmed. Winchester went into a long, elliptical orbit over the poles. It was not a stable orbit and would decay in a century or two through the combined perturbations of the Sun and Moon. That, however, was a problem for their children.

Later that same evening, Eldon Richardson collared Jason as technical advisor for a segment he was putting together on Winchester.

The media maven was composing on his keyboard as fast as he could call up tapes and spot the frames he wanted from the miles available out of the various orbiting telescopes. Jason noted that the format did not bother Richardson at all. Infrared, color composite, even radio and x-ray telescopy—all of the different images melted under his touch and reappeared in one "real-world" view.

Jason, following along on his computer interface, decided Richardson's was a video talent that lay somewhere between cartooning and black magic.

"We need something to highlight the explosions," Richardson said offhand. "Too bad there's no sound."

"Well, of course not!"

"Real track from the early fusion tests would be all wrong, too sustained, a sound carried in the air and through the ground. . . ."

Jason held his breath, hoping the media man would talk himself out.

"We want something with punch," Richardson murmured, "and a bit of music."

"A couple of bars from the *Dies Irae*?" Jason asked ironically.

"Maybe a Leone gunshot. Something campy for the cognos."

Richardson rewound and passed a fast rough at two-to-one through the monitor. What emerged was one smooth and dramatic flow of images: Winchester incoming like tumbling death, a series of punctuated missile flashes, then the asteroid veering into an orbit around the blue-green Earth.

If you could close your eyes to the technical flaws, Jason decided, it was artistic.

"There," said the media man, "that'll give the taxpayers something for fifty years of bloated Defense budgets."

In scented halls, to the drone of sitar music, the Master blinked sleepy eyes and absorbed the news.

"This is a grim day, Ananda," he intoned. "Now the Americans will believe that they can do anything."

"They can," the disciple replied serenely.

The encounter with Winchester was good practice for the last days of Ceres' journey across the February sky. They returned to Cheyenne Mountain to watch the final alignment of her orbit.

Of course, if Bathespeake and the Cray had fatally miscalculated and brought Ceres into a collision with the Earth or Moon, no human power could stop it now. The planetoid was 627 miles across and massed one percent of the Earth.

If such an object were to fall on New York City, it would throw—in the instant before impact—a black shadow on both Washington, D.C., and Boston. It would strike with a dead weight of 14 quintillion metric tons, falling at approximately 6.9 kilometers per second. Neither the Earth nor Ceres would survive such carelessness.

The shoot coordinator and a talker were standing beside Jason and Grace, staring up at the main screen. They watched the round pocked ball, half lit by the Sun, half shadowed. The view was scanned in visible light from a telescope in polar orbit that would be crossing inside Ceres.

"Six minutes, forty seconds to rendezvous," the overhead said soberly.

On the screen, a superimposed grid and a timing mark showed the final approach: Ceres was solidly on the line but coming 0.3 second too fast. The planetoid's orbit would pass its intercept point with the black hole's apogee a fraction before the hole would rise to it.

"We've got twenty-eight missiles on a closing track," the coordinator said, glancing at Jason. "Total of almost 31,000 megatons. I can bunch 'em or space 'em. How do you want to hit her?"

Jason wished he could wire into the Cray and get a precise answer, but the programming would take more time than they had. Across the black hole's orbit at apogee they had a window of about one second. It was, Jason finally decided, enough room to be sloppy.

"Use them all," he said. "Space the bursts in seven groups of four on twenty-second intervals. Ceres is going to be valuable property, no sense in gouging her face too badly."

They watched silently as bursts of light erupted on the face of the planetoid, like a crowd of photographers shooting up a press conference. Ceres did not wobble or dodge.

From somewhere, down on the line of technicians at computer and video screens, a whisper started.

"Come on, baby, come and get it."

Other voices picked it up.

"Come on down, Mother. Come down. Come and get the sucker."

The combined weapons of the human arsenal might have been no more than harmless flashes of light against Ceres. Smoothly, gracefully, the transplanted queen of the Asteroid Belt slipped into orbit 55,000 miles above the Earth. She chased around into full sunlight, moving toward rendezvous with the rising spark of Hawking-1.

"Come on. Come on. Go. Go. Go."

The orbiting platforms focused their telescopes on the last seconds of the event. They sent to Cheyenne Mountain triangulating images of Hawking-1 now slowing, its arc flattening toward apogee. And Ceres fast advancing.

"Get him, Mother!"

As the asteroid came over, it touched the black hole. A new flare lit up Ceres' leading edge. Hawking-1's renewed accretion disk bit into dark rock. Then the two merged silently and Ceres passed on.

The white flower was snuffed from the sky.

A wild cheer, full throated, rang in the subterranean hall.

The news went around the world, respecting no hour.

In Moscow, late-night parties whooped and broke out another bottle of vodka. Grim watchers in the early hours whooped and did the same.

In Prague there were polkas at dawn.

In London's Mayfair district, perfect strangers spoke to each other in the streets. Householders and dustmen congratulated one another, while west in Hyde Park Corner the orators were beginning fresh diatribes against those who would fiddle with the heavens.

In New York's Times Square, the crowds were gathered once again. A snake dance started that in two hours would trample three dozen people.

Across the Pennsylvania countryside the church bells and fire sirens sounded the good news.

In Chicago, people clustered on the street corners to sing "Happy Days Are Here Again" and drink free cases of beer set out by the neighborhood saloons.

In Honolulu, there were fireworks.

In Tokyo, they simply rioted with happiness.

In Moscow again twenty-four hours later, they were still drinking and slapping each other on the back.

In San Francisco two days later, Jason stood bent over backwards. He was looking straight up into the night sky with his hands braced on his buttocks. Beside him, Grace held the same pose. They were in the tiny back yard of her house in the Haight.

Hanging in its usual quarter was the familiar Whistling Boy on the face of the Moon, now at the full. Directly overhead was Ceres, and by an optical coincidence she had the same apparent diameter. Because her orbit was canted thirty-seven and a half degrees above the equator, she was frozen in a gibbous phase, with a dark line of shadow across her northern side. Ceres' orbit was not synchronous, like the Moon's, so she showed the Earth many faces.

Among her craters Jason tried to see the mile-and-a-quarter-wide hole that Hawking-1 had cut when it was snatched. From this distance, it would hardly be visible—just a small black shadow.

He straightened and felt a crackling in his vertebrae. He imagined that hundreds of people living along Ceres' canted orbit would suffer back and neck injuries from looking too long at the Earth's newest moon, so out of place in their northern and southern skies. He would do better to lie flat on his back, but the spring grass was wet with dew.

"Will the black hole destroy her, too?" Grace asked.

"If Ceres had a liquid core, like the Earth," he

said, "then yes. It would suck the material up and then shatter the crust. But she's cold and solid rock. The hole will gouge a cavern at her center of mass and continue spalling stone flakes from the inside until the native strength of the rock resists—" Jason did a quick mental calculation. "—When the cavern is between thirty and sixty miles across."

"And it will never come down?"

He turned to look at her—a profile tipped back in the moonlight.

"The orbit is stable. Ceres is outside the Earth's tidal limits. And Hawking-1 is firmly held in her. But . . . 'never' is a long time."

"NASPFAC has dropped hints about a power facility," she said, straightening. "And Domkin says ASSAA wants an in-depth study of the black hole's gravity field. We haven't heard from Elias and his people in Defense, but he's probably still working on a way to have Ceres retroactively classified . . . unless he's busy trying to break our pact with the Russians so he can start to hit them with their arsenal down. . . .

"But still, I wonder if anything we might do would happen to disrupt the orbit."

Jason held his breath. It was hard to imagine how any human meddling could budge Hawking-1 out of its nest. But then he himself had pulled down a moon. By accident or design, others might do as much or more.

"Let them fight it out," Grace said to the night. "I just don't want that *thing* to put our one and only Earth in danger again. It's like the Sword of Damocles up there."

"There will always be danger," Jason whispered.

"I knew all along the world wasn't gonna *die*," the Cincinnati cabbie said when the fare mentioned Ceres.

"It's the same gloom and doomsday every couple

of years. When I was a kid it was overpopulation. Then dollar-a-gallon gasoline. Then the ozone layer and aerosol sprays. Then AIDS. Then heat pollution. Then the oxygen cycle.

"The talk alone is always good for a scare. The idea of dying reminds us we're alive. And it's more exciting than a personal videodrama.

"But I don't ever *believe* it."

Chapter 22

Grace Porter: ACE IN THE HOLE

The call came while Grace Porter was in the middle of negotiations with Defense and the Consortium partners for a rescue mission to Mars. It was from a German herr professor doktor at Stanford University. It was a call for Steven Cocci.

"Dr. Cocci died some years ago," she explained. "I am his successor at Pinocchio, Inc."

"Ach, such a shame, because he was a good man, yes, and so young."

The silence on the line lengthened as Professor Marienkafer seemed to contemplate the youth of the late chairman.

"If there's anything I can do for you . . ." Grace finally prompted. "Maybe a talk with our contributions committee?"

"What? No, no—it's what *I* can do for *you*, but then perhaps he died before he could discuss with you his problem?"

Grace tried to imagine what medical skeleton she was about to discover. Ancient history now, anyway.

"No-oo," she said. "I don't think he mentioned any *problem*."

"Very strange . . . Steve wanted a bomb, a very special bomb, a concentration of *anti*matter, which is theoretically possible here in the laboratory, using cryogenic magnets and working under tremendous pressures, but for Steven this was not good enough, because he had to have a *portable* bomb, one he could load in a Shuttle and fly off to who knows where."

"What did he want this bomb for?" Grace felt her heart rising.

"He didn't say, just talked riddles, something about a dose of ipecac, which is medicine to make you vomit."

Antimatter? Vomit? The only riddle Steven Cocci had to work on before he died was how to deal with the black hole. . . . Then Grace was reminded of something Jason Bathespeake had said in the early days of their task force. Something about antiphotons. Or photon-antiphoton pairs. That tiny black holes *gave off* energy by absorbing the antiphoton member. Had that led Cocci to . . . ?

"I think I see, Professor," she lied quickly. "And you've found a way . . . ?""

"It's taken years, and you know how something like this can become a mind game, something you play with the grad students, pose the question more to test their powers of imagination and creativity than to solve any real problem, especially when Steven doesn't ever call back, but this one girl of mine is extremely brilliant and she finds a way to shift the orientation, fool a lefthanded atom into thinking it's righthanded. Anyway, it can be done. Are you still interested?"

"Yes! Of course we are."

"It will cost a lot of money. For a demonstration project, some millions. Then, if you decide to go ahead, perhaps hundreds of millions for a full-scale production facility. Very expensive, you'll say, but after that you can have large volumes of antimatter relatively cheaply. For whatever reason. Are you *still* interested?"

"Ahh—yes. Absolutely. Can I come down to Palo Alto? We should discuss this in detail."

"Surely. I'll write a proposal. Perhaps we can even arrange a national grant, say from—"

"No. Please. Don't arrange anything else. We should talk first. How about tomorrow at ten?"

"Very good. I look forward to seeing—"

"At ten, Professor!"

Somehow, Grace had always imagined that a "magnetic bottle" would have some physical presence in quartz glass or leaded crystal. Certainly it would be hidden under layers of steel and wire. She never imagined that you could look directly into it and see a tiny solar prominence, a twisted flare of bright gas, contained at huge pressures only by lines of magnetic force.

Of course, "look into" was a figure of speech, Professor Marienkafer explained. The radiation released along the direction of flow would blind her instantly. The view was through a beryllium barrier port, recorded with a scanning computer pickup.

Somehow, Grace had imagined that antimatter would glow with strange colors that human eyes had never seen. Eerie violets, poisonous greens, energetic oranges—those were the colors to attend a mass of material that had never before existed in such concentration. Or not in this universe.

Yet the antimatter plasma that Marienkafer exhibited was a whitely glowing gas. Like the inside of a fluorescent tube without the diffusion coating. Perhaps it was a bit more—more pearly—than stark white. But that could also be a distortion of the screen image.

"How much material is there?" she asked.

"Two grams," the chubby, animated professor said proudly.

Grace sniffed. "It looks like more."

"The plasma is very low density and occupies much more space than would a solid mass."

"I see. . . . What would happen if the power failed and your magnets—um—dropped the bottle?"

Marienkafer pursed his lips and looked down at his hands.

"Perhaps nothing, if the antimatter failed to attach itself to a sufficient concentration of reciprocal matter before it dissipated, but that would be a unique situation. More likely a significant percentage of it would join in a mutual annihilation, an explosion."

"How big?"

"We're not talking about the simple release of nuclear forces, as in a fusion bomb, you understand? We're talking about the total destruction of a particle. Pure matter to pure energy."

"How much energy?" Grace's head was hurting with this fog of words.

"Where Palo Alto is now, where the Peninsula is now, there becomes a hole. A deep one, filled with the Pacific Ocean. This compares with many megatons of explosive or a very large fusion bomb."

"If it's that dangerous, do you need some kind of permit or authorization to do this work?"

Marienkafer laughed. "You mean, like a *license*? From the town hall? To understand what we have done here, you need a doctorate in particle physics. The mayor doesn't have one."

Grace was relieved: Marienkafer's work would be secure from government busybodies, as she required. "What about the danger? If the power—"

"We run two fusion generators in tandem to cover all the load for the magnets. If they go down together, then you have all your bad luck for a lifetime in one day. Personally, I'm not worried."

"This is an interesting demonstration, Professor," she began.

"Thank you."

"As Steve may have mentioned when he first talked to you, we need a large amount of that material." She tipped her head at the screen.

"That *is* a large amount."

"Large enough to reverse the flow of matter into a micro black hole?"

"Yeee—what?"

Grace repeated the theory that she had heard, secondhand from Jason, almost five years before.

Marienkafer locked his hands behind his back and looked at her from under his bushy eyebrows. "The original Hawking hypothesis," he murmured at last. "That's why Steve Cocci was talking about *ipecac*."

"Yes."

"It might actually work. At any rate, it would certainly be interesting to try. . . . Do you have a lot of money?"

Grace swallowed. "I can get it."

"Good. Then I will begin defining the parameters of our experiment. It will be a very big bang, you know. For a second or more, Ceres will be another sun, too close to the Earth. That may be more than you want to bargain for."

"A second, against an eternity of doubt. I'll accept that."

He gave her that measuring stare again. "Then it's on your head."

It was a routine meeting of Pinocchio, Inc.'s Board of Directors. Or rather, it was the routine that had developed since Grace had begun dealing with Professor Marienkafer.

Once again Grace, as chairman, was asking them to forgo the quarterly dividend. She reflected that it had been easier in Cocci's day, when the chairman held fifty-one percent of the stock and virtually owned the company. During the heyday of the Phobos Project, however, she had sold some of that to finance first, their growing participation in the Consortium and second, new plants to build the automata the Project needed.

For a year now, since her initial interview with Marienkafer, Grace had been doing silent and dirty deals with stock, equipment, factories, and just about any Pinocchio asset that wasn't nailed down and painted emergency orange. Antimatter production was turning out to be even more expensive than the professor had predicted.

Gone were the net earnings from their regular sales of industrial automata. Gone were the bonuses Jason had earned them with his idea for the billiard game that brought down Ceres. Gone, long gone were the profits that Cocci had originally maneuvered with their participation in the Phobos Project. It had been six quarters since Pinocchio, Inc. had declared a dividend. And they had been quarters of unprecedented industrial growth, now that Hawking-1 had been tamed.

Grace was having weekly fights with the Accounting Department in addition to these monthly tiffs with the Board.

"The numbers any better this time, Grace?" That was Peterson, who was a chairman in his own right with an oil company. That made him no stranger to thin dividends.

"Frankly, I can't say that they are," she said. "But I can promise you that the turning point is in sight. We are nearing the end of the development phase of a special project that will put this company—"

"Are those your 'unidentified investments'?" Rickert said nastily from down the table. "I've had those tracked, you know. It seems you've got quite a grants program going with Stanford and Cornell. Want to tell us about it?"

"The work is scientific," Grace admitted. "And for now it must remain secret. This is a breakthrough in particle physics—"

"What does that have to do with robots?" Peterson asked.

"Let her finish," said Everson. "I want to hear this. Maybe I'll understand it, for once."

Grace could feel the sweat starting in her armpits, drop by drop. That was unusual, because in the past year she had become an accomplished liar.

"We are embarked on a diversification program. An absolutely new principle in particle physics has been made available to us through contacts of the late Mr. Cocci. The work is yielding a new substance that will revolutionize our science and our society, with applications in resource development and, um, in weapons, in—"

"This is nothing but a fan dance," said Rickert. He flicked the papers in front of him. "I see here that you want to sell our share of the Rock. Back when you got us into this 'Consortium,' you talked long and hard about how valuable a new moon in the Earth's sky was going to be. Now you've changed your mind?"

"Will you let her finish?" Everson demanded.

"I just want an explanation of why we're going down the tubes in the best goddamn year we've ever had."

"We all do," said Peterson.

"Gentlemen—lady," rumbled Blakemoor from the other end of the table. "Perhaps we should call a special meeting of the shareholders to examine the diversification program in detail?"

Grace was not ready for the publicity that a proxy fight would bring. Not yet.

"Is that in the form of a motion?" she asked,

staring down the table. Grace still held some forty-five percent of Pinocchio's stock, and she had a few chits out with the other owners.

"It could be."

"Well, when it is, you make it properly and we'll consider it. In the meantime, we will proceed on this course. You will all just have to trust me."

"I've heard that before," Rickert said sourly.

Grace and Jason Bathespeake took a commercial flight to Santa Barbara and rented a car for the drive to Vandenberg A.F.B. They were going to meet the orbiter that was bringing home Kornilov, Ariel, and other survivors of the Phobos Project.

One survivor in particular interested Grace. Deming's radio logs confirmed a child, a healthy girl, born to Dr. Ceram; rumor said it was Kornilov's child. These pieces of intelligence had danced through Grace's thoughts during many a late-night brood session.

If Jason wondered this morning why they didn't fly direct to Vandenberg in the Pinocchio corporate jet, he never asked. If he had, Grace would have told him it was being overhauled.

Truth was, she'd sold it five weeks ago. To satisfy the Board, she had methodically stripped the perks of the chairman's office and the senior executives. Actually, she had been ready to do that anyway: another payment was due to Marienkafer.

Grace had shared details of the antimatter project with Jason, of course. He best of all the Pinocchio staff could understand the theory behind a "bomb" that would, if needed, trigger a reversal of the flow into the micro black hole. He also understood Grace's fear that the "Sword of Damocles" might one day come down again and destroy the Earth. But whether Jason agreed with her on any of it, he had never said.

This morning on the long ride to Vandenberg, he began talking.

"I took a tap off the accounting system yesterday. . . . I'm not an expert, Grace, but it looks like the company's cash flow is getting critically tight."

"It is."

"All of this grief for a few pounds of—of magic stuff that's not even guaranteed to work. Photon-antiphoton pairs, the release of energy, it's all just theory, you know."

"I know."

"I'm beginning to hear people talk about you— 'bee in the bonnet,' 'voice in the wilderness,' 'crazy obsession.' It's not helping your credibility."

"So I've heard."

"Any corporation is a delicate social organism, Grace. You can't run it like a feudal barony, even if you own it. People get discouraged. They stop fighting for you, stop creating for you. They leave."

"They do."

"Then why do you go on with this business? It's not too late. You can abandon Marienkafer's project. Let God or National Space Power worry about the black hole. It's not your problem."

Grace could feel herself smiling. "Is that what *you* think, Jason? That I'm just obsessed about that thing?"

"Well . . ."

"Marienkafer is on to something pivotal in physics. Ready tons of antimatter, made cheaply and available in a stabilized environment. That has to be worth something."

"Such as what?"

"Some industrial process, perhaps. Surface scouring or molecular shaping or—or whatever. I don't quite know yet. Still, my entrepreneur's intuition says to follow it up. We're gambling big—maybe bigger than the Phobos Project—but we could end up owning the rights to a whole new industry. Doesn't anyone else *see* that?"

"You sound like Steve Cocci," Jason said quietly.

"Thank you—"

"We're not all gamblers, Grace. Some of us have families, futures, mortgages to worry about, kids to put through college, gardens to grow. Most people come to work for a company like Pinocchio, Inc. because it makes a useful product, shows a profit and gives them a steady paycheck. Big risks make them nervous. The importance of going after Phobos they could understand, but this . . ."

"I know."

"And you won't stop the business with Marienkafer?"

"No."

There wasn't much to say after that.

At the air base, they showed their VIP passes from the Secretary of Defense and were admitted to the tower area. The sleek Shuttle, a highly advanced model of the earlier, unpowered lifting bodies, touched down at 2 P.M. precisely.

Kornilov and Ariel were seventh and eighth on the ramp. He was carrying a baby-sized bundled object at an upright angle.

Grace saw Ariel bend down in the dramatic gesture of kissing the ground, but the 120-degree heat of the runway pushed her up quickly. Korny steadied her with a hand.

And then, with no conscious thought, Grace was running toward them across the field. A sentry started after her but let her go. Her expensive Italian shoes wobbled off her feet and she ran on in her stockings, burning her soles on the concrete.

Kornilov saw her coming and he straightened against the unfamiliar gravity of his home planet. He smoothly passed little Andrea to Ariel and put out his arms.

And Grace was suddenly in them, holding him up as much as he held her.

He was bony as a fencepost and gray from lack of sun. There were hollows under his eyes and a grimness to his mouth. She had heard how bad it had been on Mars after the second oh-two recycler had quit and Korny nursed it along with a jury-rigged pump and filters tied together from their suit stores. Now she saw the marks that cave living had made on him.

Ariel—when Grace had time to notice—was a stringy little girl again. Jason was supporting her under one arm, and she didn't seem to mind.

Still, none of it mattered. They had been brought safely home.

"You have to make a choice, Alex," Grace told Kornilov that night. She was sitting on the edge of his bed in the Vandenberg base hospital. She held his left hand, the flesh one, in both of her hands.

Nestled into a pile of pillows, he watched her with sad, shadowed eyes.

"I won't apologize," he said quietly. "We were stranded, no hope of returning to Earth. What we did was natural."

"I don't want an apology. I want you. Or I'll give you up. Ariel is a good person and no one for you to be ashamed of. But I will not share you. Not with anyone."

Korny gave her hand a weak squeeze.

"There are obligations," he said. "Andrea will need support—and a father."

"I won't deny you that."

"I'll need time. . . . To put things in order, to find my place here. Do I still have a job at Pinocchio?"

He smiled and she returned it.

"At least I can offer you employment. And my

love—you've had that before. It's about all I have to give, but it's still yours."

Kornilov's smile broadened. His eyes blinked once, then closed slowly. His hand was still pressing hers as he drifted into sleep.

Simon Guerraro had replaced Peter Kriegs in the liaison position at National Space Power. He wasn't any easier to deal with.

"You want to place an instrument package *inside* the cavern? I don't understand why."

Grace crossed her legs and settled lower in the chair. "We want to take readings on the gravity flux around the black hole as you feed in material."

"The hole is, as you know, fairly well shielded."

"We know that," she said quickly. "It shouldn't affect our data."

"Hmmm. And what, exactly, do you intend with this data?"

"We're always experimenting with new control systems for our automata. Pinocchio is developing a line to work in unstable, high-gravity environments. Confidentially, we're looking toward the market for probes into Jupiter and Saturn."

"That's interesting." Guerraro tried to match her conspiratorial tone. "NASPFAC could provide you with any information you need—at a very reasonable price. Perhaps even just a shared interest . . . ?"

"You make an attractive offer," Grace said, recrossing her legs and glancing at Kornilov. He sat perfectly still, watching Guerraro with his enigmatic Easter Island smile. In private moments, she called it his thousand-mile stare.

"However, our technical package is already prepared," she said. "Although we would gladly share with *you* anything we might learn about the black hole."

"Of course," Guerraro gave her a shrug, "I'll have to discuss it with my people."

"Of course."

Against her gut feelings, Grace had elected to suit up and accompany Korny and the team of null-gee Artificers on the journey down to Pellucidar. That's what some romantic had christened the cavern inside Ceres where Hawking-1 floated.

They rode down the side of the mile-plus-wide tunnel, dropping 300-odd miles from the asteroid's battered surface. This was billed as the Solar System's longest elevator, and Grace believed it. Even in the fractional gravity she could feel her stomach shrinking.

Between them on the traveling stage was strapped the flat canister of Marienkafer's bomb—or "instrument package." To bring it to Ceres had cost Grace the last of her salable assets and all of her remaining cachet. And even then they had been forced to travel on one of the regular garbage scows that shuttled between Earth and its newest moon.

At the same time she and Korny were planting the canister like a limpet mine against the cavern's inside wall, Pinocchio, Inc.'s directors were calling in their proxies. The issue of Grace's resignation would be topic uno when they returned to Earth.

She tried to think of a way to tell Korny that they might both be out of a job.

He probably could find something in the High Frontier: a good Iron Boss with an engineering degree in null-gee structurals could write his own ticket among the orbiting factories.

An ex-chairwoman of the board who'd almost plowed her company into the ground, however, might have a harder time. Maybe somebody needed a good bizad/legal with advertising experience, concept and comp, on the Avenue.

Grace shrugged inside her suit as the elevator stage bumped to a halt.

Pellucidar was an inside-out world.

A plain of rough gray stone stretched away from the elevator terminus. It loomed over their heads but looked like a miniature moonscape, complete with fissures and scaled craters, lit by a hard white sun.

Thirteen miles above—below?—them, mostly baffled by NASPFAC's photovoltaic panels, Hawking-1 shone with the glare of the world's wastes being crushed and sucked down into a bottomless hole. Spent nuclear fuels, toxic materials, metal-poisoned sludges—all went down the black hole's gullet. NASPFAC contracted to take anything that a thrifty economy could not sift and wash and make whole, anything that would have to be tagged and buried or burned at high temperature in licensed incinerators. It all made the same white light going down into the black hole.

Looking down—up?—at the black-surfaced baffles, Grace suffered a moment's disorientation. Then she decided that what gravity there was still tugged down at her feet. So the stone plain was roof, not ground. And Hawking-1 was a central pit, not a shining star.

The NASPFAC staging crew opened a port in the side of the terminus lobby, and Kornilov gave last-minute coding to the two Arties. With piton guns and suspensor hooks raised, they began to walk out over that plain—roof. The limpet mine was suspended on cables between them. About two thousand feet from the elevator shaft they would bolt it to the roof—floor—and set a series of switches to lock in its programming.

Then one of the Arties had been instructed to scramble those switches forever.

For as long as Ceres orbited above Earth with the black hole in her belly, the bomb would hang there.

Light leaking from Hawking-1 would power the photovoltaic cells on the package's flat face. That power would maintain the magnetic flux around 990 grams of stabilized antimatter. It would also power a complex of motion sensors and the arming devices they were circuited to.

If ever Hawking-1 slipped or was moved from its place at the center of Ceres, the limpet would explode outward, hurling the magnetic bottle into the black hole. Marienkafer, in discussions with Grace and Jason, had predicted that the toroid would hold its shape until the antimatter was well launched into the hole.

Would it be enough?

Marienkafer had laughed and suggested that laboratory experiments in this area were singularly difficult to equip.

But, although the black hole had gained hugely in its orbits through the Earth and now massed some seven quadrillion metric tons, less than a kilogram of antimatter would upset the flow. Hawking-1 would disgorge its matter, he had said. It would shine like a star with its own light and keep on shining.

The exhalation of energy would probably melt Ceres, turn her into a belt of slag that would cool to form a ring of tumbling pebbles around the Earth. Like one of Saturn's icy, lacy garlands.

For some years a bright beacon would light Earth's sky both day and night. And then it would fade as the hole closed forever. Or so Herr Professor Doktor Marienkafer, Grace's dealer in bootleg antistuff, had said.

She watched the Arties pick their spot and snug the limpet upward against the rock. Then they danced around it, driving pitons through its flanging. One of them paused to twiddle under the hatch in its side.

If National Space Power ever figured out that this "instrument package" really was a danger to their newest energy facility . . . Grace's thoughts came to full stop.

Energy! Of course!

Her heart rate just about doubled. She wondered if it would show up on her suit's telemetry.

Grace Porter, and through her Pinocchio, Inc., had proprietary rights to the world's cheapest source of antimatter. What NASPFAC did at Ceres, hauling deadly wastes far above atmosphere for disposal, she could do on the ground. For dimes. Anywhere the customer wanted to turn trash into energy.

With this plan, Grace could win her proxy fight. Easily. Just get Eldon to shape it into a nice action vid, and have Jason cost it out.

Then, when she was done putting the company back together, she could take on National Space Power—and beat them to pieces.

Grace took Kornilov's hand and turned away.

"Don't we have to retrieve the Arties?" he asked in surprise.

She gave him a quick kiss and shook her head. "These boys will take good care of them. Let's go home."

Grace Porter had bought her ace in the hole.

Afterthought on Origins and Consequences

As Ariel Ceram and Jason Bathespeake both knew, this story actually began at the beginning of time, which is also the center of space.

The space has no scale or dimension, no dividing emptiness, no rough or smooth, no thick or thin, because all matter is one particle of infinite density. No light or dark, no hot or cold, no color, because there is no release of energy. No time, because nothing happens.

And then one thing happened—the explosion, the Big Bang, the one event in the universe whose prior event, whose trigger, is unknown and probably unknowable.

As an event, a thing of time, the Big Bang was not infinite, not dimensionless, not *smooth*.

In the featureless density of the mono-particle, it created shock waves, overpressures, eddies, rifts, vacuums, curls, swirls, and clumps. These shapes that expanded outward from the unmarked center would hold for only a split second. The continuous energy release of the Big Bang scattered them like water drops on a red-hot skillet.

Not for three minutes, as humans would one day count time, did the universe cool enough to let the bruised fragments—quarks, gluons, mesons, neutrinos and other thingons and partinos—combine to form free hydrogen.

Not for 100,000 years, as humans would count them, did gravitational effects begin the path of association and accretion that leads from atoms to dust to stars and galaxies. To progress from there to the human universe was only a question of new-found time.

Part of the mono-particle would be gathered into normal matter in this way, but by no means all. The Big Bang's shock waves rolled the largest fraction of the universal mass over onto itself, compressing instead of releasing. These eddies cried once and disappeared.

They amounted to ninety percent of the calculated *omega mass* that, 15 billion years later, human astronomers would fail to find in star's light and galaxy's blaze, would be unable to count in the rotations of the visible universe.

These compressed eddies were of all different sizes. Some were insignificant on a human scale. Many were vast on a galactic scale. But all had the same dimension: none—in this universe. They were knowable only by their mass and their pull.

Having mass, they joined the visible universe in its outward flight. They began the journey through space, which is also a journey through time.

Fifteen billion years later a Swiss astronomer, Fritz Zwicky, would call them goblins. Later theorists, Stephen Hawking and others, would call them black holes.

How many of these objects were created?

How many wrinkles are there in the fabric of space? How many waves in the ocean? . . . They are beyond counting.

ISBN #	Title # Author	Publ. List Price
55979-6	ACT OF GOD, Kotani and Roberts	2.95
55945-1	ACTIVE MEASURES, David Drake & Janet Morris	3.95
55970-2	THE ADOLESCENCE OF P-1, Thomas J. Ryan	2.95
55998-2	AFTER THE FLAMES, Silverberg & Spinrad	2.95
55967-2	AFTER WAR, Janet Morris	2.95
55934-6	ALIEN STARS, C.J. Cherryh, Joe Haldeman & Timothy Zahn, edited by Elizabeth Mitchell	2.95
55978-8	AT ANY PRICE, David Drake	3.50
65565-5	THE BABYLON GATE, Edward A. Byers	2.95
65586-8	THE BEST OF ROBERT SILVERBERG, Robert Silverberg	2.95
55977-X	BETWEEN THE STROKES OF NIGHT, Charles Sheffield	3.50
55984-2	BEYOND THE VEIL, Janet Morris	15.95
65544-2	BEYOND WIZARDWALL, Janet Morris	15.95
55973-7	BORROWED TIME, Alan Hruska	2.95
65563-9	A CHOICE OF DESTINIES, Melissa Scott	2.95
55960-5	COBRA, Timothy Zahn	2.95
65551-5	COBRA STRIKE!, Timothy Zahn	3.50
65578-7	A COMING OF AGE, Timothy Zahn	3.50
55969-9	THE CONTINENT OF LIES, James Morrow	2.95
55917-4	CUGEL'S SAGA, Jack Vance	3.50
65552-3	DEATHWISH WORLD, Reynolds and Ing	3.50
55995-8	THE DEVIL'S GAME, Poul Anderson	2.95
55974-5	DIASPORAH, W. R. Yates	2.95
65581-7	DINOSAUR BEACH, Keith Laumer	2.95
65579-5	THE DOOMSDAY EFFECT, Thomas Wren	2.95
65557-4	THE DREAM PALACE, Brynne Stephens	2.95
65564-7	THE DYING EARTH, Jack Vance	2.95
55988-5	FANGLITH, John Dalmas	2.95
55947-8	THE FALL OF WINTER, Jack C. Haldeman II	2.95
55975-3	FAR FRONTIERS, Volume III	2.95
65548-5	FAR FRONTIERS, Volume IV	2.95
65572-8	FAR FRONTIERS, Volume V	2.95
55900-1	FIRE TIME, Poul Anderson	2.95
65567-1	THE FIRST FAMILY, Patrick Tilley	3.50
55952-4	FIVE-TWELFTHS OF HEAVEN, Melissa Scott	2.95
55937-0	FLIGHT OF THE DRAGONFLY, Robert L. Forward	3.50
55986-9	THE FORTY-MINUTE WAR, Janet Morris	3.50
55971-0	FORWARD, Gordon R. Dickson	2.95
65550-7	THE FRANKENSTEIN PAPERS, Fred Saberhagen	3.50
55899-4	FRONTERA, Lewis Shiner	2.95
55918-4	THE GAME BEYOND, Melissa Scott	2.95
55959-1	THE GAME OF EMPIRE, Poul Anderson	3.50
65561-2	THE GATES OF HELL, Janet Morris	14.95
65566-3	GLADIATOR-AT-LAW, Pohl and Kornbluth	2.95
55904-4	THE GOLDEN PEOPLE, Fred Saberhagen	3.50
65555-8	HEROES IN HELL, Janet Morris	3.50
65571-X	HIGH JUSTICE, Jerry Pournelle	2.95

ISBN #	Title # Author	Publ. List Price
55930-3	HOTHOUSE, Brian Aldiss	2.95
55905-2	HOUR OF THE HORDE, Gordon R. Dickson	2.95
65547-7	THE IDENTITY MATRIX, Jack Chalker	2.95
65569-8	I, MARTHA ADAMS, Pauline Glen Winslow	3.95
55994-X	INVADERS, Gordon R. Dickson	2.95
55993-1	IN THE FACE OF MY ENEMY, Joe Delaney	2.95
65570-1	JOE MAUSER, MERCENARY, Reynolds and Banks	2.95
55931-1	KILLER, David Drake & Karl Edward Wagner	2.95
55996-6	KILLER STATION, Martin Caidin	3.50
65559-0	THE LAST DREAM, Gordon R. Dickson	2.95
55981-8	THE LIFESHIP, Dickson and Harrison	2.95
55980-X	THE LONG FORGETTING, Edward A. Byers	2.95
55992-3	THE LONG MYND, Edward Hughes	2.95
55997-4	MASTER OF SPACE AND TIME, Rudy Rucker	2.95
65573-6	MEDUSA, Janet and Chris Morris	3.50
65562-0	THE MESSIAH STONE, Martin Caidin	3.95
65580-9	MINDSPAN, Gordon R. Dickson	2.95
65553-1	THE ODYSSEUS SOLUTION, Banks and Lambe	2.95
55926-5	THE OTHER TIME, Mack Reynolds with Dean Ing	2.95
55985-6	THE PEACE WAR, Vernor Vinge	3.50
55982-6	PLAGUE OF DEMONS, Keith Laumer	2.75
55966-4	A PRINCESS OF CHAMELN, Cherry Wilder	2.95
65568-X	RANKS OF BRONZE, David Drake	3.50
65577-9	REBELS IN HELL, Janet Morris, et. al.	3.50
55990-7	RETIEF OF THE CDT, Keith Laumer	2.95
65556-6	RETIEF AND THE PANGALACTIC PAGEANT OF PULCHRITUDE, Keith Laumer	2.95
65575-2	RETIEF AND THE WARLORDS, Keith Laumer	2.95
55902-8	THE RETURN OF RETIEF, Keith Laumer	2.95
55991-5	RHIALTO THE MARVELLOUS, Jack Vance	3.50
65545-0	ROGUE BOLO, Keith Laumer	2.95
65554-X	SANDKINGS, George R.R. Martin	2.95
65546-9	SATURNALIA, Grant Callin	2.95
55989-3	SEARCH THE SKY, Pohl and Kornbluth	2.95
55914-1	SEVEN CONQUESTS, Poul Anderson	2.95
65574-4	SHARDS OF HONOR, Lois McMaster Bujold	2.95
55951-6	THE SHATTERED WORLD, Michael Reaves	3.50
	THE SILISTRA SERIES	
55915-X	RETURNING CREATION, Janet Morris	2.95
55919-2	THE GOLDEN SWORD, Janet Morris	2.95
55932-X	WIND FROM THE ABYSS, Janet Morris	2.95
55936-2	THE CARNELIAN THRONE, Janet Morris	2.95
65549-3	THE SINFUL ONES, Fritz Leiber	2.95
65558-2	THE STARCHILD TRILOGY, Pohl and Williamson	3.95
55999-0	STARSWARM, Brian Aldiss	2.95
55927-3	SURVIVAL!, Gordon R. Dickson	2.75
55938-9	THE TORCH OF HONOR, Roger Macbride Allen	2.95

ISBN #	Title # Author	Publ. List Price
55942-7	TROJAN ORBIT, Mack Reynolds with Dean Ing	2.95
55985-0	TUF VOYAGING, George R.R. Martin	15.95
55916-8	VALENTINA, Joseph H. Delaney & Marc Steigler	3.50
55898-6	WEB OF DARKENSS, Marion Zimmer Bradley	3.50
55925-7	WITH MERCY TOWARD NONE, Glen Cook	2.95
65576-0	WOLFBANE, Pohl and Kornbluth	2.95
55962-1	WOLFLING, Gordon R. Dickson	2.95
55987-7	YORATH THE WOLF, Cherry Wilder	2.95
55906-0	THE ZANZIBAR CAT, Joanna Russ	3.50

COMPUTER BOOKS AND GENERAL INTEREST NONFICTION

ISBN #	Title # Author	Publ. List Price
55968-0	ADVENTURES IN MICROLAND, Jerry Pournelle	9.95
55933-8	AI: HOW MACHINES THINK, F. David Peat	8.95
55922-2	THE ESSENTIAL USER'S GUIDE TO THE IBM PC, XT, AND PCjr., Dian Girard	6.95
55940-0	EUREKA FOR THE IBM PC AND PCjr, Tim Knight	7.95
55941-9	THE FUTURE OF FLIGHT, Leik Myrabo with Dean Ing	7.95
55955-9	THE GUIDEBOOK FOR WINNING ADVENTURERS, David & Sandy Small	8.95
55923-0	MUTUAL ASSURED SURVIVAL, Jerry Pournelle and Dean Ing	6.95
55929-X	PROGRAMMING LANGUAGES: FEATURING THE IBM PC, Marc Stiegler & Bob Hansen	9.95
55963-X	THE SERIOUS ASSEMBLER, Charles Crayne & Dian Girard Crayne	8.95
55907-9	THE SMALL BUSINESS COMPUTER TODAY AND TOMORROW, William E. Grieb, Jr.	6.95
55921-4	THE USER'S GUIDE TO CP/M SYSTEMS, Tony Bove & Cheryl Rhodes	8.95
55948-6	THE USER'S GUIDE TO FREE SOFTWARE, Tony Bove & Cheryl Rhodes	9.95
55908-7	THE USER'S GUIDE TO SMALL COMPUTERS, Jerry Pournelle	9.95

WE PARTICULARLY
RECOMMEND . . .

ALDISS, BRIAN W.

Starswarm

Man has spread throughout the galaxy, but the timeless struggle for conquest continues. The first complete U.S. edition of this classic, written by an acknowledged master of the field.   55999-0 $2.95

ANDERSON, POUL

Fire Time

Once every thousand years the Deathstar orbits close enough to burn the surface of the planet Ishtar. This is known as the Fire Time, and it is then that the barbarians flee the scorched lands, bringing havoc to the civilized South.   55900-1 $2.95

The Game of Empire

A *new* novel in Anderson's Polesotechnic League/Terran Empire series! Diana Crowfeather, daughter of Dominic Flandry, proves she is well capable of following in his adventurous footsteps.   55959-1 $3.50

BAEN, JIM & POURNELLE, JERRY (Editors)

Far Frontiers — Volume V

Aerospace expert G. Harry Stine writing on government regulations regarding private space launches; Charles Sheffield on beanstalks and other space transportation devices; a new "Retief" novella by Keith Laumer; and other fiction by David Drake, John Dalmas, Edward A. Byers, more.   65572-8 $2.95

BUJOLD, LOIS McMASTER
Shards of Honor

A novel of political intrigue and warfare on a par with Poul Anderson's "Polesotechnic League" stories and Gordon Dickson's *Dorsai!* Captain Cordelia Naismith and Commander Aral Vorkosigan, though on opposing sides in an ongoing war between wars, find themselves thrown together again and again against common enemies, and are forced to create a separate peace in order to survive and bring justice to their home worlds.   **65574-4 $2.95**

CAIDIN, MARTIN
Killer Station

Earth's first space station *Pleiades* is a scientific boon—until one brief moment of sabotage changes it into a terrible Sword of Damocles. The station is de-orbiting, and falling relentlessly to Earth, where it will strike New York City with the force of a hydrogen bomb. The author of *Cyborg* and *Marooned*, Caidin tells a story that is right out of tomorrow's headlines, with the hard reality and human drama that are his trademarks.   **55996-6 $3.50**

The Messiah Stone

What "Raiders of the Lost Ark" should have been! Doug Stavers is an old pro at the mercenary game. Retired now, he is surprised to find representatives of a powerful syndicate coming after him with death in their hands. He deals it right back, fast and easy, and then discovers that it was all a test to see if he is tough enough to go after the Messiah Stone—the most valuable object in existence. The last man to own it was Hitler. The next will rule the world . . .

65562-0 $3.95

CHALKER, JACK
The Identity Matrix

While backpacking in Alaska, a 35-year-old college professor finds himself transferred into the body of a 13-year-old Indian girl. From there, he undergoes change after change, eventually learning that this is all a part of a battle for Earth by two highly advanced alien races. And that's just the beginning of this mind-bending novel by the author of the world-famous *Well of Souls* series. **65547-7 $2.95**

DELANEY, JOSEPH H.
In the Face of My Enemy

Aged and ailing, the tribal shaman Kah-Sih-Omah is prepared to die . . . until peaceful aliens happen upon him and "repair" his body, leaving him changed with the ability to survive any wound, and to change shape at will. Thus begins his long journey, from the time of the Incas to the far future, as protector of Mankind. **55993-1 $2.95**

DICKSON, GORDON R.
Hour of the Horde

The Silver Horde threatens—and the galaxy's only hope is its elite army, composed of one warrior from each planet. Earth's warrior turns out to possess skills and courage that he never suspected . . .

55905-2 $2.95

Mindspan

Crossing the gap between human and alien minds as only he can, Gordon R. Dickson examines the infinity of ways that different species can misunderstand each other—and the dangers such mistakes can spawn. By the author of *Dorsai!* and *The Final Encyclopedia*.

65580-9 $2.95

Wolfling

The first human expedition to Centauri III discovers that humanity is about to become just another race ruled by the alien "High Born". But super-genius James Keil has a few things to teach the aliens about this new breed of "Wolfling." **55962-1 $2.95**

DRAKE, DAVID
At Any Price

Hammer's Slammers are back—and Baen Books has them! Now the 23rd-century armored division faces its deadliest enemies ever: aliens who *teleport* into combat. **55978-8 $3.50**

Ranks of Bronze

Disguised alien traders bought captured Roman soldiers on the slave market because they needed troops who could win battles without high-tech weaponry. The legionaires provided victories, smashing barbarian armies with the swords, javelins, and discipline that had won a world. But the worlds on which they now fought were strange ones, and the spoils of victory did not include freedom. If the legionaires went home, it would be through the use of the beam weapons and force screens of their ruthless alien owners. It's been 2000 years—and now they want to go home. **65568-X $3.50**

FORWARD, ROBERT L.
The Flight of the Dragonfly

Set against the rich background of the double planet Rocheworld, this is the story of Mankind's first contact with alien beings, and the friendship the aliens offer. **55937-0 $3.50**

KOTANI, ERIC, &
JOHN MADDOX ROBERTS
Act of God

In 1889 a mysterious explosion in Siberia destroyed all life for a hundred miles in every direction. A century later the Soviets figure out what had happened —and how to duplicate the deadly effect. Their target: the United States. **55979-6 $2.95**

KUBE-MCDOWELL, MICHAEL P.,
SILVERBERG, ROBERT, &
SPINRAD, NORMAN
After the Flames

Three short novels of rebirth after the nuclear holocaust, written especially for this book. Kube-McDowell writes of a message of hope sent to post-holocaust humanity via the stars. Silverberg tells of the struggle to maintain democracy in America after the destruction of the government. Spinrad adds his special sense of humor with a tale about an Arabian oil baron who is shopping for a bomb. Edited by Elizabeth Mitchell. **55998-2 $2.95**

LAUMER, KEITH
Dinosaur Beach

"Keith Laumer is one of science fiction's most adept creators of time travel stories ... A war against robots, trick double identities, and suspenseful action makes this story a first-rate thriller."—*Savannah News-Press*. "Proves again that Laumer is a master."—*Seattle Times*. By the author of the popular "Retief" series. **65581-7 $2.95**

Retief and the Pangalactic Pageant of Pulchritude

Once again Retief stands up for truth, beauty and the Terran way—this time at the Pangalactic Pageant of Pulchritude. He escorts a Bengal tiger to the gala affair, where the most beautiful females of the galaxy gather to strut their stuff. But Retief has a penchant for finding trouble—and there's plenty of trouble ahead when he discovers that the five-eyed Groaci intend to abduct the pageant beauties, and blame it on Earth . . .

65556-6 $2.95

The Return of Retief

Laumer's two-fisted intergalactic diplomat is back—and better than ever. In this latest of the Retief series, the CDT diplomat must face not only a deadly alien threat, but also the greatest menace of all—the foolish machinations of his human comrades. More Retief coming soon from Baen!   **55902-8 $2.95**

Rogue Bolo

A new chronicle from the annals of the Dinochrome Brigade. Learn what happens when sentient fighting machines, capable of destroying continents, decide to follow their programming to the letter, and do what's "best" for their human masters.   **65545-0 $2.95**

MARTIN, GEORGE R.R.

Tuf Voyaging

On a colonial world in the far future, struggling trader Haviland Tuf stumbles across the find of the century—a long abandoned Earth Ecological Corps seedship, a repository of every bit of scientific knowledge once known—and since lost—to man, as well as the tools to recreate any form of life. Tuf turns the ship into a gold mine, but not without paying a price. *Hardcover*.

55985-0 $15.95

MORRIS, JANET (Editor)

Afterwar

Life After Holocaust. Stories by C.J. Cherryh, David Drake, Gregory Benford, and others. This one is utterly topical.　　　　　**55967-2 $2.95**

BEYOND *THIEVES' WORLD*

MORRIS, JANET

Beyond Sanctuary

This three-novel series stars Tempus, the most popular character in all the "Thieves' World" fantasy universe. Warrior-servant of the god of storm and war, he is a hero cursed ... for anyone he loves must loathe him, and anyone who loves him soon dies of it. In this opening adventure, Tempus leads his Sacred Band of mercenaries north to war against the evil Mygdonian Alliance. *Hardcover*.

55957-5 $15.95

Beyond the Veil

Book II in the first full-length novel series ever written about "Thieves' World," the meanest, toughest fantasy universe ever created. The war against the Mygdonians continues—and not even the immortal Tempus can guarantee victory against Cime the Mage Killer, Askelon, Lord of Dreams, and the Nisibisi witch Roxane. *Hardcover*.　　　　　**55984-2 $15.95**

Beyond Wizardwall

The gripping conclusion to the trilogy. Tempus's best friend Niko resigns from the Stepsons and flees for his life. Roxane, the witch who is Tempus's sworn enemy, and Askelon, Lord of Dreams, are both after Niko's soul. Niko has been offered one chance for safety ... but it's a suicide mission, and only Tempus can save Niko now. *Hardcover*.

65544-2 $15.95

MORRIS, JANET & CHRIS
The 40-Minute War

Washington, D.C. is vaporized by a nuclear surface blast, perpetrated by Islamic Jihad terrorists, and the President initiates a nuclear exchange with Russia. In the aftermath, American foreign service agent Marc Beck finds himself flying anticancer serum from Israel to the Houston White House, a secret mission that is filled with treachery and terror. This is just the beginning of a suspense-filled tale of desperation and heroism—a tale that is at once stunning and chilling in its realism.　　　　**55986-9 $3.50**

MEDUSA

From the Sea of Japan a single missile rises, and the future of America's entire space-based defense program hangs in the balance. . . . A hotline communique from Moscow insists that the Russians are doing everything they can to abort the "test" flight. If the U.S. chooses to intercept and destroy the missile, the attempt must not end in failure . . . its collision course is with America's manned space lab. Only one U.S. anti-satellite weapon can foil what *might* be the opening gambit of a Soviet first strike—and only Amy Brecker and her "hot stick" pilot have enough of the Right Stuff to use MEDUSA.　　　**65573-6 $3.50**

HEROES IN HELL™—THE GREATEST
BRAIDED MEGANOVEL OF ALL TIME!

MORRIS, JANET, & GREGORY BENFORD, C.J. CHERRYH, DAVID DRAKE
Heroes in Hell™

Volume I in the greatest shared universe of All Times! The greatest heroes of history meet the greatest names of science fiction—and each other!—in the most original milieu since a Connecticut Yankee visited King

Arthur's Court. Alexander of Macedon, Caesar and Cleopatra, Che Guevara, Yuri Andropov, and the Devil Himself face off ... and only the collaborators of HEROES IN HELL know where it will end.

65555-8 $3.50

CHERRYH, C.J. AND MORRIS, JANET
The Gates of Hell

The first full-length spinoff novel set in the Heroes in Hell™ shared universe! Alexander the Great teams up with Julius Caesar and Achilles to refight the Trojan War using 20th-century armaments. Machiavelli is their intelligence officer and Cleopatra is in charge of R&R ... co-created by two of the finest, most imaginative talents writing today. *Hardcover.*

65561-2 $14.95

MORRIS, JANET & MARTIN CAIDIN, C.J. CHERRYH, DAVID DRAKE, ROBERT SILVERBERG
Rebels in Hell

Robert Silverberg's Gilgamesh the King joins Alexander the Great, Julius Caesar, Attila the Hun, and the Devil himself in the newest installment of the "Heroes in Hell" meganovel. Other demonic contributors include Martin Caidin, C.J. Cherryh, David Drake, and Janet Morris.

65577-9 $3.50

POHL, FREDERIK, & WILLIAMSON, JACK
The Starchild Trilogy

In the near future, all of humanity lives under the strictly enforced guidance of The Plan of Man—a vast, oppressive set of laws managed by a computer security network. One man vowed to circumvent the law and voyage to the farthest reaches of space—but he has been found out and sentenced to death. A mysterious Power is on his side, however, and it demands not only clemency for Boysie Gann, but an end to the Plan of Man itself. If her rulers refuse, Earth's sun will be snuffed out ...

65558-2 $3.95

REAVES, MICHAEL
The Shattered World

Ardatha the sorceress and Beorn the thief unite with the cult of magicians to undo the millennium-old magic that shattered the world into fragments. Battling against the Establishment, which fears (perhaps rightly) that the pair can only destroy what little is left, they struggle to fulfill their self-assigned destiny of making the world whole again. **55951-6 $3.50**

SABERHAGEN, FRED
The Frankenstein Papers

At last—the truth about the sinister Dr. Frankenstein and his monster with a heart of gold, based on a history written by the monster himself! Find out what really happened when the mad Doctor brought his creation to life, and why the monster has no scars. "In the tour-de-force ending, rationality triumphs by means of a neat science-fiction twist."—*Publishers Weekly* **65550-7 $3.50**

SCOTT, MELISSA
A Choice of Destinies

Macedonians vs. Romans in a world that never was ... this brilliant novel shows what might have happened had Alexander the Great turned his eyes to the west and met the Romans, instead of invading India and contracting the fever that led to his early death. An exciting alternate history by a finalist in the 1985 John W. Campbell Award for Best New Writer.

65563-9 $2.95

SHEFFIELD, CHARLES
Between the Strokes of Night

The story of the people who leave the Earth after a total nuclear war, living through fantastic scientific advances and personal experiences. Serialized in *Analog*. **55977-X $3.50**

VINGE, VERNOR
The Peace War
Paul Hoehler has discovered the "Bobble Effect"—a scientific phenomenon that has been used to destroy every military installation on Earth. Concerned scientists steal Hoehler's invention—and implement a dictatorship which drives Earth toward primitivism. It is up to Hoehler to stop the tyrants.

55965-6 $3.50

WINSLOW, PAULINE GLEN
I, Martha Adams
From the dozens of enthusiastic notices for this most widely and favorably reviewed of all Baen Books: "There are firing squads in New England meadows, and at the end of the broadcasting day the Internationale rings out over the airwaves. If Jeane Kirkpatrick were to write a Harlequin, this might be it."—*The Washington Post*. What would happen if America gave into the environmentalists and others who oppose maintaining our military might as a defense against a Russian pre-emptive strike? This book tells it all, while presenting an intense drama of those few Americans who are willing to fight, rather than cooperate with the New Order. "A high-voltage thriller . . . an immensely readable, fast-paced novel that satisfies." —*Publishers Weekly*

65569-8 $3.95

WREN, THOMAS
The Doomsday Effect
"Hard" science fiction at its best! The deadliest object in the universe will destroy Earth in seven years— unless a dedicated band of scientists can stop it. The object is a miniature black hole trapped in our gravity field; experts show that the singularity will dive in and out of the Earth, swallowing everything in its path, until the planet collapses. But how do you stop something that is smaller than an atom, heavier than a mountain, and swallows everything that touches it?

65579-5 $2.95

ZAHN, TIMOTHY
Cobra

Jonny Moreau becomes a Cobra—a crack commando whose weapons are surgically implanted. When the war is over, Jonny and the rest of the Cobras are no longer a solution, but a problem, and politicians decide that something must be done with them.

65560-4 $3.50

Cobra Strike

The sequel to the *Locus* bestseller, *Cobra*. In *Cobra Strike*, the elite fighting force is back, faced with the decision of whether or not to hire out as mercenaries—under the command of their former foes, the alien Troft. Justin Moreau, son of the hero of *Cobra*, finds that it take more than a name to make a real Cobra.

65551-5 $3.50

A Coming of Age

The planet Tigris had a bizarre effect on its human colonists. Children are born with telekinetic powers. Until they reach adolescence, they can fly, move objects without touching them, etc.—and are carefully watched so that none use their abilities illegally. A scientist attempting to extend the strange powers into adulthood kidnaps a child for use in research, and it's up to detective Stanford Tirrell to catch him before Tigris faces chaos again. "Reads fast and pleasurably."—*Fantasy Review*.

65578-7 $3.50

talents writing today, *Heroes in Hell* ® offers a milieu more exciting than anything in American fiction since *A Connecticut Yankee in King Arthur's Court*. As bright and fresh a vision as any conceived by Borges, it's as accessible—and American—as apple pie.

EVERYONE WHO WAS ANYONE DOES IT

In fact, Janet Morris's Hell is so liberating to the imaginations of the authors involved that nearly a dozen major talents have vowed to join her for at least eight subsequent excursions to the Underworld, where—even as you read this—everyone who was anyone is meeting to hatch new plots, conquer new empires, and test the very limits of creation.

YOU'VE HEARD ABOUT IT—NOW GO THERE!

Join the finest writers, scientists, statesmen, strategists, and villains of history in Morris's Hell. The first volume, co-created by Janet Morris with C. J. Cherryh, Gregory Benford, and David Drake, will be on sale in March as the mass-market lead from Baen Books, and in April Baen will publish in hardcover the first *Heroes in Hell* spin-off novel, *The Gates of Hell*, by C. J. Cherryh and Janet Morris. We can promise you one Hell of a good time.

FOR A DOSE OF THAT OLD-TIME RELIGION (TO A MODERN BEAT), READ—

HEROES IN HELL®   THE GATES OF HELL
March 1986   April 1986 Hardcover
65555-8 • 288 pp. • $3.50   65561-2 • 256 pp. • $14.95

WE'RE LOOKING FOR
TROUBLE

Well, feedback, anyway. Baen Books endeavors to publish only the best in science fiction and fantasy—but we need you to tell us whether we're doing it right. Why not let us know? We'll award a Baen Books gift certificate worth $100 (plus a copy of our catalog) to the reader who best tells us what he or she likes about Baen Books—and where we could do better. We reserve the right to quote any or all of you. Contest closes December 31, 1987. All letters should be addressed to Baen Books, 260 Fifth Avenue, New York, N.Y. 10001.

At the same time, ask about the Baen Book Club—buy five books, get another five free! For information, send a self-addressed, stamped envelope. For a copy of our catalog, enclose one dollar as well.